PRAISE FOR JACI BURTON A[...]

"Jaci Burton's stories are full of heat a[...]
—#1 *New York Times* bestselling author Maya Banks

"A wild ride." —#1 *New York Times* bestselling author Lora Leigh

"Jaci Burton delivers."
—*New York Times* bestselling author Cherry Adair

"One to pick up and savor." —*Publishers Weekly*

"Jaci Burton's books are always sexy, romantic, and charming! A hot hero, a lovable heroine, and an adorable dog—prepare to fall in love with Jaci Burton's amazing new small-town romance series." —*New York Times* bestselling author Jill Shalvis

"A heartwarming second-chance-at-love contemporary romance enhanced by engaging characters and Jaci Burton's signature dry wit." —*USA Today*

"Captures everything I love about a small-town romance."
—Fresh Fiction

"Delivered on everything I was hoping for and more."
—Under the Covers Book Blog

"A sweet, hot small-town romance." —Dear Author

"Fun and sexy." —Fiction Vixen

"The perfect combination of heat and romance."
—Heroes and Heartbreakers

HOT TO THE TOUCH

JACI BURTON

JOVE
New York

A JOVE BOOK
Published by Berkley
An imprint of Penguin Random House LLC
1745 Broadway, New York, NY 10019

Library of Congress Cataloguing-in-Publication Data

Names: Burton, Jaci, author.
Title: Hot to the touch / Jaci Burton.
Description: First Edition. | New York : Jove, 2019. | Series: Brotherhood by Fire
Identifiers: LCCN 2018053523 | ISBN 9780399585180 (pbk.) | ISBN 9780399585197 (ebook)
Subjects: | GSAFD: Love stories.
Classification: LCC PS3602.U776 H68 2019 | DDC 813/.6—dc23
LC record available at https://lccn.loc.gov/2018053523

First Edition: May 2019

Printed in the United States of America
1 3 5 7 9 10 8 6 4 2

Cover photo by Claudio Dogar Marinesco
Cover design by Sarah Oberrender
Book design by George Towne

This book is dedicated to all the firefighters who put their lives on the line in order to save others. Thank you for what you do.

PROLOGUE

AUGUST 2005

THEY'D GOTTEN SEPARATED FROM THE REST OF THE group when the downpour started, but that happened sometimes. Jackson hoped the rest of them were okay in the tents. For tonight, it was just him, Rafe and Kal.

They'd been lucky to find this abandoned piece-of-junk house so they could have a roof over their heads during the storm. Jackson was on lookout tonight, because you never knew who might be prowling for space, or the cops might come and bust them and the last thing they needed was to be dragged back into some shitty foster home worse than the last one.

Foster homes were a crapshoot. Sometimes you got lucky and they were decent. More often than not you got people who were in it for the money, or the system was so overburdened with kids you ended up shuffled from one home to another and you couldn't even remember anyone's names. They sure as hell didn't remember yours. And then sometimes you got the mean ones. At fourteen, Jackson could handle himself. Rafe was getting there at thirteen, but Kal was only twelve. As the oldest, Jackson was responsible for looking out for the younger ones. His brothers. Not by blood, but they were still his brothers.

No, they were better off on their own where they had each other's backs and no one could ever hurt them again.

Tonight they had gotten lucky and had a place to sleep out of the rain. They'd scored a whole pizza some jerkoff had left uneaten on his back porch while the dude was inside having an argument with his girlfriend, so they had full bellies. Rafe and Kal were asleep on the floor in another room while Jackson stood watch. He gazed out the living room window of the old beach house, watching lightning arc across the Atlantic Ocean. The storm was a bad one tonight and the rain was coming down hard.

He walked away from the water view and made his way to the front of the house. He scanned the street out front to make sure it was still clear. Because of the rain, no one was wandering around, which made him feel more secure.

Not that you could ever feel completely safe. Not when you lived like they did.

He pushed off the wall to wander around. Lots of windows in this place. He'd bet it was killer when the sun was out. But tonight the rain made it cold, so they'd shut all the windows earlier. His boots creaked on the worn wood floor. As he moved from room to room he could imagine a family with a couple of kids and maybe a dog running this joint. They'd probably have nice furniture, some cushy-looking couch where they'd all cuddle together and read at night.

He could still remember what it was like to have a family, though that had been a long time ago and there was no point living in the past. He wasn't gonna get that life back.

Anyway, this was a decent beach house, and maybe someday

it would get fixed up. Or maybe torn down. But tonight, it was their shelter, and they didn't have one of those very often.

Having made a circuit of the place, he returned to the living room and sat down in the corner. He leaned back against the wall and settled in.

JACKSON WOKE UP COUGHING, SOMETHING BURNING HIS lungs so badly he couldn't breathe. He tried to open his eyes, but when he did they burned.

He fought to suck in air, found his voice so he could call out for Rafe and Kal. They didn't answer. His stomach tightened as he saw flames lick up the wall across the room.

Oh, shit. Fire. He didn't want to die. He didn't want his brothers to be dead. Tears pricked his eyes as he tried to see through the thick, black smoke. He pushed himself onto his hands and knees, trying to remember where the door was, what room the boys were sleeping in. Had they been right next to him, or had he moved into another room? His brain was fuzzy and he couldn't remember.

He coughed, the smoke entering his lungs with every breath he took. He pulled his raggedy T-shirt over his mouth, trying to stifle the smoke. He had to get to Rafe and Kal. He was the oldest. It was his job to save them.

He called out to them, rasping out a cough with every few words. But he kept at it. They had to hear him. If he could hear them, he could get to them. Then they'd figure a way out. Because no way were they dying in this piece-of-shit building today.

Finally, he heard voices. The sound was faint, but he wasn't imagining it. He'd definitely heard it. It was them. It had to be them. Which meant they were alive. He crawled toward the sound, his own voice hoarse as he yelled out in response.

"I'm here! Hang on." The smoke grew thicker and he could feel himself slipping away, but sheer determination kept him conscious. He was their brother. They'd been through so much together, had survived so much together. This fire wasn't going to get them.

When he saw the light and the tall shadow looming over him, he thought maybe it was too late. He was dead and this was some dark angel come to take him away. But then strong arms scooped him up.

"It's okay, buddy," the dark angel said. "I've got you. You're safe now."

Jackson shook his head and gripped the angel's arm, barely able to stay conscious. "My . . . my brothers."

"They're safe, too. They're outside. Come on. Let's get you out of here."

Jackson sighed in relief and let himself fall into the darkness.

CHAPTER 1

PRESENT DAY

JACKSON DONOVAN WAS HAVING THE BEST DREAM OF HIS life. It involved his favorite spot on the beach, a spectacular blonde in a barely-there bikini, and hot sex on a Jet-Ski. He was just about to maneuver her onto his lap while they were simultaneously bouncing across the waves, because, hey, in a dream anything was possible, when a loud noise sent him jolting off the sofa in the firehouse.

He'd thought it was the firehouse alarm, so he was instantly alert.

"Calm down," Rafe said, not even looking up from the video game he was playing. "Just Rodriguez dropping shit in the kitchen."

Jackson blinked, that sweet dream vanishing instantly. He rubbed his eyes and stretched. "Oh. Okay."

"So, good dream?" Rafe asked, grinning as he kept his attention on the TV.

Now that he knew he didn't have to gear up, Jackson leaned back in the chair. "None of your business."

His other brother, Kal, laughed. "That means it was about a girl."

Sometimes working with your brothers was great. Other times it was annoying because they knew him too well.

They'd been together for longer than Jackson could remember. Jackson had hit the streets at ten. It didn't take long to grow streetwise when you were running from either cops or social services, or whatever other dangers lurked out there for kids. You found yourself a homeless community, which he'd done, and then found other kids. He'd hooked up with Rafe a few years later, then Kal. After that, the three of them had been inseparable. They might not be real brothers, but they had all shared similar circumstances. And all those years they'd lived on the streets they'd looked out for each other, had each other's backs and had vowed to never be separated.

That had never changed.

Which didn't mean his brothers weren't a constant pain in his ass.

"You three intending to spend this shift sitting on your asses?"

Their father, Battalion Chief Josh Donovan, glared down at them. Off duty he was loving and protective and fun. Everything Jackson had always wanted in a father. Off duty he was Dad. The guy who'd saved their lives that night in the house fire.

And the man who'd adopted them, along with his wife, Laurel. Their mom.

But on shift? On shift he was their battalion chief—demanding and strict. He expected a lot of every firefighter who worked at Station 6. His own kids got no preferential treatment.

"No, sir," Kal said, giving their father the respect he was due.

"Good. Because the fridge smells like something died in there. Go investigate."

"Oh, come on, Chief," Kal said. "Let the probies do that."

Dad shot Kal a look that said there'd be no argument.

Kal sighed. "Yes, sir. I'm right on it."

But just at that moment the alarm went off, calling for both Ladder and Engine 6, along with the EMTs, who were at the hospital but acknowledged they'd be on their way. It looked like cleaning the fridge would have to be put off—at least until after the call they were headed out to.

They all ran out to the engine room. Jackson climbed into his bunker pants and jacket, grabbed the rest of his gear and scrambled into the truck. Despite having been on this engine for the past seven years, he felt a thrill every time he heard the sirens, every time the engine roared out of the house. The sounds and vibrations filled him with a sense of belonging, of knowing that this was right where he was supposed to be.

All those years he lived on the streets, he never thought he'd feel this way.

The night that firefighter Josh Donovan rescued him and Rafe and Kal from that house fire changed his life. Changed all their lives.

"Dude, you even listening?" Rafe asked.

He blinked. "What?"

"You dreaming about that girl again?"

Jackson shook his head. "No. Just thinking."

"No wonder you looked so pained."

He glared at his brother. "Fuck off."

This was one of those times he was glad both of his brothers didn't ride the same fire truck with him. One was bad enough.

They arrived at a strip shopping center a couple of blocks from the beach. Smoke poured out of the open door of a tattoo shop with a sign on the window that said *Skin Deep*. He didn't see smoke rising from the second story.

Yet.

"No flames visible." Jackson did a quick review as they pulled up in front of the building. Nothing shooting out of the roof, which didn't mean the place wasn't fully involved on the inside, or ready to burst into flames any second. Smoke was sometimes more dangerous than flame. It held secrets that could explode any second.

They'd have to be on guard.

Jackson gave out assignments, even though everyone already knew their jobs.

"Get up on that roof and check things out," he said to Kal and Ethan Pressman on the ladder team. "I need a report stat."

Kal and Pressman nodded, and they set off to get the ladder in place.

"Let's get inside and see what's going on."

"Rodriguez, you and Hendricks get the hoses."

They jumped out and immediately went to work, gearing up with their SCBA and regulators so they could breathe through the smoke. Jackson was first in, calling out to see if anyone was inside.

He hoped no one was in there. But he hadn't seen anyone outside, and the door was open. Hopefully no one was in here.

But then he heard the sound. It was faint, but he heard it.

Coughing. That thick cough that came from breathing in smoke. He knew that sensation all too well. Even though it had been fourteen years, he could still remember what it had felt like to breathe in that smoke, to fight for air. He remembered the overpowering panic. He never wanted to experience it again. He never wanted anyone else to feel it, either, so he had to get to whoever was in here.

"Fire department," he hollered. "Anyone in here?"

No answer, but he heard the coughing again so he followed the sound.

"Someone's in here," he said into his mic. "I'm heading farther back in to investigate. Still no sign of flames."

"I'm right behind you," Rafe said.

He knew his brother would have his back. One or both of them always did.

He was about to turn the corner into a room when he was met face-to-face with a short, masked . . . he had no idea. Woman, maybe? Yeah, definitely a woman. There were boobs and she was wearing skimpy shorts and a crop top and he saw a swinging ponytail. She had a bandana tied around the bottom half of her face and he wasn't sure if she was the owner or if she was looting the place, because she had her arms filled with what looked like tattoo equipment.

"Fire department. You have to get out now."

"Out of my way, Darth," she said, then erupted into a heavy cough.

Darth? He frowned, then caught on when he realized she heard him breathing into his SCBA. Something she should be doing because it was smoky as hell in here.

He'd figure out the owner-versus-looter question after he got her out of there. "You have to vacate the premises."

She shook her head and pushed at him to move him out of her way. "Screw you, Vader. I need to get my stuff."

He wasn't budging. "Nope. Out. Now."

"I'm not—" She stopped, racked by spasms of coughing. "Leaving."

He didn't have time to argue with her, so he started to pull her toward the exit. She resisted, turning back inside. He tried to draw her in the right direction, but it was obvious they were going to play tug-of-war and the smoke was getting thicker back there.

He had no choice but to hoist her over his shoulder and carry her out. Everything she'd had in her arms clattered to the floor.

"What the hell are you doing?"

He didn't bother answering her since what he was doing was obvious. He passed Rafe and Tommy Rodriguez.

"Found the source of the smoke," Rafe said. "An electrical outlet short. We've got electrical turned off. They're breaking into the wall now to make sure there's no fire in the walls."

Jackson nodded. "I'm getting her out of here. I'll be back."

"Okay."

"Put me the hell down." She was wriggling, which didn't make his job any easier.

He also didn't intend to let her win this battle no matter how much she fought him.

He made it outside and set her down. She started back inside again. He grabbed hold of her arm and dragged her over to the truck. He pulled his mask off and opened the door where the portable oxygen was located. The EMTs should be showing up soon, and then she'd be their problem. Until then, he needed to give her oxygen.

He put the mask on her face. "Breathe."

"I'm fine." But her body betrayed her with a spasm of coughing, and her voice was raspy from the smoke.

"Breathe."

She took a couple breaths of oxygen, then pushed the mask away. "Okay. I'm good now."

She tried to get up but his hand on her shoulder kept her on the bumper of the rig. "You're not going in there."

Her face was smudged gray from the smoke, but her angry blue-eyed gaze shot daggers at him. "And you can't stop me."

"Actually, I can. What the hell were you thinking not evacuating at the first sign of smoke?"

"I was thinking that everything I own is in there, and I was trying to get as much of it out as I could before the fire broke out. I would have run like hell if I'd seen flames. I didn't see flames."

She let out a series of deep coughs, so he put the mask on her face again.

"Smoke can kill you, too."

She pulled the mask away and glared at him. "I'm alive, aren't I?"

He shook his head. She was one hell of a smartass. But at least she was right about one thing.

She was alive.

REBECCA "BECKS" BENNING GLANCED IN MISERY AT HER ruined shop. She was glad she didn't own the building. Of course, if she had, it wouldn't have had the faulty wiring, which had led to this massive disaster of a day.

She'd had three appointments for today, and, since it was Saturday, it was a beautiful day to be at the beach. Who knows how many walk-ins she would have gotten for ink or piercings? All that beautiful income literally up in smoke. Likely along with a lot of her inventory. She could already imagine how difficult it would be to clean the soot off her equipment. Her ink was closed tightly in bottles so maybe it would be okay, but the cleanup was going to be a nightmare.

And since she lived in the small apartment above the shop, chances were everything in there was also covered in that gray ashy crap.

She'd deal with it. Hadn't she always managed with whatever happened to her? She'd find a way to come out of this. And if worse came to worst, she'd couch-surf with some friends until she could get back into her apartment again. It was the work that was going to be a problem. And where was she going to store all her stuff? Sleeping on someone's sofa was one thing. Storing her equipment and finding a place to set up shop in the interim? That was going to be the big issue.

God, she had so much to deal with. Her mind was whirling and right now she felt a little dizzy. She leaned forward, letting her hands rest on her knees while she breathed in the oxygen from the mask that the EMTs insisted she keep on. She rested on the bumper of the ambulance while she watched the firefighters walk in and out of her shop. And with every minute she felt her livelihood slipping away more and more.

"You feeling better, miss?"

She gave a thumbs-up to the very nice EMT with the soft voice whose name tag said *Acosta*. His partner was a cute perky blond chick named Smith.

Grumpy Firefighter, the one who'd dragged her out of her shop as if he were some kind of caveman, seemed to be semi-in-charge of the other ones, because she noted that he pointed and gave instructions to the other guys.

She blamed a lot of her woes on him. She'd had nearly all of her tattoo machines and was on her way out of the shop with them when he'd intercepted her. Then he'd had the audacity to pick her up and toss her over his shoulder like she was some damn damsel in distress or something.

She knew what she'd been doing, and she had tied a wet bandana over her face to keep from breathing in the smoke. Or at least much of the smoke. And okay, maybe she'd been coughing— a lot. But she'd been on her way out the door. She wasn't stupid. She knew breathing in smoke was dangerous.

She sat up and watched Grumpy Firefighter more closely. Hard to tell what anyone looked like under all that gear. He was nothing more than a yellow-and-red blob right now. But earlier, when he'd jerked off his mask, she'd gotten a glimpse of dark hair and extremely intense gray eyes. He had a nice mouth, too.

Not that she was interested in him or his very fine mouth. But he reminded her of someone from way back when. The old days. The bad days.

One of the other firefighters came up to her. "We need to get some information from you, ma'am," he said.

She grabbed the clipboard and filled out the form, then handed it back to him, studying him as she did. This guy looked familiar, too. Hispanic, dark hair, tan skin, soulful brown eyes and the most amazing thick, long eyelashes. She used to tease Rafael about his eyelashes all the time. She looked at the firefighter's name tag. It said *Donovan*. Not that they had ever known last names back then.

"Ma'am?"

"Oh. Sorry. I was just thinking you look a lot like someone I used to know."

The firefighter smiled, his teeth bright and even. "Yeah? Who's that?"

"A homeless kid I used to hang out with. I'd tease him about his long eyelashes. You have those same long eyelashes."

He frowned, then looked down at the form and back up at her. "Rebecca. You ever go by Becks?"

Her stomach dropped. "All the time. Your name wouldn't be Rafe, would it?"

"It would. But this can't be. You sure look different. It can't be you, Becks, could it?"

She knew who she was, but this had to be the weirdest coincidence. She and Rafe had been tight—like the closest friends. She couldn't begin to hope. "We didn't go by last names back then. You sure don't look like a Donovan."

He laughed. "I got adopted."

Adopted. Something they'd all hoped for but knew would never happen. "You did? That's awesome, Rafe. And Benning really is my name. Never adopted."

"Damn, Becks, that sucks."

"Nah, it's fine." She was having one hell of a surreal day. First the smoke-out, now running into a blast from her past. "Wow, I can't believe it."

"Neither can I. It's really you, Becks?"

Tears sprang to her eyes. "It's really me, Rafe."

He pulled her against him, and a hug had never felt so good. It was like she'd just found her long-lost family.

"Hey, we don't hug the victims, Rafe."

A tall, well-muscled guy had come around the side of the fire truck. Becks looked at him, and damn if he didn't look just as familiar. Skin the color of deep, rich chestnut, eyes that mesmerizing green with golden flecks. She couldn't see his hair because he was wearing his firefighter helmet, but she wondered if it was still long and curly. It didn't matter. She'd know that face anywhere.

It was Kal. It had to be Kal. And if it was, she might be hallucinating.

"Kal, it's Becks."

Becks studied the guy as he removed his helmet and saw that his black hair was cut shorter than he used to wear it. They'd been the same age when they'd hung out. Last time she'd seen him he'd been a gangly preteen. He'd grown up. Filled out. Damn, he was handsome now.

"Kal." She smiled.

He grinned. "Becks? Wow. You grew up."

"So did you." She couldn't believe two guys she'd been so close to had rescued her today.

Rafe threw his arm around her. "Talk about kismet, huh?"

"Rafe, what the hell are you doing?" Another voice interrupted them.

Rafe pulled away. "Jackson, this is Becks. You remember Becks, don't you?"

Becks turned to stare at Grumpy Firefighter. This was Jackson? The one guy who'd made her twelve-year-old heart go pitter-patter?

This could not be possible. All three of them had stayed together. And now they fought fires together.

Only Grumpy Firefighter's—Jackson's—brows knitted in a frown and he said the words that made her heart sink.

"No, I don't remember her."

Well, damn.

CHAPTER 2

JACKSON STARED AT THE SMUDGED BLONDE.

"Who is she?"

"Becks used to hang out with us when we were kids."

He looked over at her, searching for recognition but finding nothing but fuzzy memories of that time in his life. "She did?"

"Yeah. I can't believe you don't remember her," Rafe said. "She was with us until the night of the fire."

"Fire?" Becks asked. "What fire?"

Kal leaned against the ambulance. "We got separated from the group one night when a big storm hit. I think Greg took all of you to the adult camp. Said there was a woman with a tent that he trusted but there was only room for four. So he took you and Amy and Littles."

"Oh, right," she said. "And you and Jackson and Kal were going to tough it out or find other shelter."

"Yeah," Rafe said. "We found an abandoned house right off the beach. But a fire broke out while we were asleep."

Becks had a look of horror on her face. "Oh, no. That must have been the last night we ever saw you three. What happened?"

"Fire department showed up and rescued all of us," Kal said as he came around the corner. "The firefighter who rescued us, he's the man, Becks. He and his wife took us all in, which is why we never met up with all of you again."

"I'm so sorry about that, Becks," Rafe said. "We never had the chance to make it back to check on all of you. We were kind of swept up into the system. The Donovans became our foster parents and then adopted us."

"Okay," Becks said. "That explains a lot about what happened after the storm. We were so worried about you guys. We thought you had been picked up by the cops or social services and that's why you never came back."

Jackson had sat back and watched this reunion, racking his brain for memories of Becks.

Nothing. Then again, the past was all a distant blur to him. Kids had come and gone into and out of their lives all the time. The only constant had been him and Rafe and Kal.

Because he was the oldest, it had been his job to watch over all the kids in their group. But his main tie had been to his brothers. Everyone else was peripheral. He never bonded with the other kids because they came and went. Some were runaways from parents, some in and out of foster care. Typically, none of them stuck so he never bothered to think of them as permanent. He just watched over them as long as they were part of the group.

He stared at Becks, trying to remember her. She wouldn't have looked then like she looked now, anyway. Now she was tall and had a woman's body. Plus she had a lot of tattoos. So trying to figure out who she'd been back then was a waste of time anyway.

She sure was pretty now, though. Even with smoke smudging her face and body and hair.

"Sorry about your shop, Becks," Kal said.

She shrugged. "It's okay. But I need to get in there and get my stuff."

"It should be safe enough soon that you can do a walk-through," Rafe said. "Shouldn't it, Lieutenant?"

Jackson nodded. "As long as there's no more smoke lingering inside and no chance of a fire sparking."

Becks gave him the kind of head-to-toe inspection that made him wonder what was on her mind. She was still probably pissed off about him hauling her outside. What else could it be? He really couldn't tell from her expression.

Not that it should matter to him if she was angry. He'd done his job.

"What about upstairs?" she asked. "I live up there."

"Don't know," Jackson said. "I'll take you up there."

"I can go up on my own."

Again with the attitude. "No, actually, you can't."

"Lieutenant's right," Rafe said. "It's not safe for you to be anywhere in the building on your own right now."

"Rafe, grab Rodriguez and do a walk-through of the building and make sure it's clear for Ms.—"

He realized he had no idea what her last name was. Which fell in line with not remembering her.

"Benning," Rafe said.

Okay. At least Rafe was on the ball. "Ms. Benning to get in there and gather up her possessions."

"Yes, sir." Rafe turned to Becks and did a quick grab of her hand. "It's all gonna be okay."

She nodded and smiled at Rafe. "Sure. Thanks."

After Rafe and Tommy went inside, he started to turn away to direct the guys for cleanup.

"You really don't remember me."

He leveled his gaze on her. "It was a long time ago."

She didn't look hurt, just curious. "There weren't that many of us. And we always stayed close."

He sighed. "Look. Kids came in and out of our group all the time. Some stayed for a week, some for months. But eventually, you all moved on."

"And what you're saying is you didn't care about any of us enough to remember."

"I didn't say that."

"So you do remember all the other kids, and it's just me?"

"I didn't say that, either."

"Then what *are* you saying, Jackson?"

What was it about this woman that made every conversation with her an argument?

"I'm saying it was a tough time for all of us back then, Becks. And I'm sorry, but I don't remember you."

"All clear inside and upstairs," Rafe said as he came back outside. "Windows are all open and smoke has cleared out."

"So I can go in?" Becks asked.

"Yeah," Rafe said. "But I need to warn you it's kind of a mess. You should prepare yourself."

"I'll take her," Jackson said. "You and the other guys can wrap up out here."

Rafe nodded. "Yes, sir."

He turned to Becks. "You ready to go in?"

"Sure."

He started, and she hesitated. So he turned and saw her staring into the giant black hole of the doorway.

He realized everything she owned was probably in there, and probably damaged. He'd seen people crumble when faced with that reality. Becks was still standing. He walked back to her.

"One step at a time. You can do this."

She gave him a quick nod. "Yeah."

He led her through the door and turned on his flashlight to high beam. "Power's been turned off and will stay that way until the electrical has been repaired. A short inside the wall somewhere caused the smoke. You're lucky a fire didn't break out. This could have been a lot worse, you know."

Becks surveyed the room. Since the windows were now open, at least there was some light. Not that it helped much since everything seemed to be covered in dark gray ash.

"This isn't as bad as some places I've seen," Jackson said.

"Really? Because it looks shitty to me."

"I'm sure it does. But the damage is mostly to the structure. Walls, and internally. The owner will have to have it fixed."

Becks snorted. "Yeah, I'm sure he'll be all over that. Like never." That asshole Dave wouldn't even replace a broken light fixture. This? He'd never fix this. She doubted he even had the place insured.

As she took in a breath, the smell of smoke permeated the air. That same smoke had likely coated everything in her shop.

She'd clean it up. And fortunately most of her equipment was kept in containers, so hopefully it had been spared the smoke damage.

She opened the door leading to the stairs, hoping the loss would be limited to the business. But the odor of smoke and the gray clingy ash continued up the stairs. When she opened the door to her apartment, it was better, but the smoke had made its way up here as well.

"Not as bad," Jackson said. "But smoke rises and infiltrates. You still have damage up here."

She could see that. She picked up her favorite sweater that she'd tossed over the back of the kitchen chair. She lifted it to her nose and immediately threw it down. It reeked of smoke.

Rafe had made his way upstairs. "Hey, how's it going?"

Becks turned to face him, then gave a casual shrug. "Everything I own smells of smoke."

He nodded. "I know how to get that smoke smell out of your clothes. It's easy."

"Thanks. What about everything else?"

"It's just smoke damage, and all of it can be repaired. You have insurance, right?"

She nodded at Rafe. "For my business, yeah. But I don't own the building, and right now I have no place to work." She looked around at her apartment. It was small, but it had been perfect for her. "And apparently no place to live, either."

"Oh, that sucks," Rafe said, then offered up a fast smile. "Hey, you could bunk with us for a while, couldn't she, Jackson?"

Jackson blinked. "Uhh . . ."

Rafe turned to Becks. "One of our roommates just got married and moved down to Miami, so we have an extra bedroom available. We have a big house with a huge garage where you could store all your stuff. And it's got three bathrooms, so you could have one to yourself."

Becks shifted her gaze over to Jackson, who looked as if he'd just swallowed something that tasted terrible. Which meant he didn't want her there.

"I don't think that would be a good idea," she said. "You don't even know me."

"What? Come on. We've known you forever, Becks. We used to all camp out together. I mean, yeah, it's been a while, but you can trust us."

She laughed. "I wasn't talking about me trusting you."

"Why? Are you untrustworthy?"

She looked over at Jackson. "No. But . . . never mind. This will never work."

Jackson shrugged. "Up to you."

She didn't know how much more not into it Jackson could be. But what she did know was that there was no way she was moving into their house.

Then again, as she looked over her apartment, a sense of utter desolation rained over her.

Where did she plan to sleep tonight? She knew people who would probably let her stay a night, maybe two. That would solve her immediate problem. But she'd constantly be hopping from one place to another. And her number-one plan needed to be finding another place to set up her shop. She couldn't do that if she was homeless.

She'd been homeless before. It wasn't her idea of a great time.

She had an offer, and she needed to be smart enough to take them up on it. It wouldn't take her long to find a new shop and a new place to live, especially if she didn't have to worry about a roof over her head.

"Come on, Jackson," Rafe said. "She needs us."

Jackson looked at her.

She would not beg. She had never begged and she wasn't going to start now.

"Come stay with us," Jackson said.

"Fine. I'll take you up on your offer. Thanks."

Rafe grinned. "Awesome. It'll just be like old times again. Only this time, we're not sleeping outside. It'll be fun, Becks."

"Yeah, just like old times."

Only this time the guy she'd had a crush on when she was a budding teenager didn't remember her.

So fun.

CHAPTER 3

AFTER PACKING UP WHATEVER SHE THOUGHT WAS NEC-
essary for both work and personal survival, Becks loaded up her
truck. Kal had given her their address and directions. Fortunately,
her phone had been in the back pocket of her shorts, so at least
she'd managed to salvage that.

She stopped at the grocery store, figuring the least she could
do was buy some food for the guys as a way of thanks. After that
she headed over to the house.

It was a sprawling two-story house with cream-colored brick,
dark blue shutters and a nice-sized front lawn with tall trees. The
wide front porch was welcoming. This place wasn't at all the
shitty frat-boy-type house she envisioned them living in.

She pulled into the spacious drive and parked, got out and
grabbed her backpack. She took out her phone and punched in
the code Kal had given her to open the main garage door since it
was a three-car garage. When the door went up, she cracked a
smile.

There was plenty of room and the garage was well organized.

No junk was tossed around. Obviously the guys took care of their space. She appreciated that since she did the same with her stuff.

She went back to her truck and grabbed the boxes she'd put all her work equipment in, tucking all of them against one of the walls where her things would be out of the way of anything the guys would be doing in the garage.

She'd already moved her chairs and tables and some of the bigger items to a storage building, since they'd take up a lot of space. Hopefully they wouldn't be there more than a month since she didn't want to pay for the storage longer than that.

She took out the bags of groceries and went into the house.

Wow. The house was open, with a nice kitchen, a big living room and a good-sized table where plenty of people could crowd around and eat.

Considering the outside of the house, this wasn't a new build, but everything inside spoke of having been remodeled. She wondered who had done that.

Bedrooms were upstairs, but the first thing to do was unpack the groceries. She was surprised to find the fridge and pantry fairly well stocked, and not with junk food. There were vegetables and meat and some fairly nice seasonings. These guys weren't at all like she expected. Most dudes she knew lived sparsely, food-wise. Clearly these guys liked to eat. So did she, so they'd get along just fine.

She unpacked the groceries and put them away, then went out to her truck to grab her bag of clothes. She found the laundry room just inside the garage, so she started a load immediately since everything smelled like smoke. Hopefully the concoction that Rafe had told her about would remove the smell.

In addition to the address, the directions and the keypad code, Rafe had texted her the layout of the house, including which room would be hers. She made her way upstairs, turned left and opened the first door. She opened the shutters to let some light in. The room wasn't huge, but she didn't need much. It had a dresser and a nightstand and a decent-sized closet. There was a bathroom attached to this room. Convenient and private.

She liked that, and it was way more than she expected.

The queen-sized bed was stripped bare, but she found pillows, sheets and a quilt in the linen closet in the hall. After she made the bed, she went downstairs to grab her toiletries and set those up in the bathroom. There was no tub, but she never took baths anyway. The stand-up shower suited her just fine, plus it had a nice rainfall showerhead.

She went back downstairs and wandered, finding another living space with multiple leather sofas, a huge TV and some gaming equipment.

Sweet.

From the kitchen, French doors led to a covered patio that contained a shiny grill. Chairs were scattered around one hell of an amazing pool.

Wow. She had no idea if the guys owned this place or just rented it, but it was nicely renovated and had beautiful dark wood floors, good furniture, an abundant amount of windows to let in lots of light and plenty of usable living space so that four people wouldn't feel like they were constantly running into each other.

This place was exceptional, and nothing like what she'd expected. There were even living plants scattered around the house. And the best part about that was that they looked well-tended.

Their mom, maybe? Because she'd never known a guy who took good care of houseplants.

She could get used to living here. But it would only be temporary. The first thing she had to do was find a new workspace, because she knew her landlord. It took him months to get a light fixture repaired in the shop. Between his laziness, his cheapness and however long it would take insurance to settle the claim, she couldn't be out of work that long. She knew she was probably going to lose that location for her shop, which meant she'd have to look for a new permanent location.

That would be her first priority. Since the guys—or Rafe and Kal at least—had offered up this place as a temporary landing spot, she had a roof over her head for the moment. Not having to worry about where she was going to sleep at night was helpful.

She knew how to stay out of people's way. She'd learned that long ago in foster care. The smaller you could make yourself, the less likely you'd get noticed. And if they didn't notice you, you might not get in trouble, and even better, you might not get booted out onto the streets again.

But for tonight, at least, she had a bed to sleep in, and a washer and dryer to clean her smoke-filled clothes.

And speaking of smoke, she reeked of it, so the next thing on her agenda would be to take herself up to that very nice bathroom and scrub herself clean. She'd stopped at the convenience store first thing to wash the smudges off her face, just so she wouldn't scare anyone in the grocery store. But now she craved a shower and a hard-core loofah so she could scrub the top layer of her skin off and probably do several hair washings to get the smoke smell out.

Then she could get some things done.

CHAPTER 4

AFTER SHIFT ENDED THE NEXT MORNING, JACKSON DE-
cided to head home to check on their houseguest. Kal and Rafe
were going out to breakfast with a few of the other guys, so they'd
show up sometime later.

He pulled into the driveway and saw Becks's truck parked
there. He assumed it was her truck since he didn't recognize it. He
was assuming she hadn't invited her crew of friends over to party
while they were on shift—or at least she better not have.

He walked into the garage and laid his bag down, then opened
the door into the house and smelled something cooking. Whatever it was, it smelled good. He supposed she'd made herself at
home and took advantage of the well-stocked fridge.

Figured.

Becks was just pulling something out of the oven. When she
turned and saw him, she jerked in surprise.

She laid the casserole on the kitchen island and pulled the
earbuds out of her ears.

"Jesus, Jackson. I almost dropped this."

"Sorry. I didn't mean to scare you."

He noticed the house was empty. So no crew of hers crashing at his house.

"It's okay." She looked around him and down the hall. "Where are the other guys?"

"They stopped to eat."

"Oh. Well, before I came here yesterday I went to the grocery store, figuring you didn't have a lot of stuff in your fridge. Clearly I was wrong about that. Anyway, I made you breakfast." She cleared her throat. "All of you."

Okay, so he'd been wrong about her using up their food. "You didn't have to do that."

"I wanted to. You were all so nice about letting me stay here. I appreciate it." She swiped her hands on her shorts. "I thought you'd come off shift hungry. Are you hungry?"

His stomach growled so loud at the smell of whatever it was Becks had made, he was surprised she hadn't heard it. "I could eat. But I need a shower first. We just came off a call right before shift ended. Do you mind?"

"Of course not. I'll just slide this back in the oven to keep it warm."

"Thanks. It won't take me long."

He went into his room and shut the door, staring at the closed door for a minute.

Yeah, he'd misjudged her. No crew. She hadn't eaten all their food. In fact, she'd bought food. And cooked for them.

But still, having Becks here was . . . weird.

Not because she was a woman, but because she was part of his past. She seemed all right. Normal. Not fucked-up like a lot of them got after living on the streets.

Then again, he'd known her for a sum total of about twenty minutes and had shared nothing more than a handful of words with her, so what did he really know about her?

Nothing. And yet he'd let his brothers convince him to let her stay at their place.

Stupid move.

He stripped and got into the shower, scrubbed down and rinsed off, then got out, dragging his fingers through his hair as he stared at himself in the mirror, searching for answers about Becks.

"Only way you find out anything about her is to go talk to her."

He hoped like hell she didn't want to talk about the old days. Because as far as he was concerned, that shit was in the past.

He didn't like talking about the past. Or thinking about it.

He pulled on a pair of shorts and a T-shirt and left his room. When he came downstairs he noticed she'd set the table. It looked nice. Smelled even better and there were all kinds of food. Like . . . a lot of food. Becks was sitting at the kitchen island, legs crossed. She hadn't noticed him yet so he took a few seconds to ogle her long legs. She had tattoos running down both arms and a couple on her neck that he couldn't really see all that well since her blond hair was down and loose and damn, was her hair pretty now that she'd cleaned up. It fell in loose waves around her shoulders and he wondered if it was as soft as it looked. For some reason he itched to run his fingers through her hair.

He shook his head and came into the room.

She looked up from her phone. "Oh. Hey." She caught him looking at the food extravaganza she'd set up. She slid off the bar stool. "Sorry. I know guys like to eat a lot and fighting fires probably makes you really hungry. And I thought it would be the three of you."

She was nervous. He could tell by the way she bounced up and down on the balls of her feet while simultaneously chewing on her bottom lip. This couldn't be easy for her.

"It's okay. It's great, really. I'm hungry. What can I do to help?"

"Nothing. Let me pull the casserole out of the oven and we're ready to eat. Go ahead and take a seat wherever it is you usually sit, of course."

Yeah, she was really nervous. And she hadn't run off with the big-screen TV overnight, so he supposed she was okay. So far. He pulled out a chair and then waited while she brought the casserole over and set it in the center of the table.

She stared at him. "You're not sitting?"

"I'm holding this chair out for you to sit."

Her brows lifted. "Oh. Well, that's gentlemanly of you."

"My mom taught me—all of us guys, really," he said after she took her seat and he took his. "When we showed up at their place it wasn't like we came loaded with manners. Like, any manners. We were pretty much uncivilized."

She gave him a knowing smile and nodded. "I know. My foster parents—the ones who took me in after you all disappeared—did much the same for me."

He wanted to ask, but at the same time that was the past. And the past was always better left there since you couldn't do much to change it. So instead, he scooped up some casserole onto his plate and said, "This looks really good. Thanks for cooking."

"You're welcome. I don't mind cooking, by the way. It relaxes me."

He filled his plate with fruit salad and an English muffin. "And, what? Tattooing makes you tense?"

She had put food on her plate, too. "Not tense, really. I love what I do. It's just detail work, so it's time-consuming and creates tension in my shoulders and neck. Cooking is a way for me to let go of all that bodily tension. That and yoga."

She had a lean body. She was currently wearing shorts and a tank, showcasing her long, tan legs. He could imagine her stretched out on the floor doing all those stretchy moves. Not that he was thinking about her body at all.

"I've never tried yoga. I don't think my body bends that way."

She laughed, and the sound was like beautiful music.

"A lot of guys say that. You don't have to be bendy, Jackson. The more you get into it, the more flexible you'll get."

He took a forkful of the casserole, chewed, then swallowed. "I'll pass. This is really good. There's spinach in here?"

She nodded. "Yes. Eggs, sausage, along with mushrooms, Gruyère and Parmesan cheeses and garlic."

He could have eaten the entire casserole himself. In fact, he went for a second helping.

"Now I'm glad my brothers aren't here."

"Why?"

"More food for me."

She smiled. "I'm so happy you like it."

He leaned back in the chair. "So now that you're out of your shop, what's next for you?"

She laid her napkin on the table. "I have some appointments set up today to look at storefronts to rent for my business."

"That's good."

"I appreciate you letting me stay here. I promise not to take advantage. Obviously getting my business back up and running is my first priority. As soon as I can get that going, my next job will be to find a new place to live."

She rattled that off as if he'd busted in here demanding she pack up and get out tomorrow. Having been homeless and fostered before, he knew the feeling of being unsettled, of feeling like you didn't belong.

It sucked.

"Becks, the bedroom's yours for as long as you need it."

He caught the way her shoulders dropped, as if she'd been tight with tension.

"Thanks. But still, I'll try to get this done as soon as possible."

"Get what done?"

Kal came in, Rafe a few steps behind him.

"Hey, who cooked?" Rafe asked.

"Becks did."

"No kidding? It smells amazing." Kal grabbed a plate from the cabinet and brought it to the table, then scooped some of the casserole onto it.

Jackson frowned. "Didn't you just eat?"

"Yeah. So? This looks great."

Jackson shook his head, then got up and started clearing his and Becks's plates from the table.

Becks went over to the kitchen and started cleaning dishes.

"Stop," he said. "You cooked. I'll clean up."

"I'm just earning my keep here," she said, taking the plates from him to load them in the dishwasher. "By the way, I can pay rent while I'm here. Though I don't intend to stay long. Like I said earlier, as soon as I find a new shop, I'll look for a place to live."

He picked up a pot but she wrested it away from him.

"I said I've got this," she said.

He pulled the pot away from her, then looked down at her. "If you're going to live with us, you need to learn the rules of the house. Everyone shares duties. From grocery shopping to cooking to cleaning. No one person does it all. Got it?"

She swiped her hands on the towel. "I was trying to be helpful."

"Don't try so hard."

She shrugged. "Whatever. Fine. I'll get out of the way."

She left the kitchen.

"The casserole is great, Becks," Kal said, hollering after her as she left the room.

Kal brought his plate and some of the dishes to the sink.

Rafe had been leaning against the island. He stared at Jackson, who was putting away the pot he'd just washed and dried.

"What?"

"What's your beef with her, man?" Rafe asked.

"Nothing."

"Then why do you have to act like such a dick? She was just being nice."

"Yeah," Kal said as he finished loading the dishwasher and closed it. "Plus, she cooks. Better than you or Rafe."

Kal shook his head and left the room.

Rafe looked at him. "True that. And you were harsh with her for no good reason. Or do you have a good reason for being uncomfortable with her being here?"

"No. I don't know. Maybe I just don't know her."

Rafe slanted a look at him. "Or maybe you've just conveniently forgotten who we all used to be back then. There were more than just the three of us, Jackson."

Rafe pushed off the island and left the room, leaving Jackson alone in the kitchen.

Jackson shook his head. Rafe didn't know what he was talking about. He knew exactly who he was then. Who they all were. He just didn't want to think about it, didn't want to constantly relive every damn minute, week, month and year of their lousy existence.

Why should he, when life now was pretty great? All he ever wanted to do was forget about the life they'd lived back then. Was that so bad?

He looked around the kitchen, thinking about everything Becks had done for them this morning.

She could have just come here, tossed down her shit and crashed. She could have been gone this morning when he'd gotten here, off to do her own thing. For herself.

Instead, she'd grocery shopped. Cooked. Served him breakfast.

She didn't really know them, either. She knew who they used to be, but not who they were now. Other than the guys inviting her to stay with them, for all she knew they were a trio of total assholes now.

But she'd still cooked them breakfast. Paid for out of her own coin.

He folded the towel and draped it over the sink.

Okay, fine. Maybe he really was acting like a dick.

He went looking for her and found her in the laundry room, transferring clothes from the washing machine to the dryer.

"Hey, Becks."

She adjusted the setting on the dryer and pushed the button. "What."

"I'm sorry for being such an asshole just now."

She kept her focus on her task, pulling clothes out of the nearby basket to fold them. "It's fine. I know you don't want me here."

"That's not it."

She straightened and gave him a direct look. "Then what is it?"

He floundered for an answer, so he let his gaze drift to the empty trash bag. "Is that your luggage?"

She frowned. "What?"

He pointed to the small empty trash bag at her feet. "That bag."

"Oh. Yeah, sort of."

He looked around, but other than what she was pulling out of the dryer and what she'd just shoved in the washer, he didn't see anything else. "Where's the rest of your clothes?"

"I did a load yesterday. This is the last of it."

He blinked. "That's it?"

She looked at the trash bag and then up at him. "I travel light."

"I thought most women had deep closets filled with all kinds of clothes."

Her lips curved and she leaned into him. He inhaled the sweet scent of strawberries.

"I'm not most women, Jackson."

She skirted around him and walked away. He enjoyed the view of her incredibly sexy long legs and one very fine ass.

She was right about that—she was definitely not at all like most women.

CHAPTER 5

BECKS HAD SPENT TWO DAYS SEARCHING FOR COMMER-
cial space for her tattoo shop. Everything she'd looked at so far
had been either too small, the wrong location or too expensive.

She was starting to feel like Goldilocks. When she'd found the
original spot it had been a decent fit. Not perfect, but she knew
she'd never find perfect. All she wanted was a decent traffic location where she could pick up some walk-ins from the beach, some-
place that had parking for her customers and was in a good area
so her clients wouldn't feel like they'd get jumped late at night.

That wasn't too much to ask, was it?

So as she pulled up in the shopping center to check out the
latest location, she hoped this one was the right one.

She got out of her truck to check out her surroundings. It was
hot as bejesus, a bright sunny day so she kept her sunglasses on.

This place wasn't on the beach, which wasn't great. But it had
potential. There were other businesses surrounding it. She wandered up and down the center to see an insurance office, a bail
bondsman—okay, not awesome, as she realized the police station
and county jail were just down the road. She made a mental note

of that. She also saw a jewelry store, one closed shop, a craft store and a hair salon on the south side. Anchored in the middle was a grocery store, which meant good foot traffic. As she wandered toward the north side she noticed a fire engine pulling in.

Uh-oh. She felt a sense of déjà vu. She glanced around for smoke or a fire or, God forbid, someone sick or injured but didn't see anything. She really hoped no one was hurt.

When the engine pulled up next to her, she saw Jackson in the passenger seat.

She hadn't seen much of him—or the other guys—in the past couple of days. She'd tried her best to not be around while they were, instead either keeping to her room or staying out shopping around for a commercial rental.

He rolled the window down.

"What are you doing here?" she asked.

"Rafe saw you wandering. You checking a place out in this center?"

"I am."

Rafe leaned over. "Hey, Becks."

"Hey. Are you all doing something in this area?"

"We just worked a car wreck a few blocks over," Rafe said. "We were headed back to the station when we decided to stop for groceries and happened to see you. But we have a few minutes to help you check out a place."

"Oh. That's unnecessary."

Rafe looked to Jackson, who shrugged. "Sure, we can help you."

She had no idea what they thought they'd be looking at, but she supposed a second or third opinion wouldn't hurt.

"Sure."

She headed down the path toward the available building, not wanting to miss her appointment with her friend Margie who worked in commercial real estate rentals. She was so thankful she had Margie to help her find a new place.

So when she walked up to Margie Vasquez with her two-man firefighter escort, the woman's eyes widened.

"Uh, hi, Becks."

"Hey."

Margie motioned her head to the two hot men dressed in firefighter blue behind her, as if Becks didn't know they were there. Or that they were hot.

Not that Becks thought they looked hot or anything.

Oh, who was she kidding?

She tossed her thumb over her shoulder. "Margie, this is Jackson on my left and Rafe on my right. Guys, this is my friend Margie Vasquez."

Margie was a very attractive brunette with soulful brown eyes and a rocking curvy body. Men always gravitated to her because she had a killer smile to go with her dynamite rack and amazing legs. She was also one of the few people Becks trusted enough to call a friend.

Margie graced the guys with one of those smiles. "Nice to meet all of you. Shall we go inside?"

"Sure," Rafe said, leveling one of his own smiles in Margie's direction.

Jackson nodded and held the door as they walked in.

Margie hurried up next to Becks.

"Oh. My. God." Margie gave her the look. The one she gave her whenever one of them spotted an unbelievably good-looking guy, typically at a bar.

"I kind of know them from before."

"Before what?" Margie whispered.

Since both the guys were within earshot, she said, "I'll tell you later."

"I'll hold you to that." Margie turned so she faced all of them. "This is a nice-sized shop with a good front window to attract customers, plus excellent storage in the back and enough space for you to do your work and even hire additional help if you're interested."

Becks pictured her reception area in the front. She didn't hire any staff since she was a one-woman operation, but she kept a table in the front to give the appearance of having someone run the administrative operation of her business. Typically she kept a planner there to write down walk-in appointments she made that she couldn't fulfill that day. Then she'd move those appointments into her phone calendar once she got home. Plus she kept all her paper and sketching stuff at the desk because walk-ins often wanted the opportunity to draw their tattoo ideas.

Behind that she needed a room for her chair and the client's chair and an area to move. And then storage.

"The space is decent," she said. "But I don't know, Margie. The feel is off."

"The lighting is crap," Rafe said. "This place looks like it hasn't been updated in ages."

Jackson nodded, then crouched down to check out the wiring that ran along the baseboard. He pulled out his voltage detector.

He straightened. "Wire's frayed across here. And it's a live current. It's a fire hazard."

"I had no idea," Margie said. "I'm sorry, Becks. I would never show you a space that wasn't up to par."

"I know you wouldn't."

"I'll notify the owner of the space," Margie said. "And I'll let him know the fire department was here to inspect it."

"Oh, we'll let him know, too," Rafe said.

"Good. He should know better than to offer up shoddy property. Believe me, I'll make it known around my circle as well. This guy owns several properties, so my associates and I will be doing more careful inspections of his spaces."

"Anytime you want us to take a look, just let us know," Jackson said.

Margie looked surprised. "Thank you, Jackson. That's very nice."

"We don't mind at all," Rafe said. "Saves us from having to put a fire out later. And possibly saves lives."

Becks thought it was so nice that Jackson offered to check over the properties. Then again, like Rafe said, if it prevented fires breaking out, then it benefited everyone.

"Okay, so a big fat no on this property," Margie said. "Sorry, Becks."

"It's okay."

"I'll keep looking for you. Hopefully I'll have more places you can check out this afternoon."

"That would be great. Thanks."

She turned to walk out, but Margie grabbed her hand. "Oh, and that thing we need to discuss?"

Becks frowned. "What thing?"

"You know."

Margie absolutely failed at trying to be subtle when she motioned with her eyes and her head toward Jackson and Rafe, which totally mortified her.

Then again, her friend had never learned the use of subtlety.

"Oh. Right. Sure. I'll text you later."

"You'd better."

She hugged Margie, then walked out, Jackson and Rafe behind her.

"I'm sorry it didn't work out for you," Rafe said.

Becks shrugged. "Thanks. Something will come along. I'm looking every day."

"What was the thing Margie was referring to that had to do with Rafe and me?"

Jackson had to ask, didn't he? Becks wasn't big on subtlety, either, so she figured she'd just blurt it out.

"She thinks you're both hot and she wants the lowdown on

how I know both of you. Since it's kind of a long story, I told her I'd fill her in later."

Rafe laughed. "Awesome. She thinks we're hot, huh?"

Jackson rolled his eyes. "Come on, Romeo, time to join the rest of the crew at the grocery store."

"Yeah, yeah. Later, Becks."

"Later, Rafe. See you, Jackson."

He gave her a nod and what one might call a partial smile. She didn't know. Did the guy ever smile?

"Bye, Becks."

She had to find a place soon. The guys had been generous in letting her stay at their place, but she didn't want to take advantage. Which reminded her, she needed to discuss paying rent. Because she wasn't a freeloader.

Jackson's gaze lingered on hers, questioningly. She wondered why. Maybe he was thinking she was taking advantage of her current living situation. God, she hoped not.

But finally he turned around and walked away. She exhaled, though she didn't know if she'd held her breath because he was hot and he made her nervous, or because she didn't want him to think the wrong thing about her motivations. Likely a combination of both.

She had to wait there and watch them walk away, but admittedly, it was only Jackson's butt she stared at.

CHAPTER 6

JACKSON WANDERED THE GROCERY STORE AFTER THEY caught up with the rest of the team. He'd gone up and down three aisles before he figured out he'd missed six items because his mind had been on Becks and not on the grocery list.

Damn.

He could still see that worried look on her face right before they'd left her. What was she worried about? He could guess that it had something to do with finding a place for her business. That was logical. She'd been displaced, forced out not only from her home but also from making her living. That would scare anyone.

But was it also something more?

He shook it off and checked the list, making himself pay attention to the aisle he was in. He tossed pancake mix into the cart.

What the hell did it even matter if she was upset about something? Becks wasn't his responsibility. She was just someone staying at their house for a short—very short—period of time. He shouldn't even care about her.

Except there was something about the way she'd looked at him. It had been almost . . . a plea.

But a plea for what? For help? For understanding?

What the fuck. She'd probably just shot him a Go Fuck Yourself look and all this was in his head. Because in the short time he'd known Becks, the last thing she seemed to need from anyone was help.

The best thing to do was forget about her and focus on groceries. He whipped around the corner to find Rafe and the other guys all piled up in—of course—the cereal aisle.

He shook his head. "You can't live on Rice Krispies and Cocoa Puffs."

Rafe arched a brow. "Maybe you can't. But we could. As long as there's also mac 'n' cheese."

The diet some of these morons followed was ridiculous. "Did anyone buy meat?"

Rafe nodded. "We got pork chops and potatoes to mash for tonight's dinner."

"Plus fresh spinach," Mitchell said.

"Sounds good to me. Let's get out of here before any more boxes of cereal find their way into the cart."

Ginger Davidson, one of the firefighters, made her way alongside Jackson. "You do realize you can never have enough cereal."

Since Ginger was nearly six feet tall, he didn't have to look down to meet her gaze. "Et tu, Ginger?"

She shrugged. "I've got four-year-old twin boys at home. We know our cereal."

He laughed. "I'll just bet you do."

They checked out—fortunately with just two boxes of cereal—and loaded the groceries in the truck. Typically they'd leave the grocery shopping up to the ladder crew since they also did most of the cooking, but the ladder team had a fire call first thing this morning. Plus, Jackson wasn't always fond of their food choices.

When they got back they unloaded the groceries. Jackson went into his office to do some paperwork while the rest of the crew put the groceries away. As lieutenant, he was lucky to get out of some of the more menial chores. Not so lucky was the amount of paperwork that went into the higher rank. He had staffing issues to deal with along with requisition orders for supplies and equipment and coordinating all of that with the two other shifts that worked at Fire Rescue Station 6.

And in addition to his duties as lieutenant, he also had leadership responsibilities. When he'd been promoted to lieutenant he'd welcomed all those obligations, no matter how heavy that load often felt on his shoulders.

He'd come up with a lot of these men and women, had started as a probationary firefighter at age twenty. Now, at twenty-eight, he'd worked his ass off to be where he was. So sometimes he had to be an asshole to the people he called his friends, his coworkers and his peers, as well as his two brothers. But that was just the way it was.

When his dad had first offered him the promotion after their lieutenant had been promoted to captain, it had felt both exhilarating and horrifying. The last thing he'd wanted to do was alienate his brothers, or in any way make them think that Dad preferred one of them over the other. Because Jackson absolutely knew that wasn't the case.

He should have known better than to worry. Dad had sat down with both Rafe and Kal and told them that Jackson had more experience and had earned the job, and he loved them all equally. And that their time would come.

Neither Rafe nor Kal had an issue with Jackson's promotion. And they'd all gone out to celebrate the night he'd officially received his lieutenant's bars.

At home they treated him like a brother, with all the accompanying irreverence, as they should. On the job, they gave him the respect that went with the position.

He couldn't have asked for better brothers.

Once he finished his paperwork, he came out to the kitchen. Something smelled good.

"What's for lunch?" he asked.

"Tuna salad sandwiches, kale chips or potato chips, cottage cheese and mango slices." Ginger slid a sandwich his way.

The ladder squad had returned, so they sat as well. He was hungry so he filled his plate and took a seat at the long dining table along with everyone else. The chatter was nonstop, as always. This was where he liked to listen to his team dig into their personal lives.

First they got a rundown on the call the ladder squad had taken, and then it was a free-for-all of personal convo. Most of them were either married or in a relationship, with the exception of Jackson and his brothers and one of the guys who was in the middle of a divorce. Fortunately, Mitchell Hendricks had a strong family support system that was getting him through the divorce. And though their marriage broke up in a bad way, Mitchell and his wife both loved their two daughters and neither of them wanted to drag their kids into it. Jackson hoped they could work out their other issues and finalize the divorce before either Mitchell or Deb got hurt any more than they already had been.

Then he listened to his two EMTs, Miguel Acosta and Adrienne Smith, talk in roundabout ways about the fact that they absolutely were not dating each other, when everyone in the firehouse damn well knew they were. So that was fun. Uncomfortable for Acosta and Smith, but fun for everyone else to see the two of them squirm.

His team was a pro squad and they never let personal issues get in the way of getting the job done. He knew that whatever was going on with Miguel and Adrienne would stay outside the firehouse. They'd never do anything to jeopardize their jobs. If it did, he'd intervene. Right now he didn't have to. If it got serious or led to marriage, one of them would have to switch to either another shift or a different firehouse.

He made a mental note to keep an eye on the progression of that relationship in case he needed to step in and have a talk with them. He probably wouldn't have to. His team was professional. He didn't doubt for a second that if Miguel and Adrienne got serious, they'd come to him.

His dad never took lunch with the team, because he said he always felt like he intimidated them and they'd clam up. He wanted his lieutenant and captain to take a leadership role and bond with the firefighters, and the battalion chief would just get in the way, so Dad always ate in his office. It took a few years on the squad for Jackson to realize his dad must have the loneliest job in the firehouse.

After listening to their tough-as-nails captain, Kendall Mathias, gush about how his one-year-old little boy had taken his first steps the other day, Jackson got up and took his plate down the hall and knocked on his dad's office door.

"Come on in."

His dad was just finishing up his sandwich.

Jackson laid his plate on his lap. "Thought I'd keep you company."

His father frowned at him. "You think I'm lonely in here?"

"You eat by yourself in here every day."

"Most times your mother keeps me company."

"She does?"

"Yeah. We try to synchronize our lunch hours so we can eat together and FaceTime on the phone. Today, though, she has court."

"Hopefully changing another kid's life like she helped change ours."

His dad laughed. "You know your mother. She's been tirelessly advocating for children as long as I've known her."

And the reason that Jackson, Rafe and Kal had amazing parents. If it hadn't been for Laurel Donovan's connections as a social worker, and the way she'd relentlessly advocated for all of them to become a family, first as foster kids and then through adoption, they might never have been adopted by Josh and Laurel.

They got lucky, and not a day went by that Jackson wasn't grateful for it.

He looked over at his dad, who still looked as robust and young as he had that day fourteen years ago when he'd swept in and scooped a scrawny teenaged Jackson out of that blazing house.

Never one to get close to people, Jackson could still remember clinging to Josh, not wanting to let go of him. Josh had stayed with him as the EMTs had given him oxygen and checked him over.

He'd been tough on the streets, but at that moment, Jackson had been a scared, lonely kid, frightened for his brothers as well as himself.

On the street, they'd managed. In the system and separated, who knew what would happen to them?

Josh had told him he'd be there for him. He'd held his hand and he'd shown up at the emergency room. So had Laurel.

Jackson had told them about Rafe and Kal and how they were brothers—only not related by blood. How they had no one but each other. And how long they'd survived on the streets. Laurel had patted his shoulder and smoothed her warm hand over his cheek and told him not to worry, that she'd take care of everything.

He could still remember the way Laurel had looked at Josh that day in the ER. And Josh had nodded at her and she'd smiled at him.

Laurel had the sweetest smile, the kind of smile that could put anyone at ease.

And then suddenly all three of them had ended up at Josh and Laurel's house. Foster kids at first. And then the adoption came, and it had surprised the hell out of Jackson. It had also changed their lives forever.

"You falling asleep over there?"

Jackson blinked. "Oh. No. Just thinking about the day I met you."

His dad smiled. "A bad day that ended up being a good day for all of us."

That was always how his dad described it. "Yes, it was."

The alarm sounded, and Jackson got up. He went through the kitchen, dropped his plate into the sink and headed into the vehicle bay. He stepped out of his shoes and slid into his boots and turnout gear, then climbed into the truck. Sirens blaring, they headed out the door.

Jackson studied the report coming in so he could relay it to his team. "Multivehicular accident on I-95. Injuries reported and passengers may be trapped in vehicles. Get your game faces on."

"You got that, Lieutenant." Tommy made the turn onto the interstate.

Navigating traffic after an accident was always a pain in the ass. Getting there in a hurry was critical, but Tommy was the best at getting it done. He didn't let anything or anyone get in his way.

They got to the accident scene in record time. Jackson jumped out to do a quick triage so he could make assignments. First thing they needed to do was rescue anyone who might be pinned inside a vehicle.

"Davidson," he shouted to Ginger.

"Sir."

"You and Hendricks check for hazardous fluids and get that cleaned up."

"Yes, sir."

There was one upright vehicle with front-end damage. "Rodriguez, bring Acosta and Smith with you and check that other vehicle."

Tommy gave him a quick shout of acknowledgment.

Jackson was already on his way to the other vehicle lying on its side. "Rafe, you're with me."

Rafe quick-stepped up in time with Jackson.

They both crouched down on the driver's side. The windshield was cracked, but intact. The young male driver was unconscious. He didn't see anyone else in the vehicle.

"We aren't getting to him this way."

"We need to pull out the windshield to get into the vehicle," Rafe said. "Climbing on top to get to the driver's side would be too dangerous."

Jackson didn't like that idea because there was no way to cover the driver to protect him from the shattered glass. But sometimes there was no best-case scenario. They had to get to the victim as quickly as possible but also immobilize the victim's neck and spine in case he had a c-spine injury.

Evaluation on the scene had to be done in a matter of seconds. Jackson didn't have the luxury of time to stand around and ponder the situation.

Unfortunately, in this instance, every solution sucked.

"Let's get this vehicle upright," Jackson said. "We need to get inside and stabilize the victim first. Rafe, break into the backseat passenger window and climb in there to stabilize the victim."

"On it," Rafe said, darting off to get the ladder.

The clock was ticking. Every second the victim stayed unconscious in that car, there was more of a chance of further complications.

"Evac helicopter has been notified and it's on the way," Smith said. "The other victim is stable and a secondary ambulance is already here to transport her."

He nodded to Adrienne. "Thanks. You and Miguel stand by.

As soon as we turn this car over and get the door open, I want you to be ready to extricate the victim."

"We'll be ready."

Fortunately there were plenty of highway patrol officers at the scene to keep traffic away. Miguel had notified the officers that a helicopter was en route, so a landing area had been cleared.

Rafe and a few of the others set up the ladder. Rafe busted the back window and climbed in while the others prepared to move the vehicle back into its rightful position. This involved struts and chain and a lot of man- and womanpower.

In the meantime, Rafe assessed the victim, communicating his vitals to Adrienne.

His vitals were okay. Not great, but manageable and nowhere near the critical stage, which gave Jackson a lot of relief. The victim was starting to come around, which was a good sign.

Rafe attached the c-collar and the team was in place. All they had to do was push the vehicle back enough to get to the driver's-side door. Then they could pull the door and the roof and get him out.

Now that he was at least partially conscious, Rafe was talking to the injured passenger. No idea if the guy could hear him, but a reassuring voice could sometimes calm an accident victim.

All the pieces were in place.

"Now," Jackson said. "Start the winches and pull the car."

The struts and winches did their job and started moving the vehicle, lifting it toward his team, drawing the driver's side off the ground.

"Slow and steady," Jackson said, keeping an eye on Rafe, who had shifted to the far side to provide counterbalance to the vehicle.

Once they had enough clearance to get to the door, he halted the winches and they dove in and did the rest of the job, cutting the roof and spreading the door open. After that it was easy to get the driver out in a safe manner. An IV was started, vitals were checked and they stabilized him enough that Jackson felt like the guy would make it. It looked like his leg was broken and who knows what was going on internally, but they got him out of the car alive, and considering what a clusterfuck that accident had been, Jackson called that a win.

Now he could exhale.

By then the medevac chopper had arrived and the victim could be transported to the hospital.

They finished cleanup and loaded the truck, then headed back to the fire station.

"Inventory all the supplies, clean up the truck, and I want to see a report on the rescue truck," he advised the team. "We need to refill the meds before the next run, so do an inventory for me so I can grab those for you."

Everyone nodded and dispersed to do their assigned tasks.

Standard procedure upon every return, and they all knew their jobs. He didn't need to tell them what to do. But it was also his job to tell them what to do.

Jackson, on the other hand, had reams of incident reports to write, so he stopped in the kitchen to grab a tall glass of ice water, then headed to his office, took a seat and started his paperwork.

Kal popped his head in the door. "Heard you had a gnarly rescue."

"Yeah. Could have been worse. Victim survived."

"That's good."

"How about you? Any action?"

"Yeah. I kicked Vassar's ass in Ping-Pong four times."

Jackson shook his head. "How about you spend some time in the training room?"

"Did that, too. Vassar and I checked off on three videos and one virtual training exercise. Then I kicked her ass in Ping-Pong."

He knew better than to think Kal would waste time. At least not all of his time. "Good."

"Pressman and Law are cooking up those pork chops," Kal said. "Should be ready soon. I'll give you a heads-up."

"Thanks."

He went back to his paperwork, burying himself in getting the reports done and signing off on the refill of the meds in the rescue truck. Before he knew it, Kal was popping his head in again to let him know dinner was ready.

At least they hadn't had another call and he'd finished his paperwork.

The one thing about his job that he liked was that the day went by fast. Even though a lot of that day consisted of filing reports and doing paperwork, it was still a job he loved doing.

He'd never thought he'd end up like this. Hell, when he was a kid he never thought he'd make it to adulthood. Yet here he was, taking a seat at the table with his fellow firefighters.

No place he'd rather be.

CHAPTER 7

WHILE THE GUYS WERE ON DUTY, BECKS HAD SPENT ALL of yesterday cleaning the house from top to bottom. Despite how nice the house was, it desperately needed a thorough cleaning. She could tell the guys only did the surface stuff, and she had much higher standards. So she'd swept, mopped, dusted and scoured the kitchen and all the bathrooms. The only thing she hadn't done was change the sheets on the guys' beds. They could wash their own sheets. She did notice, however, that they all made their beds, an admirable quality since a lot of dudes she knew didn't bother.

This morning she got up and grabbed a cup of coffee, then headed to the bathroom and took a nice long, hot shower, letting the water rain down over her. Her muscles were sore from all the scrubbing yesterday so she stayed in the shower longer than she normally would, but by the time she got out, she felt a lot more relaxed.

She combed out her hair and left it wet, put on a pair of shorts and a tank top and went downstairs, intending to drink her coffee and scroll through some of the properties Margie had said she would e-mail her this morning.

She was sitting at the island doing just that when she heard the garage door go up. The door opened and all three of the guys walked in.

"Morning, Becks," Kal said.

Rafe took a deep breath. "Hey, it smells fresh in here. What did you do?"

She scrolled through the links Margie had e-mailed her. "I cleaned the house yesterday."

"You really cleaned the house," Rafe said. "It sparkles."

"Didn't know we were that dirty," Jackson said, his voice low.

She lifted her attention from the list she'd been perusing. "I like a house superclean. Is that a problem?"

He shrugged. "No. But we do scrub things up around here."

Defensive much, Jackson? "I wasn't implying otherwise. And I'm sorry if you thought I was."

"Give her a break, Jackson," Kal said. "She cleaned. How about saying thanks? Or it looks great? Which, by the way, Becks. It does. So thanks."

Her lips lifted as she caught Kal's not-so-subtle dig. "You're welcome."

Rafe came downstairs. "The bathrooms look brand-new, Becks. You're a rock star."

"No big deal. It's my way of saying thanks for letting me crash here."

"And you think we're pigs."

She shot a glare at Jackson. "You're just not going to let this go, are you?"

"Let what go?"

The worst part was, he didn't even see it. She shook her head and slid off the bar stool, grabbing her phone. "I'm going to get dressed."

• • •

JACKSON WATCHED AS BECKS WALKED UP THE STAIRS, listening as she closed the door to her room. When he turned, he faced his two brothers, both of them sporting extremely pissed-off looks on their faces.

"What?"

"You're an asshole," Kal said.

"What did I do?"

"Why do you have to give her shit about everything she does?" Rafe asked. "She cleaned the house. Why is that such a big fucking issue with you?"

"And the other day it was her making breakfast," Kal said. "Like her cooking is some kind of a felony? Come on, Jackson, what's your beef with her?"

"I don't have a beef with her at all. I just thought the house looked fine."

"Yeah, we clean." Rafe ran his finger over the kitchen island. "Obviously she wanted to scrub it up even better than we do. So that's some crime?"

Kal went to the fridge and grabbed the orange juice. "It's like you've got a personal vendetta against her." He poured the juice into a glass and took a long swallow, then leaned against the counter. "Or maybe you're trying to get her mad enough that she'll split."

"No, that's not what I'm doing." He couldn't believe Rafe and Kal would even think that.

But he could see where they were coming from. First thing he'd done both mornings they'd come off shift was jump all over Becks. So maybe they had a point.

"Okay, fine," he said. "I'll go talk to her."

"You do that," Rafe said. "I'll make breakfast. Unless you've got something to say about that, too."

He grimaced as he made his way up the stairs. He'd deserved that one.

When he got to Becks's door, he paused before he knocked. Maybe she was taking a nap.

Bullshit, Jackson. It's eight thirty in the morning and you're stalling.

He sucked in a breath and knocked lightly. "Hey, Becks, you in there?"

It was a long few seconds before she answered with, "I haven't tied up the bedsheets and climbed out the window, if that's what you're thinking."

He cracked a smile. She had some sass. He liked that about her. He liked a lot of things about her. Walking through the door this morning and seeing her in her short shorts and tank top with her tanned skin showing off all those damned interesting tattoos made him want to get to know her body in ways he shouldn't want to.

But he still wanted to.

And maybe that was the problem.

"Can we talk?"

"Isn't that what we're doing?"

Still with the sass. "How about face-to-face?"

"Fine."

He heard her footsteps approaching the door, so he took a step back. When she opened it, she stared at him.

"So I thought about—"

"Really?" Becks shook her head. "A doorway conversation? I did shower this morning, Jackson, and I won't bite unless you ask me to. Come on in."

She turned her back on him and walked into the room.

No biting unless he asked her to? What the fuck was she trying to do to him? Now there were images rolling around in his head of her mouth on his . . . everything.

And then she invited him into her room?

Goddammit.

Get it together, Jackson.

He took a step into the room, surprised to see she'd totally changed everything in it. Then again, before there'd been an empty bed and a dresser. Now there was a pretty pink-and-yellow quilt and several pillows on the bed, and on the dresser there was a collection of—was that Princess Leia and Han Solo?

He stared, utterly transfixed at the objects on her dresser. "You collect *Star Wars* figures?"

Her chin lifted. "Is that something else you'd like to complain about?"

"No. I love *Star Wars*. Everything about *Star Wars*."

She walked up to the dresser to stand beside him. "Me, too. Except the prequels, which were utter crap."

"Agreed." She even had a mini Millennium Falcon. And a Death Star. It took everything in him not to pick up the figurines and play with them. So instead he turned to face her. "You constantly surprise me."

She opened her mouth, then closed it, the two of them locked in some kind of staring contest. Finally, she said, "I'm trying to decide if that's a compliment or an insult."

"It's a compliment. And considering the life I've led, no one and nothing surprises me."

"Oh. Then thanks." She moved around him and climbed onto the bed. "Come on, sit down and tell me what's on your mind."

Since there were no other places to sit, he assumed she was inviting him to sit on the bed with her. And considering the thoughts that he'd had about her a few minutes ago, he decided keeping his distance was a good idea. So he grabbed a spot on the far edge of the mattress.

She noticed, smirking. "I mentioned I don't bite, right? Or do you just not like women?"

"I like women just fine."

"Then it's me you don't like."

Why was she always so damned frustrating? He dragged his fingers through his hair. "Look, Becks. We got off on the wrong foot, and that's my fault. I'm protective over my family. We're tight. I guess I just wasn't prepared to have you stay here and I handled it badly. I'm sorry."

She studied him. Apparently she liked to do that and he found it . . . unsettling.

Then she shrugged. "It's okay. We have the same background, you know. So I get it. It's hard for people like us to trust strangers."

He settled in on the mattress more. "We're not exactly strangers."

She let out a soft laugh and picked up a book and a pencil from the nightstand. "Aren't we? You don't even remember me."

"But you remember me."

She had picked up a notepad and was busy writing or drawing something, so she didn't even look up at him when she said, "I remember everything about you, about that time." Then she lifted her head and their gazes met. "Every minute, every hour, every day."

"Tell me your clearest memory."

"Winter was always the worst. Not that we had the harshest winters here in Ft. Lauderdale. We were lucky. But some nights got cold and we'd huddle together. You guys would gather wood to start a fire in a trash can. Melinda was a few years older than me and she'd braid my hair so I could lean in closer to the fire without singeing my hair."

The first time he'd seen her that day of the fire at her shop, her hair had been covered in soot, her face partially covered by a bandana. Now her hair lay damp over her shoulders, the color a wild strawberry blond. Her eyes were a stunning blue and her lips were full. She wore no makeup and she was still the most beautiful woman he'd ever laid eyes on.

But who she was now wasn't who she'd been back when they were kids.

A memory struck him of a skinny little girl with her hair in a long blond braid down her back. She wore a beanie and an old tattered Dolphins hoodie. She loved that hoodie and said some day she was going to go to a football game as soon as she found parents.

"You ever get to go to a Dolphins game?"

Her lips curved, and her smile made the sky blue of her eyes sparkle.

Or maybe that was just his imagination.

"You do remember me."

He shrugged. "It's coming back to me. Parts of it, anyway."

"Did you suffer some kind of memory loss? Were you in an accident or something?"

"No. I just . . . don't think about it. The less I think about it, the less I remember of the time back then."

"So you deliberately chose to forget the past? Why?"

"Because it was a shit time in my life. Why would I want to relive it?"

She scooted forward, her top gaping open to reveal not only the creamy tops of her breasts but also a tempting glimpse of a heart-shaped tattoo. A broken heart.

"Who broke your heart?"

"What?" She looked down and then sat up straight. "Oh. That. The people who threw me out because they thought I was worthless."

His gut tightened. "Your parents."

"Yes. And you've evaded my question. Why would you want to throw away your past? It shaped you into who you are today."

"Actually, my adoptive parents shaped me into who I am today."

"Oh, I see. So before you were rescued in that fire you were, what? Shapeless? No personality? No background? No baggage?

No hurts, no emotions, no feelings? And after you were adopted by the Donovans your entire persona formed?"

He frowned, not liking the direction this conversation was going. He stood. "Anyway, I wanted to apologize for making you feel like you weren't welcome here. You are. And your cooking and your cleaning. Make yourself at home here. Do whatever makes you happy, Becks. Stay as long as you like. And I'll stay out of your way."

He turned to walk out but Becks met him at the door, her hand on his biceps. "I didn't take you for a runner, Jackson."

He looked down where her hand touched him. He realized the feel of her warm fingers on his flesh did things to him that he wanted more of. He also realized he wanted to kiss her. Which would be a huge mistake, because Becks was a part of his past. And other than his brothers, the past was dead to him.

"I'm not a runner, Becks. I just left the past where it belongs. Maybe you should think about doing the same thing. You can't move forward if you're continually looking backward."

She held his gaze. "And you can't create a place for yourself today if you haven't dealt with yesterday. I can make up bullshit platitudes, too."

Despite the fact he was royally pissed, he still wanted to kiss her. Which meant it was time to leave. He walked out of the room, realizing as he headed back downstairs that he was sweating.

What the hell was wrong with him? And what was it about Becks that always seemed to piss him off so much?

She was staying at their house and obviously she was going to be there for a while. So whatever it was that bothered him about her, Becks was right about one thing.

He was going to have to deal with his past. At least the Becks part of his past.

CHAPTER 8

AFTER HER CONFRONTATION WITH JACKSON, BECKS changed into jeans and a T-shirt and slipped on her sandals. When she got downstairs she saw that Rafe had made breakfast, and he invited her to eat with them. She wanted to say no, but it wasn't Rafe she was mad at, so she accepted and took a spot at the table with the three guys.

But the entire time she ate and made nice conversation, all she could think about was Jackson, who was doing his best to ignore her.

He mainly stared down at his plate and shoveled food into his mouth, responding only when a question was asked of him. That meant she engaged with Rafe and Kal, who fortunately asked her a lot of questions about her search for a new shop.

"I have a few spots to look at today that Margie set up for me."

"Want us to go with you?" Kal asked as he finished up the last bite of his spinach omelet.

"That's not necessary. I'm sure you guys have plenty to do on your day off."

"I told Mom I'd get her car brakes replaced," Rafe said. "And Kal, you have to get that speeding ticket taken care of, don't you?"

"Oh, crap, that's right." Kal looked over at Jackson. "Jackson doesn't have anything going on today, though. He could go with you and look over the properties, making sure they're safe. Can't you?"

Jackson looked up and frowned. "What?"

"Go look at properties with Becks today," Kal said. "Rafe and I have other stuff to do."

"Oh, uh . . ."

"It's okay," Becks said, noting the reluctant look on Jackson's face. "I can do this on my own."

"But we said we'd help," Rafe said. "And we never go back on a promise, do we, Jackson?"

Becks glanced in Jackson's direction, expecting him to say no.

"We never go back on a promise," Jackson said. "I'll go with you."

Jackson looked about as thrilled as someone about to have his leg cut off.

"Are you sure?"

He nodded. "I'm sure."

"Don't you have things you have to do today?" she asked.

"Nothing. Just let me know when you want to leave."

She wasn't certain that was the case, but if she turned him down she'd have to explain to Rafe and Kal why. Better to just get it over with. Plus, she didn't want to have to go through the whole electrical nightmare again, so she wouldn't mind an expert set of eyes.

"Right after breakfast will be fine. Thanks."

"No problem."

His voice was flat and she knew that despite what he'd said, he'd rather do anything than spend the day with her.

Wasn't this going to be fun?

CHAPTER 9

THE FIRST TWO SHOPS THEY LOOKED AT WEREN'T GOING to cut it. One was way too big and much too expensive, and the other one was in a location that wouldn't garner Becks any customers.

She had high hopes for the third location.

Jackson had decided to drive—insisted on it, actually, saying he had a couple of errands to run. She'd argued with him that if he had stuff to do she could look at spaces on her own, but he told her his errands wouldn't take long, anyway, and unless she had places to go after they looked at properties, she could go with him. So she'd agreed.

Though the silence in the truck had been hard to bear. It was obvious he wasn't comfortable around her.

So on the drive to the third spot, she turned in her seat.

"I know you're uncomfortable around me. I don't know why you agreed to this."

"I'm not uncomfortable."

She couldn't see his eyes behind his dark sunglasses, and she could always tell when someone was lying by their eyes. But she sure could tell from his body language. He sat straight and stiff as a board in his seat, instead of relaxed.

"What is it about me that distresses you?"

He finally glanced her way. "I feel something when I'm near you."

She had mentally prepared herself for any type of negative answer from him. Like she was too bossy or he didn't like the way she took over his kitchen. Or she cleaned too much. But this? This was unexpected. She didn't have a prepared reaction other than a skipped heartbeat.

"Feel . . . what?"

"I don't know. A connection to you. And before you say something, no, it's not about our shared past."

Huh. Okay, that had been her first thought. Time to think of something else. "Maybe because you saved me from the smoke?"

He shook his head, keeping his focus on the road. "Not that. I don't get emotionally connected to victims. It's something else. I mean, you're pretty, Becks. Obviously. And I'm trying to avoid thinking of you as someone I'd like to . . ."

Her brows rose. Like to what? Ask out to dinner? Date? Fuck? Admittedly, she'd be okay with any of those scenarios. She mentally tried to calm her rapidly racing pulse. "Go on."

"I like you. And you're living in my house. I just don't want you to feel like there's any expectation there."

"I'll start paying rent right away."

"You get yourself situated in a new location and start working again. Then we'll talk about you paying rent. In the meantime, I'll keep my wayward thoughts in check."

He had wayward thoughts about her? Now things were getting really interesting. She resisted the urge to smile.

Wayward thoughts. Huh. This was a very thought-provoking development. She leaned back in her seat and looked out the window, trying to process what had just happened.

Jackson was hot. Like . . . smoking hot. Since she'd reconnected with him, she'd tried to ignore that part of him, but it was hard. Indeed, everything about him was hard, and sitting next to him in the truck was a test of her endurance. She'd had no idea he felt the same way about her.

He'd been everything she'd ever wanted when she had been just on the cusp of budding puberty.

It had been a lot of years since then. She'd grown up. She'd tucked more than a few lovers under her belt. But seeing Jackson again had awakened those first feelings of infatuation she'd felt all those years ago.

Is that what she felt now? She took a quick glance over at him. Infatuation? No. She'd long ago grown out of heart-eyed crushes.

Lust, though? Most definitely yes. She was a woman now, and went after what she wanted. She neither needed nor wanted love and marriage. But sometimes—hell, more than sometimes—a girl needed sex.

She'd bet Jackson was really good at sex. He had that fuming, smoldering intensity that signaled pent-up sexual frustration. And wouldn't she love to be the woman he expended all that frustration on?

She inhaled a deep breath and let it sail out on a long sigh.

"You okay over there?"

She turned her attention on Jackson, drawing her sunglasses down her nose. "Fine. Just wrestling with my own wayward thoughts."

"About?"

"You, of course."

He gripped the steering wheel so hard she saw his knuckles go white. As he made a right turn, she caught the way his jaw clenched.

"See, this is what I'm talking about."

"What are you talking about, Jackson?"

"First, you invite me into your bedroom this morning, and then you talk about not biting unless I want you to. And now you're insinuating you have wayward thoughts about me. I'm trying to be good here, Becks. But you're not making it easy."

She let out a soft laugh. "I don't know where this chivalry came from, Jackson. But I haven't asked you to withhold any sexual desire you might feel for me. If you want me, state your intentions."

He pulled into the parking lot and shoved the truck into park, unbuckled his seat belt, then leaned over and got very much into her personal space. She breathed in the utterly masculine scent of him, reaching out to grasp one extremely well-muscled biceps.

"You know what I want?" he asked.

She was breathing so fast she might pass out. God, she hoped she didn't, because this was getting really good.

"No. Tell me."

"Right now my dick is so hard it's about to split the zipper of my jeans. I'd like to throw you down onto your back, kiss you until both our lips are numb. I want to get you out of those jeans and eat your pussy until you're shivering all over. Then I want to take my cock out and fuck you until you scream because I've made you come so many times you've lost count."

She swallowed. Or tried to, anyway, because the visuals he'd conjured up made her nipples tingle and her pussy quiver.

"That all sounds really good and I'm totally down for that. Unfortunately we're in a public parking lot and Margie just drove up next to you."

He straightened and backed away. "Fuck."

Her lips quirked. "Yes, I'd like to do that, too."

"I'm gonna need a minute, Becks," he said, dragging his fingers through his hair.

She'd like to have all those minutes he just suggested to her. "Well, put a pin in what you just said, because I want all of it."

He shot a look at her. "I'm gonna need more than a minute if you keep talking about it."

She smiled. "Okay. I'll get out and talk to Margie."

She slid out of the truck, her legs quivering when she hit the ground. She felt as if her entire body were on fire and all she wanted to do was climb back in the truck, straddle Jackson's lap and act upon everything he'd just suggested. But since Margie was approaching, she did a mental cooldown, forcing herself not to look back at Jackson.

"Hey, girl," Margie said. "Let's hope third time's a charm."

She planted on a smile, trying to calm her heart rate down to normal and get her mind on business instead of the steamy conversation she'd just had with Jackson. She inhaled, let it out, and smiled at her friend. "I have a good feeling about this one. The location is perfect." Becks glanced up and down the shopping center. There was a scarf shop on the corner, a surf shop, a vape place, a couple of restaurants and other assorted retail establishments. This was the only vacant spot, which spoke well for the location.

"It just opened up and I don't think it'll last long," Margie said. "Hopefully this is the one for you."

"I hope so, too."

Margie paused and looked toward the truck. "Is Jackson coming?"

She'd like to see Jackson coming. And if she didn't stop that line of thought she'd blush through the entire tour. "He'll be along shortly. He . . . uh . . . had to make a phone call."

"Oh, sure. Let's go on in, then."

She followed Margie inside.

The reception area was accommodating and spacious. It was nice and cool inside, which meant the air-conditioning worked. There was a built-in L-shaped front desk and plenty of room for chairs in the waiting area.

The floors were pristine and clean, and the walls were freshly painted.

Perfect.

"This is nice, isn't it?" Margie asked.

Becks nodded. "It is."

"And the rent is reasonable, too. Well, as reasonable as you're going to get this close to the beach."

That was the drawback. She wanted to be close to the beach, and as far as locations went, this place was a dream spot. But the rent was higher than anything she'd ever paid before.

She turned as the door opened and Jackson walked in.

"Oh, hey, Jackson," Margie said. "I was just telling Becks about how much room there is in the reception area."

He barely made eye contact with Becks but instead gave the room a once-over. "Yeah, it's good."

They walked down a hallway. "There are three rooms in here. I know you only have yourself, but two of the rooms are big, and I know you've talked about hiring out space for another artist. With the rent being high, you might want to consider it."

"It's a good idea. And this space is ideal. I'd have no problem attracting talent." It was a decent-sized room and she could set up her chairs and supplies. "It would work."

Plus there was plenty of storage space and room in the back for a small eating area. She stood in the center of the space and looked around.

"I like this. It feels good."

Jackson had disappeared. Had he left? She'd been so immersed in looking at the space she hadn't even noticed him leaving.

But then he came out of the back room, using a rag to wipe his hands. "Electrical checks out. Looks like they did an upgrade recently. You're good to go here."

Elation filled her. "Really? It almost feels too good to be true."

Jackson cracked a smile. "Okay, Cinderella. Put on your glass slippers and sign the papers."

Oh, wow. Grumpy Jackson was a force to be reckoned with on the Sexy Meter. But Smiling Jackson? His smile made the sides of his eyes crinkle and turned her on in a very unexpected way.

Eye crinkles are a turn-on? Really, Becks?

"So this is the place?" Margie asked.

"I don't know, Margie. It's ideal, location and size-wise. It's everything I want. But the rent will be tough for me to manage. I still need to find a new place to live, which means first and last months' rent and a deposit."

Margie nodded. "We can keep looking."

She nodded. "It's probably for the best."

They turned to head out, but Jackson grasped her wrist.

"You can stay with us as long as you need to," Jackson said.

Becks shook her head. "I don't think that's a good idea."

Jackson turned his attention to Margie. "Give us a sec?"

"Sure. I'll be right outside, making a few calls. Just wave at me when you're ready."

Margie left, and Becks wanted to be sure to put an end to this right away.

"I appreciate the offer, Jackson, but I can't take advantage of you all like that."

He shrugged. "You're not taking advantage. We're not there all the time, so we won't be in your way."

"That's hardly what I was talking about. I'm the one who's in your way."

"No, you're not. The room was empty anyway."

"Don't you typically rent it out to firefighters?"

"Yeah, but—"

"But nothing. I only intended to stay a few days. And I'm taking a firefighter's spot."

He let out a short laugh. "Rafe and Kal and I decide who lives there. I can guarantee they're not going to want to push you out. Plus, you're pulling your weight at the house. You wanted to pay rent, so you'll pay rent. Right now you can pay what you can afford. When you can afford more, you pay more. Then, when you're ready, you can find another place."

She wanted to argue, but she also desperately wanted this shop. "I don't want you to think I'm taking advantage of you. You didn't want me there in the first place."

"I changed my mind."

She stepped closer. "Why?"

"Because you should rent this shop. Margie's right. The location is good and the shop has a lot of space. Plus, I think you'd have a lot of success here."

She felt a buzz of warmth that he wanted her to succeed. Not many people had cared about her in her lifetime. That Jackson did meant a lot to her.

"Okay. But on one condition."

"Shoot."

"If you need to rent out that room to a firefighter who needs it, you tell me and I'll vacate."

"Done deal." He held out his hand.

She took it, and she felt a zing of electricity cross from his hand to hers. There was a definite hot spark of attraction between them. And from the smile on Jackson's face, he'd felt it, too.

This wasn't the time, and with Margie practically sticking her nose to the glass in curiosity, it definitely wasn't the place.

So, instead, she shook his hand.

"Done deal. And thanks."

Margie peeked her head in the door. "Does this mean we can do the paperwork now?"

Becks grinned. "Now we can do the paperwork."

CHAPTER 10

AFTER SIGNING THE LEASE AND SENDING MARGIE OFF with a check for deposit and rent, Jackson and Becks ran Jackson's errands, first to the auto parts store and then to the garden store.

She gave him a look of surprise when he picked up potting soil along with some fertilizer, but for indoor plants.

"So you're the plant guy?" she asked as they headed back to his truck.

"Huh?" He looked at her and frowned.

"There are beautiful houseplants at your place. Those are yours?"

"Oh. Yeah. I like greenery. Plus plants are good for the house. They give off oxygen."

"You just got ten times more interesting, Jackson Donovan."

They climbed into the truck and he looked over at her. "So does that mean I wasn't interesting before?"

"Oh, parts of you definitely interest me."

He laughed.

They stopped at the store to pick up some groceries. Becks said she wanted to cook dinner for them tonight in celebration of finally being able to go back to work. Jackson told her that wasn't necessary. She gave him a look that told him it wasn't open for debate, so he shrugged and let her have her way. Which really wasn't a big deal.

Jackson pushed the cart while Becks tossed food into it. He wasn't sure what she was fixing, but he liked all food, and everything she chose looked good to him.

They piled the bags into the back of the truck and headed back toward the house.

"When will you open the shop?" he asked.

"I have to get set up first. Since it's vacant, I'll get the keys the first of the month, which is this weekend, so that's great. I can get in and start putting all of my gear in there."

"You got everything cleaned up from the smoke?"

She nodded. "I did. Thanks for letting me use your garage to store some of my things."

"Not a problem. I'm just glad it's all working out for you. And, honestly? Your new location is way better than the old one."

"Thanks. I think so, too. Once I get settled I'll have to get the word out to my clients with an e-mail blast and on my social media pages. I had a few appointments the day of the fire that had to be canceled."

"Hopefully they'll reschedule."

"They were all with repeat customers. They all said they'd wait on me."

He pulled off the highway and said, "You're that good, huh?"

"Got any tattoos?"

"Not yet."

He felt her gaze on him, so he glanced quickly over at her.

"What?"

"You should let me tattoo you. Then you could see how good I am."

"Are any of the ones on your body ones you did yourself?"

"Yes."

"You should get naked and let me decide if I want you tattooing me."

She pulled her sunglasses down and regarded him. "You'd let me use my naked body as advertising?"

"Hell, yes."

She laughed. "We'll discuss that option."

He liked that she considered it an option. He'd been thinking about her all afternoon. She was smart and sassy, and he liked smart and sassy women. He wanted to know he was going to get as well as he gave. Plus, that sassiness was given from an incredible mouth. He wanted to kiss her so badly it made him ache. While they'd been looking at the new shop, he found himself looking at her mouth, wondering what her lips would feel like under his. Then his gaze had traveled south and he found himself inspecting her butt.

He was an ass man, and Becks had a well-defined butt. He itched to grab a handful of it and see if it was as firm as it looked.

And then there were her breasts . . .

But since they were pulling into the driveway, he shut down any further mental inspections of Becks's body.

"I don't see Rafe's or Kal's cars," Becks said as they grabbed the bags out of the back of the truck.

"They might not be back yet from running their errands."

They took the groceries into the house and unpacked them together. While Jackson was in the fridge, he lifted his head.

"I'm having a beer. Want one?"

"Sure."

He grabbed two beers and popped open the tops, handing one to Becks.

"Thanks." She took a long swallow, then set it down and washed her hands. She took out the cutting board and started working.

"Anything I can do?"

"Not if you have something else you need to be doing."

"I don't. What do you need?"

"You can stay and talk to me while I work."

He went to the sink to wash his hands, then grabbed a knife from the drawer and came up beside her.

"I'm handy with a knife, you know. I can do some cutting."

"Fine. You can slice onions and jalapeños."

He gave her a sidelong look. "Punishing me, huh?"

She laughed, then nudged her hip against his leg. "No. But if you think it's too hard . . ."

"Didn't say that. You just do your thing."

"I was planning to."

They worked side by side. Jackson chopped while at the same time watching Becks. She was fast and efficient, slicing tomatoes and avocados and mangoes like a pro. He also noticed she wasn't much for conversation.

"You're used to being alone."

She jerked her head up. "What?"

"You're not talking."

She frowned. "I'm working here."

"I don't know about you, but I can slice and talk at the same time."

She resumed her cutting. "So talk. I'm listening."

He shook his head. "You're very independent."

"Didn't we all grow up having to be that way?"

She had a point. Being on their own most of their childhood meant they all had to learn to rely on themselves. "True. But I had Rafe and Kal. Who did you have?"

"My smarts and my ingenuity. And really fast feet."

He laughed. "Yeah, outrunning the cops meant you had to be quick."

"Plus carve out some exceptional hiding spots. In our area, I had ten that no one knew about."

He stopped slicing and leaned his hip against the counter. "Ten?"

"Yeah."

"Damn. That's impressive."

"I didn't want to get caught and be hauled into foster care."

"But didn't you end up there anyway?"

She nodded. "After you and Kal and Rafe disappeared, the rest of the group mostly scattered, which meant I was alone. It was harder to find food and shelter without you."

She had continued to chop, her head down and focused. He grabbed her focus by laying his hand on her forearm. "I'm sorry."

"It's okay. If the situation had been reversed I'd have jumped on the opportunity to have a family. Plus, it worked out okay. I lucked out and got put with decent foster parents who I ended up staying with until I aged out of the system."

"I'm glad for you. That doesn't always happen."

"Tell me about it. I had some nightmare foster families."

He wanted to know more, but he understood a lot of people didn't like talking about the experience. He sure didn't. "Want to talk about it?"

She shrugged. "You know the various situations. There was one couple only in it for the money. In that house there was me and three other kids, all roughly the same age. One had mental deficiencies and needed serious attention. Not that Bethany and Henry cared. We could all have been running around with sharp knives in both hands and those two couldn't have cared less, as long as we didn't cut our own throats—or each other's. Because that would have meant they'd lose out on a paycheck. Otherwise, they didn't give a shit about us. Unless the social worker was there for a visit."

"Of course."

"But it wasn't as bad as the other place I stayed in when I was—" She lifted her gaze to the ceiling. "Nine, ten, maybe?" She made eye contact with Jackson. "Foster dad who liked to cuddle the girls a little too much."

His stomach churned. "Oh, fuck that. Did he touch you?"

"No. I was good at screaming for him to keep his fucking hands off me, and the wife would beat him over the head with a magazine and threaten to kill him if he didn't stay away from us. So I made sure to be loud enough every time he crept into the bedroom at night. I didn't sleep much, but while I was there he didn't touch any of us. And as soon as the social worker visited I made sure to mention that he kept putting his hands on me and I was afraid to sleep at night. When they interviewed one of the other girls and she said the same thing, everyone got removed from that house in a hurry."

"Jesus. I'm sorry, Becks."

She shrugged like it was no big deal, when Jackson knew damn well it had been.

"It is what it is. We all went through it. I'm sure you had your fair share of nightmare scenarios in foster care, too."

"It wasn't great, that's for sure. That's why I preferred living on the streets."

He finished scooping the onions and jalapeños into a bowl, then went to the sink to wash his hands. He dried them on the towel and when he looked up, he found Becks staring at him.

"What?"

"That's it? I tell you my horror stories and you don't share yours?"

"Oh." He lifted one shoulder in a shrug. "Not much to tell. A lot like yours. Shitty foster parents. They were all nightmares. You know."

"Yeah, that's really specific, Jackson. Thanks for giving me a glimpse inside your life."

She put the bowls in the fridge and washed her hands, then disappeared down the hall. He followed her to the laundry room, watching her pull clothes from the dryer and cram them into a basket.

"What exactly is it that you want from me?"

She shut the door and brushed by him. "Nothing. I don't want anything from you that you're not willing to give."

She went upstairs. He thought about staying where he was to sulk and drink his beer, but he hated leaving things unsettled, so he followed her into her room.

She lifted her head and shot a glare at him. "Do you mind?"

"I do, actually. So what if I don't want to talk about the past? Some people like digging into that shit. I don't happen to be one of those people."

"And some people like to get to know other people by finding out who they were and how they feel about what happened to them when they were younger. We share a past, Jackson. One you keep wanting to forget about. I'd like to know why."

Why did everyone want to keep drilling down into a past that was best kept buried? "There is no why. There aren't any deep, dark secrets I'm keeping. You know everything about me, Becks. We lived on the streets when we were young. Then I got lucky and was adopted. I became a firefighter. And here I am now."

She folded a shirt and laid it on the bed. "And that's it. That's all there is to know about you."

"Pretty much, yeah."

"I call bullshit on that." She picked up the shirt and turned to put it in a drawer.

He skirted around her bed and moved in next to her. "No, it's not bullshit. It's who I am. I don't want to talk about my past. That doesn't make me some kind of monster."

She closed the drawer and straightened. "Of course it doesn't make you a monster. I think you're avoiding dealing with the ghosts of your past. And I know better than anyone that it will haunt you until you address it."

He laughed. "There's nothing to address, Becks. Honest. I'm a happy guy. I have an amazing family, a job I love and a great place to live. My life is pretty damned perfect."

She cocked her head to the side. "Is it?"

"Yeah." He sat on the edge of her bed.

"Then why do you refuse to talk about the past?"

"I . . . don't know. I guess because it's over and I'd like to forget about it. You were there. It wasn't the best time of our lives. I don't like reliving it."

"But there were fun times, too. And you made friends. Come on, Jackson. You ended up with two brothers out of it. How could that not be an amazing time in your life? It couldn't have been all darkness."

She didn't understand. He could never make anyone understand why he didn't want to go back there. "Yeah, you're right. Rafe and Kal were the best thing that ever happened to me back then. All of you were. If not for our group I never would have survived."

"None of us would have made it alone. And you were our leader. You were the one who made sure we got fed and had a place to sleep at night."

He felt that stab of guilt that hit him every time he thought about how he'd left all the kids behind. And Becks had been one of those kids.

"You know if I could have done this any other way, I never would have left."

She laid a hand on his shoulder. "Jackson, I don't blame you. You had no choice. And you got lucky. Any one of us would have leaped at the opportunity."

She didn't know, couldn't possibly know how much willpower

it had taken not to go back, the choices he'd had to make both for himself and for his brothers.

"When we ended up with Josh and Laurel, I tried to go back. I told them I needed to check on my friends. They wouldn't let me."

"That's understandable. Plus they were probably afraid you'd bolt."

"Probably."

She looked at him, and he saw the sympathy in her eyes. He didn't deserve it.

"We waited for all three of you to show up. Littles was so scared when he couldn't find you."

Goddammit. He hated knowing that. Littles had always been attached to him. He knew the kid thought of him as a father figure. He dragged his fingers through his hair. "It was my job to protect all of you. And I let you down. If we hadn't gotten separated the night it rained . . ."

"Then we would have all been in that house with you, right?"

"Yeah. Believe me, I've gone over the scenario a thousand times in my head. My dad tells me it was hard enough getting the three of us out of that house. It was pretty consumed when they got there. We were lucky."

She sat on the bed next to him. "And if the rest of us had been there, Jackson, some of us might not have made it out. You and Rafe and Kal might not have made it out. Stop feeling guilty about that night. We were fine. Mason and I took care of Littles and the others. We found shelter and food that night and we were all okay."

He looked up at her. "You ever wonder what happened to everyone?"

"Yes. When I decided to go into foster care, I convinced Littles to go with me. We were even in the same house for a while. Littles had the same social worker I did, so I found out he got adopted. Amy found some other group to hang out with. I don't know what happened to her. Before I got into the system, Greg just disappeared one night and never came back. I don't know why. Mason stayed out on the streets, so no idea where he ended up."

This was why he didn't delve into the past. The knot in his stomach tightened as the weight of that responsibility he'd felt for all the kids sank deeper inside him. Part of him still wanted to know where they all had gone. If they were okay. If they were happy and safe. But there'd be no way to get those answers, and it ate away at him. The best thing to do was not think about it.

"I'm glad about Littles," he said.

"Me, too. Look, Jackson . . ."

He stood, needing to put an end to this conversation. "Anyway, I should probably get back downstairs."

"Are you all right?"

"I'm fine. I just have a couple of things I need to do. And the guys will probably be back soon."

"Okay. I'll be downstairs in a minute. I just want to finish putting the laundry away."

"Yeah, sure."

He left her room and went downstairs, feeling unsettled and wishing they could have been doing anything in her bedroom other than talking about their past lives. And maybe he should have showed Becks that the present was way more satisfying than the past.

So why didn't he linger? Change the subject? Kiss her?

Why in the hell didn't he kiss her? That sure as hell would have been a topic changer.

Because you have your head up your ass about the past.

He blew out a frustrated breath and opened the fridge to grab the iced tea. By then Rafe walked in.

"What's up?" Rafe asked. "How did the search go with Becks?"

"Fine. She got a place."

Rafe grinned. "Great. Is it a good spot?"

"It's fine."

"Oh, so it's fine. What's up your ass now?"

"Nothing."

"That sounds like a bad-mood kind of nothing."

The one thing that both irked him and that he respected about Rafe was his ability to read people. That ability could be helpful in an emergency situation. As it related to Jackson? Annoying as shit. Rafe could read Jackson's mood by one word.

"I'm fine."

Rafe brushed by him to pull a glass down from the cabinet. "Uh-huh. Sure you are. What happened with you and Becks today?"

"What makes you think this has anything to do with Becks?"

Rafe slanted a look at him. "Because she's a woman and you suck at dealing with women. Plus you like her."

He took a drink of tea and set it down on the counter. "I never said I liked her."

"You don't have to. Ever since you dragged her out of her smoke-filled shop, the chemistry between the two of you has been like a constant heat source around here. And the two of you are either sniping at each other or giving each other looks."

Jackson frowned. Looks. Whatever. He wasn't looking at her.

"You're full of shit."

Kal walked in and tossed a bag on the counter. "No, you're full of shit. Actually, you both are, but why's Jackson full of shit?"

"About Becks and the way the two of them are doing this sex dance around each other."

Kal gave a quick nod. "Oh, that. Yeah, you totally are."

Jackson glared at both of his brothers. "For fuck's sake. We are not. And quit watching us."

Kal dug into the fruit bowl on the counter and grabbed a peach. "Dude, no one even has to watch. It's like the temp goes up ten degrees whenever you're both in the same room."

Rafe shoved Jackson. "Ha. See? See? What did I say? I said the exact same thing."

Just then Becks reappeared. "Hi, guys. Have a good day?"

"Outstanding, Becks," Kal said, grabbing a paper towel to catch the juice from the peach. "How about you?"

"It was good. I leased workspace today."

"Hey, great," Rafe said. "The one by the beach?"

She nodded. "It's a perfect location, with plenty of space for a waiting area and multiple rooms for storage and doing ink, so it's exactly what I was looking for."

"I'm happy for you." Kal came over and drew her against him for a quick hug. "When do you move in?"

"My friend Margie texted me when I was upstairs. I'll pick up the keys tomorrow. I officially start paying rent on Monday, but since the place is empty the owner said I can start moving in this weekend."

"Perfect," Rafe said. "We can help you move."

"You don't have to do that. I know you guys have your own things to do."

"Hey, we're like family," Kal said. "And family helps family. We'll pitch in."

She looked over at Jackson, who nodded and said, "Yeah, we'll help."

"Great. Thank you. Oh, and I don't know if Jackson told you or not, but he said I could continue to stay here. The rent's higher on the commercial space than I can really afford right now, so he said you all wouldn't mind. I'll still pay rent here, of course."

Rafe shot him a knowing look before slanting a sweet smile at Becks. "You're welcome to stay here as long as you like, Becks."

"Agreed," Kal said, looking over the top of Becks's head to smirk at Jackson.

Both of his brothers could go straight to hell.

CHAPTER 11

THERE WAS NOTHING LIKE SERIOUS MUSCLE TO REDUCE what Becks thought would be an all-day job to just a couple of hours. With Jackson, Rafe and Kal's help, they had everything placed in all the right spots in her new space by mid-afternoon.

She knew the guys had to be tired coming off shift first thing Saturday morning, but they pitched right in and loaded stuff into their trucks without complaint. She had fixed them sausage and egg burritos and had those ready when they first came home, so they gobbled those up and got right to work.

They went with her to her storage locker and did all the heavy lifting, taking the chairs and tables and loading those into their trucks. She could have done it herself but she hadn't minded ogling their muscles while they did the heavy lifting.

Okay, so it might have been Jackson's muscles she'd ogled the most. He'd changed into shorts and a sleeveless shirt. He was tanned and had amazing shoulders and she'd had a hard time concentrating while watching the man sweat.

She'd cleaned the storefront window on Friday and painted a new Skin Deep logo on the window, and had her sign guy come by and put all the date and time details on her door, but she was still surprised to have a couple of people stop by while they were moving in and talk to her about getting tattoos. She made two appointments for Tuesday and one for next Saturday.

Outstanding. She'd had a good feeling about this place the minute she had walked in. And it had turned out she was right. This was going to be a great studio. She couldn't wait to get started on Tuesday.

Kal swiped his hands on his shorts and surveyed the room. "It looks good."

"Yeah, it does," Rafe said.

They'd helped her paint the back wall in the reception area a bright turquoise, where she intended to put her art. In the main tattooing room she'd gone with a pale gray.

"It's perfect."

"And it's dry," Kal said. "So let's put up some art."

She surveyed her drawings and paintings and some of the photographs of her favorite tattoos. "You guys didn't need to hang all my stuff on the wall. I can do that."

"Hey, we're here, hammers and drills and all," Jackson said. "Might as well use us."

She'd have liked to have Jackson drill her in so many different ways, but she tucked that dirty thought away for the time being. So she directed and they hung the art. Then they helped her put supplies away.

She swiped her hands on a paper towel. Other than making a few calls to clients and prospects, she was ready. And oh, so eager. "We're done."

"And you're ready to go," Jackson said.

She looked them over. "Okay. Which one of you is going to be my first customer?"

Kal laughed. "Hey, I'll show up and let you put some art on me, but not right now." He pulled his phone out. "Got plans."

"With Tandy?" Rafe asked.

"Mind your own business."

Rafe shot a grin over at Jackson and Becks. "It's with Tandy."

"And who would Tandy be?" Becks asked.

"She's a trainer at the gym," Rafe said. "Incredible body. Great work ethic. She's also a physical therapist. Super amazing at both of her jobs. No idea what she's doing with a dumbass like Kal."

"Fuck off, Rafe."

Rafe laughed. Jackson let out a snort of laughter.

Becks shook her head. "This is probably why Kal doesn't want to tell you who he's dating."

"He does the same thing to both of us when we're going out with someone," Jackson said.

"Truth." Rafe nodded. "We all do. It's a brother thing. Plus, we're only looking out for each other, to make sure one of us doesn't end up with a hose chaser."

Becks choked out a laugh. "A . . . what? Did you say hose chaser?"

Jackson nodded. "Yeah."

"You can't be serious."

"Oh, we are," Rafe said.

Becks leaned against the front desk and crossed her arms. "Really. And what constitutes a hose chaser?"

"They're only after the uniform," Jackson said. "They get off on telling their friends they're hooking up with a firefighter. Or a cop."

"The ones who date the cops are the badge bunnies," Kal said.

"Oh. My. God," Becks said. "So just because you wear a uniform they want in your pants? I don't get the appeal. No offense."

"None taken," Jackson said.

"Don't get me wrong. What you do for a living is admirable," Becks said. "But as far as I'm concerned it doesn't make you any more fuckable than any other guy."

Kal laughed, hard. "I see you haven't changed much at all, Becks. Still saying exactly what's on your mind."

She shrugged. "No reason not to, is there?"

"Nope. Anyway, I gotta go see my girl. Who, by the way, is not a hose chaser."

"Thank God for that. And thanks for helping today, Kal."

"Anytime, honey." Kal kissed her on the cheek and left.

She turned to face Jackson and Rafe. "How about some late lunch? My treat since you both helped me out so much today."

"I'd love to," Rafe said. "But I need to go get an oil change on my truck and then I've got a date, too, that I need to get ready for."

Becks frowned. "You could have done the oil change this morning instead of helping me."

"Hey, we're family, Becks. You needed me. Besides, I've got plenty of time to get my stuff done. So don't worry about it."

She heaved a sigh. "Okay. Thanks for helping me today. I never could have gotten it done so fast without all of you."

Rafe hugged her. "You're welcome. We'll always be here for you anytime you need us."

He walked out, leaving Becks alone with Jackson. She lifted her gaze to his.

"For some reason I get the feeling the two of them did that on purpose."

Jackson raised a brow. "Nah. They're always running off doing something or another."

"So you don't think they're trying to set us up to be alone?"

"No, I don't. But I'm not complaining about having you to myself."

She liked where this was going. "Really. Because I got the distinct impression the other day in my bedroom that you couldn't get away from me fast enough."

"The timing was off that day. I didn't want my brothers to come home and walk in on us in your room."

She moved closer to him, needing to gauge if his interest was all talk and no action. "I see. Well, that is kind of the drawback to all of us living together, isn't it?"

When she was only inches away from him, he drew her against him. "Yeah, it's gonna be a problem. But right now it's just the two of us."

She laid her palms on his chest, loving the feel of his rock-hard body against her skin. "Yes, it is. In front of a very large and extremely revealing picture window."

She motioned with her head to the approximately eight-year-old boy leering at them through the window.

"Shit," Jackson said, pulling back right away. The kid outside laughed and ran off. "There's got to be a place we can be alone."

"Surely we can do that at home. Your brothers bring women home, don't they? You're all respectful of each other's privacy, aren't you?"

"Yeah."

"And I'm certain they'd be respectful of mine, say, if I had a guy in my room."

"I know they would be."

She shrugged. "Problem solved, then. We'll meet in my room whenever we want to do . . . whatever it is that we want to do."

She saw him look toward that big window. Then he took her hand and led her to the back of the shop. He backed her up against the wall and pressed his body against hers. "I have a pretty good idea we're on the same page as far as what we want to do. But you need to let me know if it's what you want."

As if she hadn't made her intent . . . and her consent . . . perfectly transparent to him?

She wound her hand around his neck. "Jackson. I want sex. With you. In a bed in my room. Or in your room. Or in my truck. Or your truck. Or even right here. On a chair. On the floor. Or up against the wall. Just so we're clear."

A low growl came from his throat.

"Very damn clear, thank you."

He pressed his lips to hers and a burst of heat sizzled across her skin. The softness of his lips, his breath mingling with hers, and the hot taste of his tongue far exceeded all of the prepubescent fantasies she'd had of kissing him all those years ago. Back then she'd imagined a soft kiss, murmured endearments and hand-holding.

Childish daydreams.

She wasn't a kid anymore, and neither was Jackson.

Her need for him now was very, very adult.

His hands were masculine and large and rough as he moved them over her, getting to know her body as he slid his hands down her arms and around the front of her body. He slipped one hand under her shirt, teasing her stomach with his palm. She released a moan of utter pleasure at feeling that skin-to-skin contact.

This kiss was an adult kiss with lips and tongues and roaming hands that promised hot, fiery passion and even steamier sex. She wanted the opportunity to strip him down and explore him all over.

But then he pulled away. "This just isn't good enough, Becks."

She cocked her head to the side. "I don't know, Jackson," she said, trying to catch her breath. "But from where I'm standing, it was getting really damn good."

He dragged his fingers through his hair. "I know. But I want to get naked with you and touch you and kiss you and lick you and fuck you. For hours. And we can't do that here. And I don't know how you feel about it, but a quickie just isn't gonna cut it for us. Not the first time."

She was bowled over by how sweet that declaration was. "Okay. So we need a bed in a bedroom with a locked door. Appointment sex?"

"I'm okay with it if you are."

She was more than okay with it. "So let's go have something to eat, because other than sex with you, food is definitely a priority right now. Then we can put our calendars together and make an appointment."

"I'm good with food." He gave her a devilish smile. "As a second choice."

She locked the shop and they climbed into his truck.

He started the engine and turned to her. "What are you hungry for?"

Him. She was hungry for him, but she had to shift mental and libidinal gears.

"Fish tacos."

He grinned. "Excellent choice."

They ended up at the Drunken Taco because it was right on the beach. One of the reasons she liked to work nearby was so she could soak up the ocean view whenever possible. The salt spray and fresh ocean air never failed to revive her after a long day of inking and piercing. She often either drove or walked to the beach to just stick her toes in the sand or take a walk along the beach, lost in her own thoughts.

But now she was sitting next to Jackson after having her fill of fish tacos. She'd had a couple of refreshing glasses of beer while watching the mesmerizing waves as they crashed in, then pulled back out. The water always beckoned her.

"You're staring at it like you'd like to plunge in headfirst."

She smiled at Jackson. "It is hot today. Wouldn't you like to do the same thing?"

He took a long pull of his beer, then set it on the bar. "The thought's crossed my mind."

"Do you have your board shorts with you?"

"Anyone who lives around the beach should be ashamed if they don't carry their swim stuff in their vehicle."

She nodded. "So true."

"Which means we're going for a dip, right?"

Her lips curved. "Definitely."

"Great. Then I can check out more of your tattoos."

"You could see all of them if you'd just get me naked."

He took another swallow of his beer. "I don't mind waiting. And imagining."

"You're not like any guy I've ever known before."

"Is that right? In what way?"

"Most of them want to get me undressed right away."

"I never said I didn't want to fuck you right away. I think about it a lot. But I also want to get to know you, not just your body."

She took a long swallow of beer and slid the empty bottle across the bar. The bartender handed her another. She swiveled in her seat to face Jackson. "For the record, I would also like to get you naked. And get to know you as a person as well."

"Thanks. I'd hate to think you were just using me for my moving skills. And my magnificent dick."

She snorted out a laugh. "Oh, now you're just boasting."

"I wouldn't boast about it if it weren't true."

"We'll see, Mr. Magnificent."

He nodded. "Yeah, you'll see all right. And feel. Everything."

She could not believe they were having this conversation. Though she had to admit she was amused as hell.

"And probably scream," he added. "Maybe even faint."

"Laying it on a little thick, aren't you, Jackson?"

"Did I mention it was thick?" He arched a brow. "Have you been peeking?"

She rolled her eyes. "You do go on, don't you?"

His gaze was direct. "All. Night. Long."

She was on fire. But she couldn't admit it to him. So she gave him a nonchalant shrug. "Now I'm no longer interested."

He leaned into her to whisper in her ear. "Bullshit. You'd take me down right now if we weren't in public."

That was absolutely true, but there was no way she was letting him know that. "Hmm. Maybe. So, are you ready for a swim?"

His lips curved upward, as if he knew he'd ignited a flame in her.

Bastard.

"Sure. Let's go."

Jackson went into the public restroom to change into his board shorts. Becks had grabbed her backpack and was off doing the same. He tucked his clothes in his truck and waited there for Becks so he could store her clothes.

While he was waiting, he answered a few text messages and e-mails, including a group text from his mom inviting him and his brothers over for dinner tonight. She said Dad was smoking some ribs. She'd also added that they should include Becks, if she was available.

Someone had told her about Becks.

Kal, probably, since he was closest to Mom and told her everything. Jackson texted her and told her that he might stop by, and that he'd talk to Becks about coming, too.

He winced as soon as he sent the text, realizing that implied Becks was with him. Which she was, of course, but his parents didn't need to know that.

Then again, they might just think he was at home and so was she. Hopefully they'd think that.

Both Kal and Rafe said they'd be there. He'd have to see how Becks felt about going to dinner at his parents'. It wasn't like they were dating. Plus his brothers would all be there. It'd be fine. No pressure.

He hoped.

"Here."

He looked up from his phone and his jaw dropped.

Becks stood there, clothes draped in her hand. But it wasn't what was in her hand that made his breath catch. She wore a turquoise-and-black bikini top and black boy shorts that molded to her amazing body. She had curvy hips and gorgeous breasts along with tattoos scattered here and there. She had almost an entire sleeve of ink covering her right arm, several on her left arm, that heart above her breast, and more ink on her abs.

"You're beautiful."

Her lips curved. "Thanks."

"Turn around."

She'd pulled her hair into a high ponytail, revealing more tats on the back of her neck that he'd already had a glimpse of once or twice. There were flowers there, something pink and pretty. She also had one stunning tattoo of a tree on her back. It was encased within a circle, with twining branches and leaves that filled to the edges of the circle, and roots spreading across the bottom. The tattoo was devoid of color, which made it that much more interesting.

"What is this?" he asked, tracing his finger across the tattoo.

"The tree of life."

"It's amazing." He couldn't help but want to run his fingers over all of her ink. Up and down her arm there were all these sea creatures, and she had various words with vines and flowers entwined around them on the other arm.

"Your body tells a story."

She smiled at him. "Not many people get that."

"Score one for me, then."

She laughed and held out a bottle of spray sunscreen. "You can ask all the questions you want about my ink later. It's hot and I'm anxious to get in the water. How about you get this sunscreen on me?"

"Sure." He sprayed the sunscreen all over her, then did himself as well. She tucked the bottle in her bag and he put the bag in the truck and locked it up. He grabbed a couple of boogie boards from the back of the truck and they headed down the pier toward the beach.

It was a perfect day. Ocean breezes kept it from being too hot, but Jackson didn't much care about the heat. He intended to stay in or near the water. He hoped Becks felt the same way.

Apparently she did, because as soon as they got to the water's edge she slid belly first on her board into the water, the wave taking her for a long ride across the sand until another surge poured over the top of her. She laughed, grabbed the board and did it again.

He realized he could stand there and watch her, mesmerized, because her body was so in tune with the board and the waves. Some people never understood how you needed to relax into the board, ride the waves easy. He'd sat back and watched folks stand on a boogie board or a surfboard all stiff and unyielding, and then wonder why they toppled over. If they'd only loosen up, the ride would be so much more fun.

He could tell how relaxed Becks was. Even when she stood, there was no tension in her body. She was all fluidity in motion, her wet ponytail flying behind her as she skidded across the water.

Since the hot sun was bearing down on him and sweat ran in rivulets down his back, he decided it was time to get wet. He slid his board into the next wave and did a half flip, gliding into the air and diving into the wave. The cool water felt great. When he surfaced, Becks was right there, board in her arms.

"You really don't half-ass anything, do you?"

He grinned and shrugged. "No idea how much time any of us has, so might as well live the hell out of our lives."

She stared at him. "Did you lose someone close to you?"

At one point in his life, he'd lost everything in one shattering moment. One minute he'd been a happy, carefree kid. The next . . .

But that was the life he'd lived before, the part of his life he didn't want to recall. "Nah. But, you know, the work we do reminds us every day how fast it could all disappear."

"Of course. We've all been there. It's good to have fun, to appreciate life every day."

He liked that she understood, and of course she would, because she'd been where he'd been. Maybe their backgrounds weren't the same, but like his brothers, she'd lived down those dark alleyways. She'd gone hungry and had spent nights with the stars as a roof over her head. So to be where they were now? They'd gotten lucky.

"So let's get to appreciating this day."

"I will if you get out of my way." She shoved him aside and went running, attempting the same flip-over dive that he had done. The results weren't exactly the same, but she did a decent flip.

When she came out of the wave, she cast a brilliant smile at him.

"Okay, how was it?"

"I'd grade it a C minus."

"C minus? Bullshit. I flipped all the way up."

"You dove into the wave. Not above it. Want some lessons?"

"Sure."

He showed her how to propel the board along the wave, then over it. It took her quite a few tries—okay, a lot of tries. And he did it, too, to show her the body mechanics.

He gave her credit for not giving up, even when wave after wave slammed into her.

She might think he was fearless, but she was the same.

They finally took a break and sat at the water's edge, letting the waves lap over their legs.

This was where Jackson was most content. He liked that Becks seemed happy to just sit next to him and not talk. Some women—guys, too—felt the need to fill the void with chatter. But they soaked in the atmosphere together with silence.

Check off another thing that worked between them. It might be a small thing, but it was still important.

Which reminded him of a big thing.

"Oh, I almost forgot. My mom invited you over to dinner tonight."

She blinked. "Really. Meeting the parents, already? I had no idea we'd moved into that territory so fast."

He slanted a look at her. "It's not like that. I guess Kal must have told them you were living at the house, so Mom invited all of us over for dinner, and then said if you're available you should come, too."

She laid her head on his shoulder and batted her lashes at him. "Oh, Jackson. You don't have to hide your true feelings from me. I know you want to get married and have three babies in three years. I can't wait to tell Mom and Dad."

"Funny." Sense of humor. No tension or freak-out about having dinner at his parents' house. He liked that about her, too.

She laughed and straightened. "I'd love to come to dinner. It's nice of your mom to include me."

"Yeah, she's nice like that. She's also probably curious about you, so be prepared for a deluge of questions."

"I think I can handle it. After all, we're just friends. And roommates. Until we get married and have those three babies in three years."

She wiggled her brows and he laughed.

"You have a beautiful laugh, Jackson, and your whole face lights up. You should try it more often. It suits you better than your grumpy face."

He frowned. "I do not have a grumpy face."

"Oh, yes, you definitely do. You're doing it right now."

"I am not."

"Yes, you are." She laughed, which only made him frown again, then made him aware that he was frowning.

"Goddammit."

She smoothed her hand over his brow. "Frowning causes wrinkles. And life is short, remember? Smile more."

He liked her hand on him. She made him relax. "I'll take that under advisement."

They played in the water a while longer, until it was time to head back to the house to get ready for dinner.

After he showered, he stared at himself in the mirror, both frowning and smiling.

He did not have a grumpy face. He was generally a happy guy. Wasn't he?

Now he was going to think about his stupid face all night.

Dammit, Becks.

CHAPTER 12

BECKS SHOWERED AND CHANGED INTO A PAIR OF BLACK shorts and a red-and-white cotton short-sleeved shirt. She slipped on her canvas tennis shoes and then put on a touch of mascara. Summer was always too hot for makeup unless you were going somewhere fancy. She didn't think the guys' mom and dad cared whether she was made up. She towel-dried her hair, figuring by the time they got there it would be mostly dry.

When she came downstairs she found the guys in the game room, as she'd discovered they called the extra living area. They were all engrossed in some action game with a lot of explosions and warfare. She wasn't a gamer, so she had no clue what they were playing.

"Should I bring something, like a salad or salsa or a dessert? I can whip something up."

Kal shook his head while not taking his eyes off the TV screen. "Not necessary. Mom likes to cook. She says it relaxes her after a long week."

"Okay. But since I'm not one of her kids, don't you think I should bring something?"

Jackson did drag his gaze from the TV. "Hey, don't sweat it. She really will have everything taken care of and we all pitch in and help when we get there."

That, at least, was slightly more detailed information. "Okay."

"Ha. You're dead, Jackson," Rafe said.

Jackson tossed his controller on the table. "Shit."

Rafe laid his next to Jackson's. "Time to go anyway."

"Which means I kicked all your asses," Kal said.

Jackson pulled his keys out of his shorts pocket. "In your dreams. I killed you four times."

"But it's the last time that counts."

They had all headed toward the garage while they were arguing, so Becks followed.

"In whose universe?" Rafe asked. "You always make up your own rules."

Jackson nodded. "Yeah, and they're always wrong."

Kal seemed unoffended. "You're both jealous because I beat you all the time."

Jackson signaled for Becks to climb into his truck. "Someday you both might be as good as me."

She could hear Kal's loud laugh even after she closed the truck door.

As Jackson backed down the driveway, Becks glanced over at him. "Is it always like this?"

"Like what?"

"You and your brothers."

"What about—oh, the bickering?" He laughed. "That was tame. You should see when it gets physical. We can throw each other across a room."

Her eyes widened. "Oh, no. Does anyone get hurt?"

"Nah. It's all in fun. That's how we blow off steam."

"It sounds brutal."

"It's just play, Becks. We're all tough. We can take it and we all know the limits of roughhousing. So did our dad. Once we settled in with our parents and got comfortable enough to be ourselves, we really started having fun with each other."

Now that she knew they didn't actually try to kill each other, she leaned back against the seat. "It must have been amazing to grow up together."

"It was pretty incredible. Not a day goes by that I don't realize how damned fortunate I was to get adopted along with Rafe and Kal. All three of us adopted together? It's almost unheard of, especially at our ages."

"Obviously your parents saw something special in all of you."

"Yeah, I still question what that was. We were a trio of hard-luck cases. Especially me. I was bitter and angry and once the shock from being in the fire wore off, all I wanted to do was get back out on the street."

"So what stopped you?"

"Rafe and Kal. When our parents offered the option of fostering us, Rafe and Kal jumped on the idea. They wanted to stay."

Now she understood. "And you didn't want to be separated from them."

"Right."

"So you made the ultimate sacrifice and allowed the Donovans to foster you."

"Yeah. Some sacrifice. A warm bed, hot meals, a shower every day. And I got to go to school."

Most kids hated school. But for homeless kids who craved learning? Being able to attend school was like winning the lottery.

"I understand, Jackson. We had freedom to come and go as we pleased, to do whatever we wanted to do. We didn't answer to anyone, especially adults. That kind of freedom was hard to give up. And foster care was sometimes hazardous. It was like tossing a coin as to which was worse—the streets or the unknown of a foster home."

"Yeah."

He pulled into the wide driveway of a very nice ranch house. It was an older home, but Becks could tell it had been well maintained. The front yard was small but there were a couple of very pretty palm trees out front along with an extremely tall oak. She could picture the guys roughhousing on the front lawn, or riding their bikes down the long driveway.

It must have been heaven. She felt a pang of jealousy, then shoved it away.

She'd had a decent life and she was grateful for it.

"Nice house," she said as they got out of the truck.

He scanned the front of the house, then smiled. "It's home."

Home. A word not many of them had ever been familiar with. "It's a nice home."

He shrugged. "It's not so much what's on the outside that makes a place home, but the people on the inside."

She felt a rush of emotion at his words. "Isn't that the truth."

They walked in the front door, which was unlocked. Becks heard raucous noise coming from the family room, which was where Jackson led her. Rafe and Kal had already made themselves comfortable on one of the sofas, which faced another one where a very attractive black woman sat next to a striking-looking white man. Both looked to be in their late forties or early fifties.

"Hey, Becks is here," Rafe said.

The older couple stood and the woman came over to her with a smile on her face. "Becks, I'm Laurel Donovan. I've heard a lot about you."

Instead of a handshake, Becks was enveloped in a hug. It was a nice hug, too. Not smothering, but gentle and warm.

"Thanks, Mrs. Donovan."

"Oh, none of that," she said. "Call me Laurel."

"Okay."

Mr. Donovan held out his hand to shake hers. "Welcome to

our home, Becks. I'm Josh Donovan. Glad you decided to come along for dinner."

"Hi, Josh. And it's not like these guys would let me say no."

Josh laughed. "They can be persuasive."

"Come on, honey," Laurel said. "Let's go into the kitchen and have something to drink and get to know each other."

"No inquisitions, Mom," Jackson said.

Laurel pivoted. "When have I ever done an inquisition?"

"Every time we brought a friend over," Kal said.

"Hush, you," Laurel said, laughing.

Becks thought Laurel had the best laugh she'd ever heard. She felt instantly comfortable.

"Kal told me you have a tattoo business," Laurel said. "Wine or beer?" she continued as she opened the refrigerator in what was a small but very clean kitchen.

"Beer would be fine, thank you. And yes, I do. I assume he also told you how we ran into each other again after all the years apart."

"He did." She poured herself a glass of wine. "Let's sit at the table."

They each took a seat at the nicely sized wood table that took up almost all the space in the nook.

"I'm sorry about the smoke out at your place."

"It's okay. I just found a new spot for my shop and it's even better than the old one."

"Then I'm glad. Sometimes bad things happen to you so that something good can take its place."

"That's very true."

Laurel looked her over. "Your tattoos are beautiful. I have one on my hip that my boys don't even know about."

"Really." Becks cracked a smile. "What kind, if I can ask?"

"It's a leftover from my wayward youth. A spilled shot glass, of all things. I got it in Mexico one drunken night with my girlfriends."

Becks laughed. "Drunken tattoos are always the biggest regrets. But look at it this way, you had fun with your friends, didn't you?"

"Oh, it was memorable all right. Permanently memorable."

Becks let out another laugh. "Lesson learned. I've done some cover-ups for people who got drunken tattoos they want to forget ever happened."

Laurel lifted her chin. "I regret nothing. It's just funny to me now."

"That's the way to think of it." Becks took a swallow of her beer, letting the cool liquid soothe her dry throat. "I always think of mine as the story of my life. How I felt at a moment in time, my emotions, my heart, what I was going through."

"So your skin is an open book, the canvas of your life."

She loved that Laurel understood and her heart swelled. "Yes. Exactly like that."

"It's a beautiful canvas, Becks. Own your happiness as well as your sorrow. It makes you who you are."

"I intend to. Thank you."

Jackson appeared in the kitchen. "How's it going in here?" he asked as he went to the fridge to grab a beer.

"We're doing fine," Laurel said. "Getting to know each other. What are you guys all doing?"

"Talking work, of course." He stood there sipping his beer.

"Sounds great, honey," Laurel said, waiting.

Jackson continued to linger, until his mom gave him a look. When he still didn't move, she said, "Out."

He rolled his eyes and said, "Fine," then left the room.

Laurel turned to Becks and smirked. "I think he was wondering how you were faring in here, or if I was interrogating you."

"Hardly. And why would he even care?"

"Because he likes you. It's obvious."

Uh-oh. She had no idea how to respond to that. "Oh, we're just roommates."

"Becks, if we're going to be friends you need to understand that I know my sons better than anyone. Better than they know themselves sometimes. And I know when Jackson is interested in a woman. Trust me, he's interested in you."

"I see." She played with the condensation on her bottle of beer, feeling suddenly lost for words.

"If you're not interested in him, you should probably let him know that."

She lifted her gaze to Laurel. "Oh, I'm interested in him. And he knows it."

"Good. Then I'll butt out because it's now none of my business what the two of you do."

Thank God she wasn't one of those mothers who interfered in her kids' lives. Especially her adult sons' lives.

"I mean, nothing's happened between us yet. We're still feeling our way around each other. Plus I live at the house and it's kind of awkward with Rafe and Kal being there."

"You two will figure it out. It's nice to be reunited with all the boys, though, isn't it?"

"Honestly? It was kind of unbelievable. But in a very happy way. After that night in the storm when they disappeared, I didn't think I'd ever see any of them again. We were all so close back then. Losing them hurt."

Laurel cast a sympathetic look at her. "I'm sure it did. It must have been hard living on the streets."

"It was. But I ended up in foster care with some good people, so it worked out for me."

"Your choice, or did you get picked up?"

Obviously Laurel knew a lot about the system. "My choice, actually. Without Jackson and the others, I didn't have my support system."

"So you took the chance on foster care again."

She nodded. "I knew if I landed with a bad family I could run again. The streets were a known thing to me, and I'd done foster care before, too. But I was tired and hungry and I'd lost Jackson, Rafe and Kal. I just needed a roof over my head and some food in my belly."

Laurel shook her head. "And obviously it worked out for you that time."

"It did."

"I'm happy to hear that. The foster care system is imperfect, but sometimes there are so many wonderful people out there who really love and take good care of the kids."

"Yes, there are. I got lucky and ended up with a wonderful family. So did Jackson, Rafe and Kal."

She grinned. "Thank you. We love those boys and Josh and I feel as if we're the lucky ones."

Becks didn't know Laurel all that well, but what she'd seen so far told her that she really did love her sons.

Josh stuck his head in the doorway. "Sorry to interrupt the girl talk, but I'm ready to cook the chicken."

Laurel nodded. "I'll get it ready."

Laurel stood, and so did Becks. "What can I do to help?"

They ended up prepping the chicken, then made a kale salad with pomegranates and readied the corn to put on the grill along with the chicken. They also made green beans and some sweet potatoes. Becks's stomach rumbled the entire time.

"It must have been hell on you feeding three growing boys," she said as she pulled the bacon out of the oven to let it cool.

"It was a sight to behold watching those boys grow. It seemed like every time I turned around they'd each grown another few inches. And we were always out of milk."

Becks laughed. "I can imagine. They were skinny and gangly when I knew them. Of course lack of food didn't help. And Jackson always made sure the younger kids ate first."

Laurel leaned against the kitchen counter and stared into the living room for a few seconds before turning her attention back on Becks. "He did? That doesn't surprise me about him. He's always been a caretaker of his little brothers, even when they got older and didn't really need taking care of anymore."

She wondered . . . "Laurel, has Jackson ever talked to you about his time on the streets? Or before?"

"Not really. He never wanted to talk about the past."

"To me, either. I've tried to get him to open up to me, but so far I'm not getting much. He didn't even remember who I was that day of the fire at my shop. Rafe and Kal recognized me right off. Jackson didn't."

"I think he'd like to pretend his life started the day Josh rescued him and his brothers."

"I believe that." She crumbled the bacon in with the green beans and stirred, then put the lid on the pot to simmer. "This smells delicious."

"I don't know about you, but I'm starving."

"Me, too. And since everything is moving along in here, let's go see what they're doing outside. Come on."

Becks grabbed her beer and followed Laurel through the sliding door onto the back deck.

They had a small but nice backyard with a covered patio and a large deck. There were beautiful trees affording plenty of shaded space for kids to run around. It must have been great to grow up here. She could envision Jackson, Rafe and Kal as they'd been the last time she'd seen them as kids having a blast in this backyard.

Sometimes she wished she'd been able to stay connected with them throughout their childhoods. Growing up with them would have been her ideal. She could have visited them here, and maybe, if her foster parents had adopted her, they could have come over to her house.

Who knows? Maybe she and Jackson could have dated when she was a teenager. He might have even asked her to prom.

Which was totally unrealistic and foolish and childish, but hey, dreams were fun.

"How's it going out here?" Laurel asked, moving over to where Josh was manning the grill.

"Chicken's about done. How are things inside?"

"Same. Becks and I are hungry."

"All that gossiping work up an appetite?" Jackson asked.

"Oh, you are just dying to know what we were talking about, aren't you?" his mom asked.

Jackson shrugged. "Not the least bit interested, Mom."

Laurel cast a knowing look at Becks, who smiled.

She wondered if Jackson would ask her later about her conversation with his mom.

Or if he really wasn't interested at all.

DINNER WAS GOOD. GRILLED CHICKEN AND ALL THE VEG-etables had really filled him up. Plus, his mom had made ice cream for dessert. He'd had two bowls of that, which meant he'd have to run off some of these calories before he headed back to the fire station, because right now he felt like a slug.

He sat back and sipped on his glass of ice water. After that amazing dinner, beer just felt too heavy. He wandered the yard, checking out the jalapeños his dad was growing in the raised beds, along with some tomatoes and squash.

"What do you think?"

He looked up to find his dad next to him. "Everything's looking great. You're going to have a hell of a yield in the jalapeños."

"Yeah, we always end up with way more than we can use."

"And all the guys at the firehouse appreciate that."

His dad laughed. "Never mind sharing when there's plenty to go around."

"The chicken was great, Dad. Thanks for inviting us over."

His dad grasped his shoulder. "Door's always open, kid. You know that."

It was one of the things his dad had first said to him, back when Jackson wasn't sure about all of this family stuff. They'd had long sit-down talks with his mom and dad and Rafe and Kal, first about the fostering thing, and then, later on, about the possibility of Josh and Laurel Donovan adopting them.

Jackson had balked each time. Not because of Josh and Laurel. From the beginning they had been there when Jackson had needed them most. First, in the hospital while he'd recovered from the smoke inhalation from the fire. Then when he'd fought them over not being able to go back out onto the streets. It had been Laurel—his mom—who had stroked his arm and convinced him that it was best for his brothers, and better for him, to recover with a roof over his head and steady meals. And she'd told him if at any time he felt uncomfortable, he could bail and she'd look the other way.

He'd believed her. And he'd never once felt the need to run.

By the time the adoption came along, he was more than ready to have Josh and Laurel as his parents. Though that realization hadn't come easy to him. It had been a long time since he'd had real parents. So long he'd almost forgotten what his real parents looked like.

Almost.

The memories of them, of the last time he saw them, were so painful he tried his best to forget.

"You're quiet."

He lifted his gaze to find his dad staring at him. "Your comment about the door always being open made me think back about old times."

"Which ones?"

"When I first came to live here."

"So, some good times, some not so good."

He clapped his dad on the back. "All good times with you and Mom, Dad."

His dad smiled. "You're a good kid. Always were."

Jackson grinned. "Except that time when I was fifteen and I took your truck for a joyride in the middle of the night."

"Yeah, well, no kid is perfect. And as I recall, you spent a month with no TV, no phone and no video games as a result of that lapse in judgement."

Jackson winced. "That was the longest month of my life."

"You deserved it."

He laughed. "I did."

They walked along the beds, occasionally pulling weeds they saw.

"So . . . about Becks."

He knew the subject was going to come up. If not from his dad, then definitely from his mom.

"What about her?"

"Girlfriend? Roommate? What?"

"Just a roommate. I'm not in the market for a girlfriend."

"Have you ever been?"

His dad knew him all too well. "No. Not my thing."

"That's what concerns me."

This was new. He stopped, straightened, and looked at his father. "What?"

"That you don't form attachments."

"Dad, I have plenty of attachments. You and Mom and Rafe and Kal. I'm attached to all of you."

"That's family. We've been together a lot of years, and even that took an enormous amount of work to make happen, for all of us to bond together. I'm talking about a relationship. Someone to care about."

He shrugged. "I've had other things on my mind. My education. Fire training. Building my career. It wasn't exactly conducive to bringing a woman into my life."

"Maybe not in the beginning, but you've been settled into your firefighting career for a while now, Jackson. And yet you still seem to hold yourself away from forming any kind of bond with anyone."

Jackson didn't see it that way, and he was being honest with his father when he told him that his career had come first.

"I've dated plenty."

"Dating isn't the same thing as falling in love with someone. Have you ever even been in love?"

"No."

"Hmmm." His dad walked away, focusing his attention on his tomato plants.

Jackson followed. "What does that 'hmmm' mean?"

He looked up at Jackson, a warm smile on his face. "It means that maybe it's time to give that love thing a try, see how it feels."

Jackson already knew what it felt like to love people. To lose the people you loved. He wanted no part of that ever again.

"We'll see."

"Becks seems really nice."

Jackson glanced up at the porch where Becks sat with his mom. They were both drinking iced tea and engrossed in conversation as if they'd known each other forever.

He hadn't spent much time talking to Becks tonight. He didn't know why. Maybe because his mom had grabbed her right off and taken her into the kitchen to talk over . . . whatever it was the two of them had talked about.

Hopefully not him. Because while he had an attraction to Becks, that was all it was. That was all it ever could be.

"Yeah, she's nice."

"And you two have a lot in common."

He could see where his father was going with this. "I didn't even remember who she was when we first saw her again, Dad."

"That's because you try to shut out that part of your past. Maybe if you tried digging into it again you'd remember Becks more clearly."

"She was just a kid back then. I like the woman she is right now. That's enough for me."

"Hmmm."

His dad walked off, leaving Jackson feeling irritated and out of sorts.

Him and his *hmmms*. Jackson knew exactly what his dad was about. He meant that as a way for Jackson to start thinking about what he was doing and how he felt. He knew exactly how he felt. He felt just fine about the way things were going between Becks and him.

In the present. Today.

He didn't need to dig into the past to feel any differently about Becks.

And he sure as hell never needed to fall in love. With anyone. Ever.

CHAPTER 13

BECKS HAD HAD A GREAT NIGHT WITH JACKSON AND HIS family. His mother was warm and compassionate and they'd spent most of the evening together talking. Kal had joined in at one point and the two of them had regaled his mother with stories of their time on the streets. Not the bad stuff, just the fun times they'd had. And there had been a lot of fun times.

It had been fascinating to hear the story about Laurel's connections as a social worker and how she'd played an integral part in arranging for them to be placed in the Donovans' care as foster parents. Her connections had also helped pave the way for their eventual adoption.

The entire thing had been amazing and fortuitous. She'd told Kal she was so happy things had turned out for him like they had. He'd said he'd been lucky to end up with parents who loved him, considering what he'd started out with.

She knew he'd had bad circumstances with his birth parents, but back then none of them had ever delved too deeply into their pasts. She also knew she could probably ask him about it and he'd likely talk to her.

Unlike Jackson, who sat beside her on the ride home clammed up and not saying a word. Which wasn't unusual for him, but for some reason she got a vibe that he was irritated.

"Something wrong?" she asked.

"Nope."

Okay, then. Definitely pissed. She'd barely had a conversation with him all night, so it couldn't have been anything she'd done or said.

"Would you like to talk about it?"

"Nope."

"Of course you wouldn't."

He shot a glare at her. "What's that supposed to mean?"

"That you never want to talk about your feelings."

"I talk plenty about my feelings. I talked about my damn feelings all damn night. I'm just talked out."

"Okay. Sorry." Wow, definitely a bug up his ass. She intended to steer clear of Grumpy Firefighter for the rest of the night.

So she huddled against the door and checked social media, determined to pretend he didn't exist.

When he pulled into the driveway, he shut off the engine. She was about to hop out and go hide in her room when he said, "Sorry, Becks."

She turned to face him. "It's okay."

"It's not. My dad said some things that upset me and I barked at you and that's not fair. I shouldn't take it out on you. I'm sorry."

"You're forgiven. I'm sorry you're upset."

"Thanks."

They got out and went inside. She'd noticed neither Rafe nor Kal were home.

"Where are your brothers?" she asked.

He laid his keys on the hook just inside the door. "Friend of ours has a club. They mentioned they were going there after they left Mom and Dad's."

"Oh. Are you going?"

"The club scene isn't my thing. I'd rather swim a few laps and work off some of tonight's dinner."

"I'll let you get to it, then." She started to head upstairs.

"Hey, Becks."

She stopped at the landing where the stairs curved. "Yes?"

"Wanna take a swim with me?"

She tried to ignore the little flutter in her stomach elicited by his invitation. "I'd love to. I'll be right back."

She kept her steps slow and even as she ascended the stairs, trying not to run.

When she closed the door to her room, she stifled a small *Whee!* of excitement.

Honestly, girl. It's not like he asked you on a date or anything. You're just going for a dip in the pool. As roommates.

Yeah, right. Roommates who'd kissed.

Her lips still tingled from that kiss. Her sex still tingled from that kiss, and she remembered every detail he'd told her of the things he wanted to do with her.

She wanted all those things.

But for right this minute? A swim sounded great.

She changed into her swimsuit and slid into her flip-flops, threw a cover-up over her suit and went downstairs. She didn't see Jackson, so she assumed he was already outside.

He was, in the water doing laps.

Apparently he hadn't been kidding about the swimming laps part. She walked out there and kicked off her flip-flops, pulled off the cover-up and laid it over one of the chairs, then stood at the water's edge.

He apparently hadn't noticed her, which was good because she was enthralled watching the way his body knifed through the water, his arms cutting in without even making a wake. His movements were smooth and sure, the mark of confidence as he made his way to one end, dipped under and propelled his body forward before surfacing and stroking his way to the other edge.

He was mesmerizing to watch. She finally sat at the edge of the pool and dipped her legs in the water, wondering how long he'd be able to continue.

He did two more laps, then disappeared into the depths. Since it was dark outside and there were no lights on in the pool, she had no idea where he'd gone. She searched the water for him, looking for him to reappear on the other side of the pool, but he didn't.

Until she felt his hands on her ankles and he surfaced next to her, spraying her with water. She yelped.

"You scared the shit out of me," she said, kicking water at him.

He laughed. "Were you worried about me?"

"No. Yes. Dammit. Asshole."

He grinned. "You coming in?"

"I might."

"Come on. Jump. I'll catch you."

"I can swim, you know."

He gave her a devilish smile. "More fun if you let me catch you."

She got up, then jumped in, feeling his hands along her sides as she slid into the water. When she surfaced, he was right there. She swiped her hair out of her face and wrapped her legs around his waist.

"You saved me," she said.

"Yeah, you were in real danger in five feet of water."

"Hey, don't ruin my lifeguard fantasies."

He swept his hands around her back and bobbed them up and down in the nicely cool water. "Lifeguard fantasies, huh? Did I ever tell you I was a lifeguard for a couple of years?"

"Really. That explains how well you swim."

"Yeah. Dad got us all into swimming right away after he and

Mom fostered us. The first time they took us to the beach they realized we didn't know how to swim. After that weekend all three of us were signed up for swimming lessons."

"And you liked it." What she really liked was having her legs wrapped around Jackson, the two of them floating along the water while they talked.

"I liked it a lot. I'd always been drawn to the water. But, you know, it wasn't like we had family vacations at the beach or anything when we were kids."

"What about before?"

He frowned. "Before? Oh . . . I don't remember."

She'd bet he did remember, but he didn't want to talk about it. She wasn't going to push him. Not tonight. "Obviously you love the water."

"There's nothing like it. The buoyancy, that feeling of freedom you get when it's just you and the water. I always felt that. Even before I knew how to swim. You know?"

"I understand. I loved the water, too. Sometimes when I'd go off by myself, I'd sneak out to the beach on weekends when it was crowded with people and just hide out and watch, imagining myself as part of one of those happy families."

He smoothed his knuckles over her cheek. "That's like a form of self-torture, Becks."

She shrugged. "Not for me it wasn't. It was like a game of fantasyland. I liked to imagine that someday it could happen."

"And did it?"

She shrugged. "Sort of. That nice family that fostered me also liked the ocean. And they only fostered four kids, so they'd take us to the beach sometimes. They also had a pool in the backyard and my foster dad taught me to swim."

"That's nice."

"It was."

"Do you still see them?"

"My foster parents? After I first aged out I visited a few times. They always welcomed me. But they ended up having to move up north when Rosie—that's my foster mom—when her mother got sick. So they moved to Vermont."

"I'm sorry."

"It's fine. I liked her, but she wasn't my real mom or anything."

"Do you miss her?"

"Sometimes. I don't have a mom person to talk to about mom-and-daughter things. Then again, I never had that anyway, so how can you miss what you never had?"

He shifted her so he held her in his arms. "You're so matter-of-fact about it. Doesn't it hurt?"

Some people would be bothered that he was digging. She liked that he wanted to know more about her, about her past and her feelings. "Yes and no, which I know doesn't make sense. We didn't exactly have traditional childhoods. I've been to friends' houses and seen relationships they have with their parents—both good ones and bad ones. You and your brothers have a wonderful relationship with your parents."

"Yeah."

"My friend Margie? Her parents are awful people."

He frowned. "How so?"

"Always fighting with each other. Margie says it's tense there, all the time. She moved out when she was eighteen, just to get away from the constant bickering. She said they should have gotten a divorce a long time ago, but they're that couple that stayed together because of the kids. Margie has two younger siblings. Anyway, she said her parents play the blame game and she and her siblings have always been dragged into the middle of their fights."

"That can't be fun."

"No. My parents were awful people, too. But they were just

criminals and drug dealers. At least they got along. Which isn't saying much."

"So what happened with you and your parents?"

"I got in the way. Can't make money selling dope when there's always a kid who wants to be fed and taken to school and has homework. So they just up and took off one day when I was at school."

"Are you fucking kidding me?"

She shook her head and pulled away from him, letting herself float in the water, the awful memories of that day making her wish she could escape them. "Not kidding. When I got home the apartment was empty. Not that there was much there to start with."

"Christ, Becks. I'm sorry. What did you do?"

"Sat there for a really long time and cried. I was eight years old, so I didn't know what to do. Then I waited for them to come home, figuring they'd gone out."

"How long did you wait?"

"Three days. I went to school, came home, stayed alone at night, scared and huddled in my bed with all the lights on, hoping they remembered they had a kid they were supposed to come home to. I waited as long as I could, but the food ran out and I got so hungry I had to tell my teacher at school that my parents hadn't come home for several days. They called child services, who collected me and placed me in foster care."

"How long did you last in foster care?"

"I made it two years initially, then I bailed when I was ten. That was after the experience with creepy foster dad. I had a hard time trusting people after that, and one of the kids I was housed with told me you were often safer on the streets if you could hook up with a group you trusted."

"What about your parents? Did they ever come back for you or try to get you back?"

She lifted herself out of the pool and sat on the edge. "No.

Child services and the cops searched for my parents, but I was never told they'd been found."

He swam over and hoisted himself next to her. "Well, that sucks."

"Yeah."

He waited a beat, then asked, "Did you ever look for them when you were an adult?"

She nodded. "At first I didn't want to know, but once I graduated from high school I researched. My dad's doing thirty years in the federal penitentiary in Tallahassee for armed robbery with a deadly weapon. My mom died of a drug overdose ten years ago."

He drew her into his arms. "Goddammit, Becks. I'm sorry."

She'd cried buckets of tears for what seemed like days on end when she'd found out about her mom and dad. Why, she had no idea, since it was obvious they'd never cared about her. And then she vowed to never think about them ever again, to never let them or thoughts about them enter her universe again.

And they hadn't. Until tonight. Strangely enough it didn't hurt as much talking about them as it had before. Maybe because Jackson had been holding her, and their tone had been conversational. He'd never once pressed her to give up information she might not have wanted to.

And right now the comfort he gave her by holding her in his arms was all she needed to banish those ghosts from her past.

"Thank you," she said, letting her head remain on his chest.

"For what?"

"For letting me talk about it. I know you don't like to relive the past."

"Hey." He tipped her chin so she was looking at him. "This is your past, not mine. And you can talk about it anytime you want to."

"Thanks. I hadn't intended to. It just kind of . . . fell out."

He smiled. "Well, feel free to let any parts of you fall out that feel natural to you."

She arched a brow. "You mean you'd like me to get naked."

"Hey, that's not what I meant, but if you're suggesting it I won't object."

She laughed. "Whatever. I'd like a beer, though." She stood and grabbed a towel to dry herself. "You want one?"

"Sure."

After she was certain she wasn't dripping wet anymore, she went inside and made a pit stop to the downstairs bathroom, then came out and headed to the refrigerator, surprised to find Jackson in the kitchen, slicing a peach.

"I said I was going to grab the beers."

"I got hungry," he said. He took a piece and held out his hand.

She started to take the slice from his hand, but he pulled it back. "Let me."

She stared at him, at the hunger in his eyes that had nothing to do with peaches. Yes, she'd like to let him do all kinds of things. She opened her mouth and he slid the peach slice between her lips.

The fruit was juicy and some of it ran down her chin. She tilted her head back and Jackson leaned in to lick her neck.

She gasped, chewed and swallowed, then tried to breathe as his tongue mapped a trail from her neck to her jaw. Then he put a slice of peach between his teeth and brought his lips near hers.

She bit half of the peach, sucking it into her mouth while he took the other half.

God, she wanted to kiss him. He didn't draw back, just kept his gaze intently on her—on her mouth as she chewed and swallowed the peach.

She didn't wait for him to lick the juice running down from her chin. She held his head between her hands and swept her tongue across his lips, tasting the juicy peach and softness of his lips along her tongue. Sweet. Juicy. Maddeningly hot. And when he wrapped an arm around her to draw her close and fit his mouth to hers, she trembled.

He hesitated. "Okay?"

She nodded. "Yes. Kiss me."

The kiss was fire, causing her body to erupt in an explosion of heat and sensation, every nerve ending going haywire in reaction to the taste of him, the feel of his hands wandering over her skin. She licked her tongue over his, his answering groan making her weak with desire.

His fingers mapped a trail down her back, settling just above the top edge of her bikini, teasing her butt.

If they didn't get naked soon, she might not survive.

She pulled her lips from his. "Sex, Jackson. Now."

One corner of his mouth lifted. "I like a demanding woman."

He took her hand and they left the kitchen, taking the stairs. They made it halfway up the stairs to the landing when Jackson pushed her against the wall, his mouth devouring hers. Hot flames of desire lit inside her and she couldn't control her breathing any longer. The kiss went on and on until she felt drugged with pure sensual joy.

She hadn't realized she'd been missing this—having a man touch her and kiss her—until Jackson had laid his mouth and his hands on her. She'd been so preoccupied with work lately that she hadn't taken the time to enjoy these pure carnal pleasures.

She wouldn't make that mistake again, because having Jackson's hands roaming over her feverishly turned-on skin was everything.

He untied the top of her bikini and it fell forward, baring her breasts. He cupped one breast, using his thumb to slide back and forth over her nipple.

She gasped, the sensation unbearably delicious. And when he leaned over to take a nipple into his mouth and sucked, her legs nearly buckled. Watching him play with and lick her breasts and nipples while she leaned against the wall of the stair landing seemed so incongruous and ridiculous, yet utterly hot at the same time. Her body was on fire and alive like never before.

And then he dropped to his knees and dragged her bikini bottom down to her ankles. He lifted his gaze to hers.

"Step out of these."

She did, but then realized she was exposed in more ways than one.

"Jackson."

"Yeah."

"What if your brothers come home?"

"They won't. And I can hear the garage door come up, so relax."

She was going to try, but she wasn't sure she could. What if—

"Ohhh."

He'd slipped his hand between her legs and began to rub against her sex, and all thoughts of where she was vanished. Instead, she was caught mid-breath in a web of utter pleasure. She felt like she might explode.

Surely he couldn't make her come that fast. But she was already close, her body humming in tune to the expertise of his seeking fingers. He teased and stroked her with his fingers, and suddenly it was his mouth there, covering her clit with his lips. She let out a cry of delight as his warm lips sucked on her most sensitive areas.

"Ohhhh," she said again, realizing that unintelligible mumbling was all she could manage. She didn't even have to direct him where to go because she was already there. She moaned, rocked against his mouth and let go, crying out with her orgasm.

She rode his face with wild abandon, not even caring if the house came down around her at the moment, because this climax was so damn good.

"Mmmm," he replied against her sex, the low hum of his voice making her come harder. He stayed right there with her until she stopped shaking. And then he stood and smiled at her.

She shuddered out a smile while simultaneously catching her breath.

"Well, that was good," she said.

She thought now they'd continue up to the bedroom.

"Wait right here," he said.

Apparently they weren't going to the bedroom, because as she rested against the wall Jackson disappeared upstairs for what seemed like half a second, but what did she know of time, because she was in a sex-soaked daze. When he came back he dropped his board shorts. Becks barely had a fraction of a second to appreciate the beauty of his naked body before he slid on a condom, then hoisted her into his arms and pushed her against the wall again, this time entering her with a slow, easy thrust.

"Oh, yeah," he said. "Just like this."

She dug her nails into his shoulders, feeling him swelling inside her.

"*Oh, yeah* is right," she said, meeting his gaze as he partially pulled out, then slid back into her. "Jackson."

The eye contact was intense, the way he looked at her as he drove deep making her convulse with pleasure.

She might die, right here on the landing, and she wouldn't care because this felt amazing. Jackson felt amazing, especially when he moved in close and rubbed against her, hitting all her pleasure spots and dragging her ever closer to another climax.

She ran her fingertips over his shoulders and down his arms, feeling the flex in his muscles as he held her as if she weighed nothing, which wasn't true at all. But he was balancing her with one hand while increasing his pace as he moved within her, and she lost her mind, especially when he slammed his hand against the wall.

"Fuck," he said, grinding against her. "You feel so damn good, Becks."

His skin was slick with sweat as she swept her hands across his back. She knew what it was costing him to hold her, but she was so close and all she could think about now was getting there again and taking him with her. "Harder."

"Hell yeah," he said, driving into her faster and deeper, spurring her on ever closer to the edge.

She was there. Right there, tipping on the edge of the best damn thing ever.

"Come with me," she said, digging her nails into his biceps.

"Dammit, Becks. Goddammit."

He was breathing hard, and pushing both of them even harder. But she wanted him to go with her. So when he gripped her butt in a tight hold and tilted her pelvis, she lost it, shuddering as she came.

And he did go with her, letting out a loud groan as he slammed her so hard against the wall she knew she'd have bruises tomorrow. Glorious, sex-induced bruises. And she didn't care because her orgasm lasted all the way through Jackson's.

He finally let her legs slide to the floor, but she wasn't sure she was steady enough to stand. He wrapped his arm around her to hold on to her while she gained feeling in her tingling legs.

Frankly, she wasn't sure how he was still standing. She felt his arms shaking.

"Hell of a workout, huh?" she asked.

"Let's just say I'll be able to skip arms at the gym tomorrow."

She laughed.

They headed upstairs and when they got to the top, he paused and turned to her.

"Your room or mine?"

She shrugged. "Mine's fine."

They went into her room and she closed and locked the door. She followed Jackson into the bathroom and turned on the water in the shower.

She turned to Jackson. "How about a quick rinse-off?"

"Since you made me sweaty, I'm all for it."

He stepped in with her and she backed into the spray, swiping her hair back. The warm water felt good. What felt even better was having Jackson pour soap in his hands to scrub her back.

Just having his hands on her felt good. And when she rinsed, she turned him around and returned the favor.

She washed and rinsed her hair and they got out of the shower. She handed Jackson a towel and got one so she could dry herself off.

"This would be way more fun if you let me dry all your parts," he said.

"I'm more interested in getting you into bed so I can check out your naked body."

His brows popped up. "I'm game for that."

She climbed onto her bed and used the heels of her feet to push back toward the head of the bed. Jackson followed, sliding alongside her. She rolled to her side and propped her head in her hand.

"I've been waiting for this," she said.

"What's that?" His fingers whispered a trail between her breasts.

"You. Me. Naked and alone together."

"Really. Fantasized about it and everything?"

"Naturally. Didn't you?"

"Yeah. And I've been wanting to get a look at your ink."

She rolled over onto her back and tucked one arm behind her head. "Look away."

Jackson had thought about this moment for a while now, ever since he'd gotten his first good look at Becks. And though she wore a lot of tank tops and shorts and he'd gotten to see some of her tattoos, it wasn't like he'd had the opportunity to inspect them up close like he was doing now.

Her artwork was amazing. He started with her left arm, running his fingers over the purple octopus and blue dolphin to the gray humpback whale and amazing sea turtle. And laced throughout each tattoo were waves and plankton and coral and smaller fish, as if he were actually getting a glimpse into the ocean.

"Why the sea creatures?"

"I had this fantasy of living under the sea when I was a kid. That Poseidon would come rescue me and take me to live with him."

Jackson searched her arm. On her outer shoulder he found a man with white hair and a flowing beard, ocean waves rising around his legs. He held a large trident.

"Poseidon, I presume?"

She nodded.

"Does he protect you?"

"It's been working so far."

"Glad to hear it." He climbed over her to inspect her other side, where vines crawled around lines and paragraphs of words.

"And all this?"

"Poetry, one-liners of things I've found and liked over the years."

"And who have you liked?"

"Oh. The list is endless. Maya Angelou, E. E. Cummings, Langston Hughes, Dylan Thomas, Robert Frost, Keats, Andrea Gibson, Margaret Atwood. A few things I wrote."

She wrote poetry? "Yeah? Which ones are yours?"

She lifted her arm and searched the writings. "That one."

He read the paragraph. Dark lines intertwined by bleeding vines. The line read:

My pain has made me powerful. I will never be pushed away again.

He looked up at her. "Wow. That's intense. But why do I feel there's more to this?"

She shrugged. "I have a journal where I write some poetry now and again."

"So this is a line from one of your poems."

"Yes."

"Which means there's more to this one, right?"

"Yes."

He sensed her wariness, as if she wasn't sure she could trust her innermost thoughts to him. He knew exactly how she felt, but he was still curious to see more. "Can I see it?"

She gave him a dubious look. "You like poetry."

"I like you."

She stared at him for a few seconds, then got up and went to her dresser. She pulled out a notebook and clutched it close to her chest, as if it held secrets she didn't want to divulge.

"You don't have to share it with me if it makes you uncomfortable, Becks. But I'd love to read some of your poetry."

She sat on the bed, flipped some pages and handed it to him. "It's from this one."

He sat up and read the poem.

Don't push me away.
I've been to dark places, where the cold is so hot the
*   devil won't tread there.*
I've bled soul-tearing heartache that makes strong men
*   weep.*
My fury is relentless, my pain as deep as the core of the
*   universe.*
I've lived at the bottom and risen, a tower of strength
*   and resolve.*
My pain has made me powerful. I will never be pushed
*   away again.*

Jackson read the lines over and over again, breathing in the hurt in her words and wondering what had caused it. He finally lifted his gaze to find her studying him.

"These words . . . they're strong. They show how formidable you are, Becks."

She frowned. "Don't tease me."

"I'm not. The words are raw. Honest. Your writing is good, Becks. Really good."

He saw the stain of pink blush across her cheeks. "Thank you."

He handed the journal back to her and she slipped it on top of her dresser, then climbed back in bed.

"So you were in a dark place when you wrote it."

She shrugged. "Not really. Sometimes I can't help but relive dark times, go back to the place of those memories. Journaling helps remind me that I'm stronger now than I've ever been."

"See? That's why I don't think about the past. It only drags you down."

She crossed her legs over each other, and he liked that she was so comfortable about being naked with him. Plus, she was beautiful and he could look at her body for a long damn time.

"I disagree. It's okay to go back, to remind yourself of where you came from."

He drew his finger over the broken heart above her left breast. "Like this? To feel that pain again? Why?"

"To retrace your steps. To figure out how you got from there to here. What you did right, and what you did wrong."

"Oh, come on, Becks. Who the fuck wants a hard look backward at all the bullshit they had to go through to get to now?"

"Yes, there were bad times. But there was good, too. We had to climb through mountains of pain, but if it was all awful neither one of us could have survived it. I also take the time to remember the people I met along the way. The ones who helped me get here." She smoothed her hand along his thigh. "Like you."

He felt a twinge in his gut. "I didn't do anything."

"Are you serious? Don't you remember when . . ." She stopped, let go of his leg. "You really don't remember. Any of that time."

He never wanted to. Not after . . . "I remember the night of the fire, being at the beach house with Rafe and Kal. Everything from that night is vivid to me."

She didn't ask. He appreciated that. But even though she didn't, the memories of that night came rushing back. He didn't want to remember it. None of it. Not that night, none of the shit before that.

He pushed it back, far back until the rising panic went away. And instead, he pulled Becks down on her back. "I like living in the now. Where I have a beautiful woman lying next to me."

She swept her fingers over his forehead. Her fingers were cool, offering relief to the mental torture of his past twisting around in his mind.

"Those memories still linger, Jackson. Anytime you want to talk about them, I'm happy to listen."

"I think we talked enough. There are other things I want to do with my mouth now."

He loomed over her, watching her smile light up her eyes. "Really. What kinds of things?"

"Let's start here." He kissed her, a light brush of his lips over hers. He wanted more, deeper, to get lost in the taste of her so he could forget the memories that had tried to surface, but this wasn't about him. It was about playing with Becks.

So he pulled back and trailed light kisses along her jaw before sliding down to her neck.

"Or maybe here." He continued on, using both his lips and tongue to map the skin of her throat and along her collarbone, before dipping into the valley of her breasts.

The sounds she made let him know she was enjoying the direction he was going. He liked it, too. Her skin was petal soft under his lips, she smelled like vanilla soap and the sounds she made caused his dick to get hard. And when he mapped his way over her belly, he felt her abdominal muscles ripple.

He teased her right hip with his teeth and she jumped. He lifted his head. "Ticklish here?"

She gave him a pointed stare. "Yes. Are you?"

He laughed. "No."

She wriggled out from under him and pushed him onto his back. "Let's find out."

"Hey, I wasn't finished with you."

She straddled him. "I'm just getting started. I told you I wanted the chance to explore your body. You wouldn't want to deny me, would you?"

She raked her nails across his chest, and lower. His dick pounded every time she slid her sweet pussy along his hips. There was no way he was going to stop her from touching him.

"Feel free to have your way with me."

She gave him a devilish smile. "I intend to."

With her damp hair spilling across her shoulders and teasing the tips of her nipples, and the sparkle in her eyes that said she was in the mood to play, Jackson was sure that he'd fallen into some sort of dream, the kind he thought about when he had his dick in his hand to jack off. Becks leaned forward and kissed him, aligning her body on top of his. He felt the press of her breasts against his chest, teasing her feet along his legs, and it took everything in him not to take control, to flip her onto her back and plunge his cock into the softness of her pussy so he could ease the ache inside him.

But Becks wanted to explore, so he was going to lie there and let her touch him. Not that he could really consider it suffering since she was currently sliding her hands over his shoulders and down his chest.

"You have a great body, Jackson," she said after pulling her lips from his. "Not overly muscled, which I hate."

His lips quirked. "You hate muscles?"

"The guys who spend every day at the gym bulking up so their necks are as thick as their heads? Yeah, I hate those kinds of muscles."

"Some guys like to work on their bodies."

She paused in her exploration and sat up. "You know guys like that."

"Yeah, we have a couple of the guys in the department who work out pretty seriously. Nothing wrong with that, they just like to bulk up. Makes them feel strong, like they can do their jobs better. And one of them competes as a bodybuilder."

She twisted her lips, then shrugged. "I guess if that's your thing and it makes you happy, it's fine. But I'm not attracted to men like that."

He grasped her hips. "So you're saying I'm wimpy."

She laughed and ran her fingers over his abs. "You're hardly wimpy. You have a magnificent body. Lean and hard in all the right places. You have plenty of muscle, it's just not bulging like you're about to explode.

He laughed. "Well, now that you've described it that way, I'll be sure not to become a bodybuilder."

"Good. Because I love your muscle just the way it is. Which is why I've wanted to get you naked and get my hands all over you."

She scooted down his thighs and leaned over to brush her lips across his neck, her tongue flicking out to tease his skin. He closed his eyes and soaked in the feel of her tongue dragging across his neck.

He liked it. Hell, she could flay his skin from his body with her teeth and he'd probably like it as long as it was Becks touching him in some way. Whatever she was doing to him? He wanted more of it.

So when she rolled her tongue over his nipples, he groaned, unconsciously lifting his hips to drag his cock against her.

"Mmm," she murmured against his skin. "I know what you need."

Becks had everything he needed. Her sweet body, her mouth

on his heated skin and the sexy sound of her voice. Though all three of those were torture right now as she slid down his body, using her tongue to torment him.

She wound her hand around his cock and he dragged in a breath, bracing himself up on his elbows to watch as she flicked her tongue over the head of his shaft before fully bathing his cockhead with her tongue.

Christ, the heat of her tongue was unbearable, and yet he needed it more than he needed to breathe.

Then she lifted up and slowly covered his cock with her mouth. He shuddered as he watched his cock disappear into the recesses of her hot mouth. He lifted, feeding more of his shaft to her, and when she wrapped her hand around the base and started to stroke and suck, he wanted this sweet torment to last forever.

"Oh, yeah, suck it like that."

He took in ragged breaths as she wound her tongue around him, then drew him in deep. She had a wicked, sexy, hot-as-fuck mouth and he was going to lose it soon.

"Becks, I'm gonna come."

She made a humming noise and swirled the tip of his cock like an ice cream cone, then went down on him like she was starving, taking him in, urging him to let go.

He swept her hair to the side so he could watch her cheeks hollow while she sucked, felt the way she squeezed his cock.

And then he lost it, jettisoning spurts of come into her hot, greedy mouth. His orgasm blew the top of his head off, making him feel weak and dizzy and totally at her mercy.

It was fucking great.

After, he lay spent and unable to form words.

Becks moved to his side and lay next to him. When he could manage to move his limbs again, he rolled over to face her. He swept his thumb over her bottom lip, then drew her toward him to kiss her.

"I think I lost a million brain cells when I came."

She gave him a smile. "I'll be sure to quiz you with some brain puzzlers later just to be safe."

She laid her head on his shoulder and wrapped her leg around his hip.

It was nice. Probably too nice. He made a mental note to hightail it out of there in a few minutes. He didn't want things to get too close between them.

And then he fell asleep.

CHAPTER 14

BECKS WOKE EARLY TO THE FEEL OF A HAND CUPPING HER breast. She looked down and smiled.

She was surprised, actually, that Jackson was still in bed with her. But she wasn't complaining.

Easing out of his grasp, she quietly flipped over.

God, the man was beautiful when he slept. His features were easy on the eyes. Long lashes, full lips, a straight, narrow nose. Incredibly sexy beard stubble. She wanted to run her fingers over his bottom lip. She really liked his mouth. She also wanted to kiss him. Maybe wake him up. Have more sex.

Okay, he probably needed some sleep. They'd stayed up late last night. He'd passed out. So had she. Then sometime in the middle of the night he'd woken her up, hard and demanding and they'd reached for each other, no words, just passion and need, both of them in such a hurry for each other Jackson barely had time to slip the condom on. Her body flamed up just thinking about the hot, wicked tangle of limbs, the feel of his body sliding against her, the way he'd touched her and made her come in such short order.

And then they'd fallen asleep again still tangled together. She smiled, remembering the exhaustion after that bout of sex.

Not wanting to rouse him, she got dressed and went downstairs to make coffee.

No one else was up, so she took a couple of sips to help her wake up, then set the cup aside and got out ingredients to make biscuits and gravy. She started the sausage, letting that sizzle while she made the dough for biscuits. When the sausage was done, she set them aside and finished forming the biscuit dough, covering it up to let it rise.

Then she made herself another cup of coffee and went outside to sit by the pool.

She could already feel the sweat beading between her breasts. It was going to be a brutally hot day. In fact, after about ten minutes she couldn't handle being outside, so she grabbed her cup and made her way into the cool air-conditioned house.

She found Kal leaning against the counter drinking a tall glass of juice.

"Morning," she said, coming up next to him to rinse her coffee cup in the sink.

"Mornin'. I see you got breakfast started."

"I thought biscuits and gravy sounded good."

"They do. I think I'll cut up some fruit to go with it, if that sounds okay to you?"

"Kal, it's your house. You can do anything you'd like. I'm not mistress of the kitchen, you know."

"Okay. But just so you know, Mistress of the Kitchen sounds kind of badass. And should come with a whip."

She laughed. "I like this idea, especially if it means I don't have to do dishes ever again."

Kal frowned. "Maybe I didn't think this through."

"Think what through?"

She looked up to find Rafe coming down the stairs. He yawned and dragged his fingers through his hair.

"Kal said I'm now mistress of the kitchen and I get to call the shots in here. Oh, and you guys are forever in charge of doing the dishes."

Rafe shot his brother a frown. "What the . . . dude, engage your brain first before you make words."

Kal shrugged. "I haven't had any coffee yet."

"In the future, make sure you don't speak before you've had a cup."

Becks laughed. She'd missed these guys. They had been her fun when they were kids.

She poured juice and climbed up on a chair at the island. "Remember that time we snuck into the fair?"

Kal grinned. "Yeah. And then someone got a phone call and ran off and left their uneaten to-go lunch on the table."

"Yes," Becks said. "I remember it was a turkey sandwich, with chips. You and me and Rafe split it."

Rafe took his coffee cup and came around the island to sit next to her. "Best damn turkey sandwich I ever ate. It was loaded down with turkey and lettuce and tomatoes."

"And mayo," Kal added. "Plus the plate had a ton of chips."

"Don't forget the pickle," Becks said.

Rafe leaned into her. "We took turns taking a bite of the pickle."

She laughed. "How could I forget? You and Kal argued about who was taking the biggest bites."

"Hey, we were growing boys. We would always argue about food."

"We ate good that day, though."

She struggled to remember something. "Where was Jackson that day?"

"I don't remember," Kal said.

"I do," Rafe said. "He was with some girl he'd met on the beach. We asked him to come with us but he said he had a date."

Kal laughed. "Yeah, yeah. He even went to the Y to get cleaned up so he'd be all pretty smelling for her."

"Oh, right," Becks said. "Now I remember."

She remembered being crushed and devastated and all those girly things because she'd had a thing for Jackson even then.

She remembered hanging out in her tent, trying to keep from drowning in her own prepubescent sorrows. Then Rafe and Kal had asked her if she wanted to go on an adventure. At first she'd wanted to say no, but then she'd realized there was no point in feeling sorry for herself, especially since Jackson had totally forgotten about her to go on his "date," so why not?

She'd ended up having the time of her life. They had no money so they couldn't play games on the midway or ride any of the rides, but there were so many other things they could do for free. There were the buildings with animals, where the kids involved in 4-H showed off their cows and pigs and goats.

It smelled awful in there, but Becks had loved seeing all the animals and the looks of pride on the kids' faces. It must have been amazing to be responsible for raising those animals. And then they'd gone to the craft buildings to see all the handmade items.

Becks pretended all the sweet old ladies in there were her grandmother. Probably because she'd never known her grandparents.

Hell, she'd barely known her own parents.

"I've done my share of Dumpster diving in my life," Rafe said. "But that fair was like one of the biggest scores of our lives, food-wise."

Kal pointed at him. "Oh, that's right. We ended up finding a big shopping bag that someone had discarded, and then we found food all over the place and brought it back to our tents for everyone to share."

Becks smiled at the memory. "We were heroes that night. Everyone ate."

"And on a day when everyone eats," Kal said, shooting his gaze over to Rafe to let him finish.

"It's a good day." Rafe grinned.

Becks nodded. "Yes. That was a good day."

She never took that for granted, never forgot where she came from. She'd gone hungry so many days, weeks, months. She still volunteered at the food bank, still gave part of the money she earned to various organizations that helped the homeless. And she often walked around where they all used to call home and made sure they got fed and had clothes and necessities.

There was nothing so debasing as being homeless. That feeling of helplessness and hunger had made her feel less than human. She never wanted anyone to feel that way.

The door to her room opened and she saw Jackson make his way from her room down the hall to his. He didn't even look their way, almost as if he were still asleep.

Rafe and Kal looked from the second floor to her.

"We slept together," she said.

"Huh," Rafe said. "What a surprise."

"I'm hugely shocked," Kal said, then turned to make himself a cup of coffee.

She smiled and shook her head, knowing that neither of them was shocked or surprised.

She slid off the bar stool and went to the sink to wash her hands so she could start working on making the biscuits.

Kal started slicing fruit and Rafe asked what he could do, so she instructed him on how to start making the gravy using the sausage pan she'd used earlier.

"You three look busy."

She glanced up as Jackson entered the kitchen. She tried not to pay attention to the way her heart did a quick flutter, or notice how hot he looked in his board shorts and muscle shirt.

Interestingly enough, Rafe had come downstairs this morning in shorts and no shirt. The man was incredibly ripped. And Kal had an awesome body, too. She looked at both of them.

Nothing. She felt nothing. They were like her brothers.

Jackson, on the other hand . . .

She heaved out a sigh, placed the biscuits on the pan and shoved them in the oven.

"Thought we'd have breakfast together," she said. "If you're hungry."

"I'm definitely hungry." He made his way to the kitchen cabinets and grabbed a cup, turning his back on his brothers and shooting Becks a knowing smile.

"Probably from all those calories you burned having sex with Becks last night," Rafe said with a smirk.

Jackson's gaze shot to Rafe, then over at Becks. "You told them?"

"She didn't have to, man," Kal said. "We both saw your walk of shame out of Becks's room."

"Walk of shame," Becks whispered, trying to hide her amused smile.

Jackson glared at Rafe and Kal. "Just . . . mind your own business, got it?"

His look was dead serious. Becks was glad he wasn't directing that look at her.

Rafe raised his hands. "Got it."

"Ditto," Kal said.

"Good." He turned to Becks. "Anything I can do to help?"

She looked around, doing mental inventory before turning to face Jackson.

"Maybe some eggs to go with all of this?"

He gave her a quick nod. "On it."

She went to set the table while the guys finished up. Then she pulled the biscuits from the oven and placed them on a plate on the table. By then Jackson had finished the eggs and the gravy was done. The fruit salad was added and Kal had poured some mango juice for everyone.

And now Becks was hungry as well.

The eggs were creamy, the biscuits and gravy were smooth and soft and delicious and the fruit was tart and sweet. Becks devoured every bit of hers, shocking herself by how much food she ate.

"Wow, you were hungry, Becks." Kal looked at her empty plate before lifting his gaze to hers. "Just how much—"

"Don't even say it," Rafe said under his breath but enough for Becks to hear. "He'll kick your ass all the way down the block."

Jackson was too busy cleaning his own plate to pay attention to the other guys, fortunately. She'd hate for him to jump all over his brothers because of her.

Besides, she thought their comments were funny. It wasn't like they were being snide or disrespectful. She'd always thought of Rafe and Kal as her brothers—her family. It was only Jackson she'd thought of differently.

For obvious reasons.

She took the last swallow of mango juice, then leaned back in her chair, completely satiated.

"Great breakfast, Becks," Kal said.

"It was a team effort. So thank you."

"Hey, we're always a team," Rafe said. "From the beginning."

"Do you guys ever go back to where we used to stay?" she asked.

"No," Kal said. "I don't ever want to go back there."

"Too many bad memories," Rafe said.

She looked at Jackson.

"You already know my answer. Why?"

She shrugged and started stacking plates. "Before you got up this morning, the guys and I were reminiscing about some fun times we had."

Jackson piled forks onto the top of the plates. "We've talked about that."

"What have you talked about?" Kal asked.

"About how it wasn't all bad," Becks said.

"No, it wasn't all bad," Rafe said. "But I still don't want to go back. Ever."

She got up and piled the plates in her arms. "I go back often."

"What?" Jackson asked. "Why?"

She went into the kitchen and laid the plates in the sink, then turned on the water to rinse them.

Jackson was there to take them from her and stack them in the dishwasher.

"Why do you go back?" he asked.

"I take sandwiches and toiletries and clothes and hand them out to the kids who live there now. Sometimes books and toys."

"Dammit, Becks." Kal slung his arm around her shoulders, then nudged her out of the way and took over dish-rinsing duties. "That has to be rough."

She put the leftover biscuits in a container. "It hurts to know there are still homeless kids out there. But you know how it is. There likely always will be. So I do what I can to make it a little easier on them."

"You let me know next time you're going," Rafe said. "I'll go with you."

She looked over her shoulder at Rafe. "Would you really?"

"Sure I would. If you can handle it, I guess I can, too."

She looked at Jackson, hoping he'd offer to join them.

"Don't look at me," he said. "I'm never going back."

She sighed and popped the lid on the biscuits, then turned to scoop the remainder of the fruit into another container.

"I'm kind of in Jackson's corner on this one, Becks," Kal said, grabbing a towel to go wipe down the table. "I mean, we've been there, done that. Why go back and torture yourself with those memories?"

"Because there are still kids like us out there today. Still homeless, still thinking that no one cares about them. I like to talk to them, to let them know they shouldn't ever give up. So that maybe they'll see that someone does care about them, that there's hope for their futures."

Kal dried his hands, then tossed the paper towel into the trash. "Okay. When you put it that way I can see how you'd want to give back. We all got out, rose up, ended up with a better life. So what do you do? Talk to them about getting off the streets and into foster care?"

She took a seat at the island. "Oh, no. I don't try to talk them into anything. My last foster family was great. But I also experienced horror shows in the foster care system. I wouldn't dream of recommending anything those kids don't want. Plus, they'd never trust me and let me in if I steered them wrong. I just ask them how they're doing, find out what they might need, if they have buddies out there to rely on like we did. If any of them are sick I might run them into the free clinic so they can get checked out. Otherwise, I just drop off stuff."

"Sounds decent," Kal said.

"We should go shopping today, get some stuff for them," Rafe said. "Then go out there."

Kal nodded. "I'm in."

"Whoa," Jackson said. "What's the hurry?"

Rafe shrugged. "Why put it off?"

"I just think we should . . . think about it."

"I think you don't want to think about it," Rafe said. "And all of us going would make it too real for you."

Becks could tell Jackson was getting angry. His brows knitted together and he was taking in deep breaths.

"It's okay if you don't want to come along, Jackson," she said. "Rafe and Kal and I can do this by ourselves."

"Sure. Yeah." He started to walk away, but then turned to look at her, his face twisted with frustration. "You know, if you hadn't brought it up, you wouldn't be dragging Rafe and Kal with you."

"Excuse me?"

"What the fuck, man," Rafe said. "Are we robots?"

"I'm pretty sure we have minds of our own, bro," Kal said. "It's not like she's twisting our arms."

He waved his hand in dismissal. "Whatever. I just think no good comes from trying to relive the past."

She understood where he was coming from, but she had to make him understand that he had it all wrong. "Jackson. I'm not setting up a tent there to live with those kids. I'm trying to help."

"Sometimes trying to help does more harm than good. You think those kids enjoy seeing you show up smelling all sweet and looking like some golden goddess while they're dirty and living in a shithole?"

She'd tried. And now she was mad. "I don't believe they're thinking anything at all about me other than I'm the bringer of food and blankets and clean clothes and toiletries and some entertainment so they can feel better about themselves.

"You remember how it was back then, Jackson. If someone came by and gave one of us five dollars, we'd go grab a burger, fries and a drink and we'd split it. We wouldn't pay the slightest bit of attention to the person who gave us the money, other than a quick thanks."

"Right," Kal said. "Because the only thing we'd be thinking about was how fast we could get to the fast-food joint and grab some food. It's not the person so much as it is the kindness."

"Becks is right," Rafe said. "They might recognize her because she makes regular visits, but they aren't jealous of her circumstances. They're just happy that she keeps showing up and wondering what she's brought for them this time. Like us back then. All we cared about was when we'd get our next meal."

Jackson sighed. "I guess. Sorry, Becks."

She shrugged, still angry that he always wanted to take out his frustrations on her. "It's fine." She turned to Rafe and Kal. "I'm going upstairs to get changed. I'll be ready to go in about twenty minutes if you two still want to come with me."

"I'll be ready to go whenever you are," Kal said.

Rafe nodded. "Same."

"Okay." She walked upstairs and went into her room and closed the door. She noticed Jackson had made the bed. She sat on it and sighed.

Just a few hours ago they were tangled up together on this bed, embroiled in hot passionate lovemaking.

And just like that his passion had cooled and he'd accused her of . . . hell, she couldn't even make sense of what it was he'd accused her of. But whatever it had been, she didn't like it.

The man ran hot and cold like no one she'd ever seen before. One minute he acted like he wanted to take her to bed and make love to her for hours. He was hot and caring and the kind of man she was definitely interested in spending time with. And then it was like a light switch going off and he was surly and accusatory and definitely *not* the kind of guy she wanted to spend any time with at all.

She had to do some serious thinking about Jackson.

CHAPTER 15

AS SOON AS BECKS HAD GONE UPSTAIRS AND CLOSED THE door to her room, Jackson's brothers had laid into him.

"What the fuck, man?" Rafe asked.

Followed by Kal's "Are you seriously out of your fucking mind? What's wrong with you?"

He deserved it.

He paced in front of the kitchen sink. "I don't know."

When they both looked at him, he raised his hands. "I honestly don't know. It's not Becks. It's me. Or maybe it is her. Maybe it's reconnecting with her that's brought up the past and it's triggering something inside me."

"Yeah, the asshole inside you," Kal said.

Rafe nodded. "It's like every time you're around her, you act like a raging dick."

"Not every time." Though Jackson had to admit it was getting to be a pattern. A pattern he didn't like seeing in himself.

Kal shot him a look that told him he didn't buy it. "Whatever it is, man, you need to figure out how to deal with it. Because you can't sleep with her one night and then act like you just did this morning. She'll dump you fast."

"Unless that's what you want," Rafe said. "Is that what you want? You had second thoughts about the whole sex-with-Becks thing, so now you're pulling out the asshole side of yourself to get her to dump and run?"

He'd let his brothers jump on him because he deserved it. But now he was pissed. "Come on, Rafe. You know that's not how I treat women. I'm kind. And I'm always straightforward and honest."

"Fine, that's true," Kal said. "So what's this attitude all about? You know this is why Becks is currently so pissed at you."

"I just told her how I saw the situation. Which I may have misinterpreted."

"May have?" Kal threw his hands up in the air and shot Jackson a look of disbelief. "You were a douchehole, like you've been to her since the moment we met up with her again the day of the fire. It's like every time I'm around the two of you together, you can't act like a human. What the fuck, Jackson?"

When Kal blew up like that, he knew it was because something upset him. And this time, that something was Jackson.

"Okay. Okay. You're right. I'll fix it."

"You'd better. I like having her in our lives again. Don't fuck this up because you can't keep your past and your emotions and your dick separated."

Jackson hated being wrong. But he also hated revisiting the past. He had a damn good reason for compartmentalizing that part of him.

But now he realized Becks hadn't done anything wrong. She hadn't invited him to come along, hadn't asked about his past. She'd only stated what she did to return to that part of *her* past. And in return, he'd been the one to pounce, to accuse, and had made her angry right after they'd had a great night together. In addition, he'd pissed off the people he loved the most—his brothers.

Time to make amends.

So while his brothers went to their rooms to get dressed, he dashed upstairs, too, changed clothes and slid into his tennis shoes.

There were parts of his past he had no intention of ever confronting. But this wasn't about him. This he could do.

When he came back downstairs, Becks was there alone, sitting on one of the chairs at the kitchen island doing something in a notebook. Drawing, maybe? He guessed if she was a tattoo artist, she probably drew all the time. She wore shorts and canvas tennis shoes and a tank top, her hair piled up in a high ponytail.

He wanted to step up behind her and kiss the back of her neck. And if he hadn't acted like such a jerk he might have been able to do that. But he seriously doubted she was even speaking to him right now, let alone inviting him to put his mouth or any other part of his body on her.

"Hey," he said.

She looked up from her notebook. "Hey."

"So I thought I'd come with you."

She laid her notebook on the island. "Don't feel pressured into doing something you don't want to do. For me or for your brothers."

"I don't. I feel bad that I overreacted. And I'm seriously sorry I jumped all over you and made accusations that aren't true."

She shrugged. "You don't know me all that well."

He read the hurt in her eyes, and he felt shitty for being the one to have hurt her. He stepped in and picked up her hand, rubbing his thumb over her soft skin. He kept his gaze on hers and said, "I hurt you. I always seem to say the wrong things when I'm around you. I don't mean to."

Her lips gave a slight curve. "Maybe I bring out the worst in you."

"I think it's more that I bring out the worst in me. You should probably know that before you decide if you want to be around me. But I'm genuinely sorry and you should feel free to tell me to go fuck myself if you never want to see me again."

She reached up and slid her hand across his jaw. "You're forgiven. Don't make a habit of being a jerk. And maybe stop and ask me questions next time before you make assumptions."

There weren't a lot of women he knew who could be so forgiving of his behavior. That Becks was said a lot about her. He lifted her hand and kissed the back of it. "Thank you."

And then he leaned in and brushed his lips across hers. A brief kiss, but she rose up and sighed into his mouth, making him crave more.

"I guess you two made up," Kal said as he came down the stairs.

They broke contact, but the taste of her still lingered on his lips.

And when Becks smiled up at him, Jackson ached inside, because all he wanted was to pull her into his arms and hold her. Just . . . hold her.

"Okay, okay, enough," Kal said. "I might like you better when you're fighting."

Becks laughed.

Rafe came downstairs about ten minutes later.

"As always, waiting on you," Jackson said.

Rafe grinned. "No surprise. I am the prettiest, after all."

"I don't know how you can say that," Kal said. "After all, I dress better than you."

Jackson rolled his eyes. "Don't forget I can kick both your asses."

Kal laughed. "Maybe when I was twelve."

"You decide, Becks," Rafe said.

"I think you're all super strong and awesome firefighters," Becks said.

When they all continued to stare at her, she added, "And of course, you're all very pretty."

Jackson looked at her. "Hey."

She shrugged. "That is not a lie. Can we go now?"

"I guess."

He and Becks got into his truck, and Rafe and Kal took Kal's truck. Their first stop was going to be at a store to buy the needed supplies.

Jackson wasn't sure how this was going to go, but he'd agreed, so he'd see it out.

He just wasn't looking forward to going back to where he'd come from.

CHAPTER 16

BECKS COULD TELL JACKSON WAS NERVOUS. ALL through their shopping trip he'd barely said a word.

Maybe he was concentrating on the supplies they were buying, the arguments they were having about the need for clean underwear versus having a battery-operated game system.

"Guys," she said. "Underwear. Toothpaste, toothbrushes, wipes. Basic human necessities."

Kal looked at her as if she were speaking Klingon. "A game system is a basic human need, Becks."

She rolled her eyes. "No."

Kal held out the game system to her. "Kids have lots of downtime to get bored."

Rafe nodded. "And get in trouble. Especially boys."

She pondered that thought. "Okay, you might have a point. But nothing expensive that'll get stolen."

"Maybe some comics and books," Jackson suggested. "If they read or are being taught to read by some of the adults, it'll help them progress."

She looked up at him. "Great idea."

They headed to the book aisle and browsed for a while. She picked out several that would fit multiple age groups, from pre-teen to young adult books for girls. The guys took care of comics and books for young males.

They bought quite a few things. She appreciated that all three of the guys chipped in on the cost, because it allowed her to get way more stuff than she normally would. In the end, they ended up buying some rain parkas and tennis shoes in various sizes.

Lexie was hitting that about-to-be-a-teen growth spurt, so she grabbed capris and a T-shirt for her growing body, along with a sports bra so she wouldn't have to feel like she had to hide her budding breasts. Becks remembered how it felt when she first started blooming, and how embarrassing it was not to have the necessary clothing.

She also picked up quite a few sanitary items for the older girls. There was nothing worse than being homeless and on your period and having no tampons or pads available.

They picked up energy bars and prepacked sandwich items, then they hit the checkout.

They parked in one of the lots near the beach, got out and started bagging up the items, then made their way to the park. Her stomach always knotted up when she made her way to the place she'd called home for so many years of her youth.

She'd been lucky. She'd made the choice to get out and had been fortunate to spend her last five teen years with a really nice foster family. It could have been much worse for her. And as they passed the adult encampment, she looked at some of the faces of people she'd seen and known when she was a kid. Still there, spending their lives in those camps—distrustful, living day by day in a fog of hunger and helplessness. Some were alcoholics or drug addicts. Others had been put there simply by unfortunate circumstance. Becks knew as well as anyone that no one chose to be homeless.

"I thought I was the quiet one," Jackson said, coming up to walk beside her.

She gave him a half smile. "Just thinking that I remember a few of these folks from before."

He looked over as they passed old Red, who seemed to stare right through them. "Yeah. Some people just get stuck in a rut and don't know how to dig themselves out. Red got caught up in alcohol. Won't stay at the shelters. He doesn't really trust people."

She nodded as they passed a faded pink tent where dirty white tennis shoes attached to a woman's feet hung out. "And Miss Peggy . . . she used to like me to read to her when I was younger. She lost her glasses a long time ago. She was always losing her glasses. I brought some readers to her last time I was here, along with a mystery book from one of her favorite authors."

He rubbed her arm. "You're a kind person, Becks."

She shrugged. "I just know what it's like to go without your favorite things."

They moved into the deeper part of the park, the place where the kids all lived. They liked to live separate from the adults, mainly because some of the adults couldn't be trusted around kids. Most of them were okay and kept an eye on the kids to make sure they stayed safe. But you never knew who you could trust, and it was always best to stay within your trusted group.

There were homeless families that kept their kids in a tight group with them, and they were never allowed to socialize with the single kids. Becks had always wondered why their parents never let them hang out. It wasn't like Becks or Jackson or anyone else was going to kidnap them. Either way, it was okay. Those kids had parents to look out for them. They were the fortunate ones.

The place looked the same. Tents were different. Kids were different. Otherwise, nothing much had changed. Kids were still homeless, and there were still way too many of them out here.

"Where is everyone?" Rafe asked.

Becks put her bags down. "They're hiding, probably because I brought three big guys with me. They probably think you're with children's services. Let me go talk to them. You guys hang back."

She took a walk into the tented areas.

"Hey, guys. I know you're out here somewhere. I just want you to know I brought some friends with me. They used to live out here, too, so you don't need to worry about them. I'd never give you up. You know you can trust me."

She stepped out of their personal space, waiting out on the fringes.

Lexie came out first, her sweet smile always a bright spot in Becks's visits. Maybe it was because Lexie reminded her so much of herself. Tough on the outside, but kind of a marshmallow on the inside. She knew what it was like to act like you didn't need anyone, when in reality all you really wanted was someone to love you. So Lexie was special to her and she always wanted Lexie to feel as if someone cared about her.

"Hi, Becks."

"Hey, Lexie. How's it going?"

"It's been fine. Really hot out here."

"I know, baby. You staying cool in the trees here?"

"Yeah, it's okay."

"I brought you some things. I brought everyone some things."

From the corner of her eye, Becks noticed a young woman watching them. She couldn't be more than twenty at most, but she was eyeing Becks.

As Lexie came closer, the woman frowned.

"That a new friend of yours?" Becks asked.

Lexie looked over her shoulder, then smiled. "That's Aria. She's been here a while. Stays in the adult camp, but she keeps an eye on us."

"Good. I'm glad to hear that."

"So what did you bring me?" Lexie asked, eyeing the bags sitting at Jackson, Rafe and Kal's feet.

"Is it okay if I bring my friends over to meet everyone?"

Lexie glanced around her to look at the guys, then back at Becks. "You sure they're not with the cops or the services?"

"Cross my heart." And she did.

"Okay."

Becks turned and nodded at the guys. They picked up the bags and entered the camp. Becks found the bag she'd packed for Lexie. The kid rifled through it, smiled, and then her eyes widened. She lifted her gaze to Becks and she leaned in to whisper in Becks's ear.

"You got me a bra?"

"I thought you might need one."

"I do." She threw her arms around Becks. "Thanks."

Becks's heart squeezed. "You're welcome."

Soon enough, everyone appeared, seemingly from nowhere. Becks knew exactly how it was done. When you were a homeless kid, you could become a ghost, disappearing into the trees, blending into the walls, becoming invisible.

Sometimes that meant you had to run and run fast. Sometimes you got caught and you'd get stuck in a foster home. Or for some kids, what was even worse, your real home.

"How's it goin', Becks?"

Their leader was a girl, a sixteen-year-old named Georgia. She was one of the toughest girls Becks had ever known. She had her brown hair pulled back into a low ponytail.

"It's going well, Georgia. How's the group?"

"Hangin' in there. We lost Eddie the other day. Got caught by the cops snatching food from the taco truck at the beach."

"Oh, no. I'm sorry."

"Yeah, me, too. But he should have known better. He went off on his own instead of with the group. You know how it is. You run off without a plan, you'll pay for it."

Georgia made it sound like she didn't care. Becks knew better. Georgia had to guard her heart or else she'd fall apart. Losing one of their own was always tough. She'd seen it happen with kids she'd grown up with countless times. They thought they knew better, and they could do it their own way. But without backup and lookouts, it almost always ended in a failure, and that meant you'd get scooped up by the cops and sent either back home to your terrible parents or into the system.

"Tough break," Jackson said.

Georgia nodded. "Who are you?"

"Sorry. Georgia, this is Jackson. Next to him are his brothers, Rafe and Kal."

"Hey," Georgia said.

"Hey, back," Rafe said.

"Like me, they grew up out here," Becks said. "In fact, back then, Jackson here was our leader, like you are now. He kept us all safe."

Georgia looked Jackson up and down, then nodded.

Jackson nodded back.

"Brothers, huh?" Georgia asked. "You all don't look nothing alike."

Kal laughed. "Yeah, they're really sad that they're not as good-looking as me."

Georgia snickered.

"We made our own family," Jackson said. "But we're all brothers."

Lexie nodded. "They made a family, just like we do."

"We brought you some food for the group," Becks said, "along with a few other things."

"Thanks," Georgia said. "We appreciate it."

"Let's get everything disbursed," Kal said. "I know you all are hungry."

JACKSON LET BECKS HANDLE THE KIDS. HE HELPED OUT with handing out the bags, but he mostly waited and watched, knowing how hard it was for these kids to trust any adult, especially adults who didn't live like they did.

Plus, he wanted to stand back, hover in the periphery, not engage. Just being here was hard enough, made his pulse race and his stomach tie itself in knots.

He never came back here. The location wasn't exactly the same, but it was close to where they used to call home, and the encampment looked the same. Tents and boxes and anything that would keep the blistering hot sun off you. And something you could grab in a hurry in case you needed to run.

Fortunately the cops mostly left you alone unless you were causing shit.

So they never caused shit. Most of them hadn't, anyway.

Becks motioned for him, so he stepped in to help out.

Georgia was a force, for sure. The younger ones wanted to dive in and just grab stuff. She made them wait for Becks to hand them a bag. Then they all hurried off to their hideouts to eat and see what else was in their bags.

Jackson didn't blame them. Food was their number-one priority, and unfortunately a scarcity. Without it you'd die out here. Shelter was secondary. Third was a place to hide out. Cops and social services were always looking to snatch the homeless kids off the streets, so you had to be adept at covering your ass, making sure you weren't noticed.

Kal and Rafe had already made friends with some of the boys. That didn't surprise him. His brothers were friendly and approachable, whereas Jackson had chosen to stand back and observe. He knew how skittish these kids could be, especially Georgia, who felt responsible for protecting them. He didn't want to do anything to scare them and he'd rather err on the side of caution.

Right now Kal and Rafe were kicking the soccer ball around with several of the kids, boys and girls alike and varying age groups. Jackson smiled.

"So you think you're too good to get in there and get dirty with the rest of them?"

He looked up and saw a raven-haired young woman who'd come to stand beside him. She couldn't be more than twenty or so, and she was eyeing him with a look of distaste.

"I'm not too good for anything. And you are?"

"None of your business. Still waiting for you to tell me who you are."

She wasn't going to give, so he was going to have to. "A guy who pretty much grew up here."

"Yeah? You got out, huh?"

"You could say that."

"So you're slumming today, figured you'd allay some of your guilt by feeding the kiddies?"

She was smart. And she was a smartass, too. But he understood. He'd been there. "You got a chip on your shoulder the size of a mountain, don't you? And this wasn't my idea. It's all Becks's doing."

"Which means you turned your back on where you came from and never intended to come back."

Wow, was she ever irritating. And pretty damned accurate in her assessment of him. "I don't think you can have it both ways. And I didn't turn my back and I'm not here to massage away any guilt. I took care of my group when I was here. The only reason I left was I got caught up in a fire and rescued by a firefighter."

She stared at him. "Oh, so you guys are the ones who got adopted by the fireman. Everybody knows that story."

"They do?"

"Yeah. Which one are you?"

"I'm Jackson."

"No kidding?" Her entire demeanor changed. "You're like . . . legendary around here. I'm Aria, by the way."

Legendary? Why? He didn't know anyone even knew what had happened to them. Or cared.

Becks came over. "Hi, I'm Becks. I see you met Jackson."

"I'm Aria. I just found out this is Jackson. He used to lead a group here."

Becks smiled. "I know. I was part of his group way back."

Aria's bright green eyes glittered with interest. "Really? What was it like?"

Becks laughed. "Pretty much like it is now."

"People tell stories about Jackson."

Becks looked at Jackson, then over at Aria. "They do, huh? What kinds of stories?"

"About how he used to forage for food, bring back pizzas and sandwiches for everyone. How he'd steal clothes and rain gear and shoes so no one would go without. How he'd go without so no one else would go hungry."

"Huh. Just like Robin Hood of the Homeless." Becks quirked her lips at Jackson, who held up his hands.

"No idea," Jackson said.

"Seriously," Aria said. "Just like that."

"Where did you hear these stories?" Becks asked.

"From Mason. We'd sit around the circle at night and Mason would tell us all stories about when he was a kid. Jackson, you had hero status."

Jackson's heart skipped a beat. After Becks told him Mason

had disappeared from their group, he'd thought about him a lot. "Mason? You know him?"

"Sure I do."

"He's here?" Becks asked.

"Not at the moment. He comes and goes," Aria said. "He doesn't like to stay in one place too long. It makes him anxious."

"I've never seen him on all my visits here," Becks said. "Not that I'm sure I'd even recognize him now. It's been such a long time."

"He's moving around right now," Aria said. "He'll probably be back next week. He's never gone for more than a couple of weeks at a time. I think he has a couple of camps he stays at."

"Why do you think he does that?" Becks asked.

"He got arrested a few times and he hates that feeling of confinement. So he says if he stays on the move, the cops won't be able to find him."

Becks looked over at Jackson, who shrugged. "He was fine when we were younger. I don't know what happened."

Rafe and Kal had come over, just as surprised as Jackson was to discover Mason was still there.

"Wow," Rafe said. "I can't believe Mason is still here."

"I'm just glad he's okay," Kal said, then turned to Aria. "Is he okay?"

"After you and the guys left, he was fine," Becks said. "He stepped up and was strong and capable. But like I told you before, I have no idea what happened to him after I went into foster care."

Aria shrugged. "We're not sure. Everyone here thinks he's manifested a form of mental illness. He's super paranoid about everything, always looking over his shoulder. But since he won't go to a clinic to get checked out and treated, it's hard to say what's going on inside his head."

"It's not drugs?" Rafe asked.

Aria shook her head. "Never touches them. He thinks drugs

are poison and the people that deal them are trying to kill him. So we know for sure he's not doing any kinds of drugs. And he doesn't touch alcohol, either. I've never seen him drink anything but bottled water."

"Well, damn," Jackson said. He knew that a lot of homeless people struggled with mental illness. Either it put them in the position of being homeless, or sometimes they ended up manifesting symptoms because of a lack of adequate health care.

"I'll try to see him sometime when I'm out here," Becks said. "Maybe he'll remember me and I can talk him into seeking help."

"Good luck with that," Aria said. "We've all tried. I do my best to keep an eye on him, but sometimes I'm at work."

Jackson arched a brow. "You got a job? That's great."

"Yeah. Temp work and it's only part-time, but it allows me to feed myself and some of the folks here."

"Hey, getting employment is awesome," Becks said. "I know how hard it can be to get a job."

"Yeah, it's been okay. Only downfall is I can't save any money to get out of here."

"It's hard for people to get out," Rafe said. "But you're on the right track."

"I'm trying," Aria said.

"What kind of temp work?" Becks asked.

"Answering phones. Scheduling stuff. I work for a couple of bail bondsmen. I started out doing fast food, squirreled enough money away to buy some decent pants and shirts so I could step up my game and hopefully make better money."

"You know computers?"

Aria smiled at Becks. "Yeah. Aced those classes in school. I don't intend to live on the streets forever."

Becks nodded. "I understand."

"I like your ink," Aria said. "Don't have any myself yet, but someday, when I can afford luxuries."

Jackson watched the wheels turning in Becks's head. He had no idea what she was thinking about, but he knew it had something to do with Aria.

"Are you looking for a full-time position?" she asked.

"Yeah. Of course."

"Okay, I have an offer for you."

"I'm listening."

"I'm opening my new tattoo shop on Tuesday."

"Ohh, that explains all the ink. You do all those yourself?"

"Just a few."

"Are you good?"

Becks's lips lifted, and Jackson could tell she wasn't bothered at all by Aria's line of questions. "I'm damn good."

"Okay. Tell me about the job offer."

"It's about a three-block walk from here, or you could take the bus. I normally operate by myself, but I could use someone to help me out, answering the phone and keeping my schedule."

Aria's eyes narrowed, as if she didn't believe what Becks was dishing out. "Are you serious?"

"Dead. I have in mind to hire another artist now that I have the space, because that'll draw in even more business. At my other shop I always had to turn away clients and I hated doing that. Now that I have the room, I won't have to do that. Which means the shop will be even busier and I won't be able to work on clients plus answer phones plus do scheduling plus deal with walk-ins. You'll also learn all the supplies we use and how to keep track of and order them. I need a receptionist and assistant. I'll pay you a decent wage. We start at noon and close around eight p.m. I'll give you a ride back here so you don't have to walk home alone."

"Yes."

Becks paused. "Yes, as in you'll take the job?"

"Yes, as in I'll take the job."

Becks smiled. "Great. I'll give you the address to the shop. Start tomorrow so we can set everything up. Be on time."

Becks wrote down the address in a notebook Aria produced.

"Do you have a phone?" Becks asked.

"Yes."

They traded phone numbers.

"Any dress code?" Aria asked.

Becks shook her head. "No. Whatever you're comfortable with."

"I'll look presentable."

Becks nodded, then started to turn away.

"Hey, Becks?" Aria asked.

"Yeah?"

Aria nodded. "Thanks for this."

Becks didn't smile. "It's not a handout, Aria. I need the help, and you'll earn every dollar."

"Okay. See you tomorrow."

When they finished up, they said their good-byes.

Becks hugged Lexie.

"You'll come back soon?" Lexie asked.

"Very soon."

Jackson's heart squeezed as he watched the way Lexie hugged tight to Becks, like she didn't want to let go of her.

He understood the sad look on Becks's face as they climbed into Jackson's truck.

"It's hard to leave her, isn't it?" he asked.

She was watching in the side mirror as they pulled away. "Yeah. Always is."

"And that whole job offer thing. You did that for Aria."

She pulled her attention away from the mirror and onto Jackson. "Partly. But I wasn't lying about needing help at the shop. I've just been lazy about running an ad or looking for someone."

"Hopefully she won't let you down."

"She won't. People like Aria just need someone to give them a chance. We all needed a chance once."

"What did you do when you aged out of the system?"

"I was lucky. I had already been working part-time in retail and made friends who let me share an apartment with them. And I already knew what I wanted to do with my life, so I worked three jobs, paid rent on time and saved money like crazy so I could eventually start buying supplies for my tattoo business.

"Then I got a job apprenticing for this great tattoo artist. She taught me a lot about how to do ink. I worked with her for three years before I went off on my own."

He pulled onto the highway. "I'll bet it was hard to start your own business."

"At first, yeah. Working alongside Tina gave me confidence. But I knew if I didn't strike out on my own, I'd never have that independence that I'd wanted for so long. And I already had a client base, so it was slightly less scary than if I'd tried to do it on my own from the beginning."

"And look at you now, hiring an assistant and talking about bringing on another tattoo artist."

"Yeah, well, we'll see how both of those go. The other tattoo artist will help me pay rent."

Jackson exited the highway and made a right turn toward their neighborhood. "What? You're not going to mentor some young artist like Tina did with you?"

She stared at him and didn't answer. He wondered if he'd insulted her, so when he pulled into the driveway, he turned to face her.

"Did I say something to hurt your feelings?" he asked.

"Actually, no. You gave me a great idea."

"I did?"

"Yes. I should pay it forward, like you said. Mentor a young artist who needs to learn the business."

"You're already doing that with Aria."

"She doesn't want to learn how to tattoo. She just needs a regular paying job. But it's really hard to get a mentorship with a tattoo artist because they're all so busy. No one wants to take the time to bring up the new kids."

He turned off the engine and they went into the house. "Okay, so how do you find a new artist?"

She shrugged as she laid her bag on the kitchen island. "Word of mouth is big in our community. Everyone knows everyone else. If I put some feelers out there, I'll have ten apprentices at my front door tomorrow applying for a mentorship with me."

Jackson went to the fridge and pulled out a beer, holding it out for Becks, who nodded. He popped it open and handed it to her, then grabbed another one for himself. They went into the game room to sit down.

"Okay, but who's going to help you pay rent? An apprentice won't bring in money right away, will they?"

"No. I'll still have to bring in another artist. But once they're hired they can work independently. And Aria can keep track of their schedule and mine. I'll work the mentorship with the new artist, and once I get them rolling there's still ample room at the shop for another artist."

Jackson took a swallow of his beer. "So it's that simple to find someone to mentor?"

"Sure. I'll be at the shop tomorrow getting things set up to open Tuesday. I'll send some text messages and see what happens."

He leaned his head against the sofa. "You're going to have a busy day tomorrow."

She leaned back and smiled up at him. "Yeah. It's going to be a great new start."

He tipped his beer toward her and she clinked her beer with his.

"I like seeing you smile. I hope your new place works out."

She took a sip of her beer. "I know it will. I had a good feeling about the location and the shop from the first time I walked in."

She sighed and laid her head against his shoulder. Jackson figured she was tired. It had been a long afternoon. But then she sat up and turned to face him.

"I'm hungry. We should grill something. Where are the guys?"

He shrugged. "No idea."

She pulled out her phone and started typing. "I'll see if they want to come home for dinner."

Part of him appreciated that Becks thought of his brothers and wanted to include them.

The other part of him really wanted to be alone with her and wished she hadn't texted Rafe and Kal.

He estimated that the part that wanted to be alone with her was about eighty percent, and the part that appreciated her notifying his brothers was around twenty.

So maybe he wasn't as generous as Becks was.

Her phone buzzed a couple of times. She stared down at it.

"Hmm. Rafe has plans elsewhere and says he won't be home until late." She looked up at him. "Very vague."

"He probably has a hookup that he doesn't want to tell you about."

"Really. I thought he was dating someone."

"Rafe never dates anyone exclusively."

She studied him for a few seconds. "I see." She looked down at her phone. "And Kal says he's having dinner with your parents, then he's meeting up with a few of the guys from the station house at some place called Tommy's Fish House?"

Jackson cracked a smile. "Tommy Rodriguez is a firefighter. He owns a family restaurant and bar near the beach. Actually, his grandfather Tomas, also Tommy, built the place, and Tommy and his family run it now. We all go there to hang out, eat and watch sports in the bar while we drink."

"So kind of an extension of your firefighter family."

"Yeah."

She looked down at her phone, then back up at him. "Should we go there?"

"To the bar? No."

"You don't want me to meet your firefighter family?"

He took the phone from her hands and laid it down on the table. "I absolutely want you to meet everyone. But it's been a long day and we've been hanging out with a lot of people. And now we're alone here at the house. How about we take advantage of that alone time?"

"Oh. Sure." Then her eyes widened. "OhhhhmyGod I'm so dense."

He laughed. "No, you're not."

"Yes, I am." She kicked off her shoes, then climbed onto his lap and straddled him. "You know, it's been a while since I've been with a guy, so I don't want you to think I'm not into you. Which I totally am. How could I not be? I mean, look at you." She swept her hands up his arms and rested them on his shoulders.

He tried not to laugh, but damn, the ego stroke was nice. "Thanks. Look at you, too."

"I wasn't after a compliment, but thanks. I guess I was overly focused on the homeless kids today. And then making sure Rafe and Kal were taken care of. But now that everyone is, let's focus on you and me."

"You do that a lot, don't you?"

She frowned. "Do what?"

"Take care of everyone else."

"No, I don't."

"I think you do. As soon as you moved in here you started cleaning the place and making sure we were fed."

"That was more of a thank-you."

Her voice had lowered and he was afraid he'd offended her, when he'd really meant it as a compliment. He tipped her chin with his fingers so she was looking at him. "Hey, it's not an insult and I'm not picking a fight with you. You're a caregiver, Becks. There's nothing wrong with that."

"Thanks."

"As long as you don't let people take advantage of you."

"Trust me. No one takes advantage of me. I'm fully capable of knowing the difference between offering assistance and people taking too much. I learned that the hard way."

"Good." He started to touch her, then stilled. "Wait. Taking too much? What does that mean?"

She rolled off him and slid onto the couch next to him. "No, not physically. But someone did use me emotionally. Someone I thought was a friend. Only it ended up being a one-sided friendship. She'd come to me for advice and counsel and to rant, but when I needed to do the same she wasn't there for me."

He hated that someone had hurt her that way, especially knowing what a giving person Becks could be. "Well, that's bullshit."

Becks nodded. "I didn't notice it at first because she was always so sweet to me. And we spent a lot of time together at a time when I really needed someone in my life. It took me a while to realize that all that time we spent together she was doing all the talking, and I was listening or offering advice. I never got to tell her about my bad day or a lousy date or when I had problems with my boss. It was always about her."

"That's not a real friendship."

"No, it's not."

"It should be two-sided. Someone to listen to you vent, to offer you advice and a shoulder to cry on when you need one."

"Yeah. I finally had to end the friendship."

He smoothed his hand along her arm. "Bet that was hard."

"It was really hard. We were friends during one of my first jobs as an adult. But our relationship had grown toxic and I just couldn't do it anymore. I felt bad about it because she didn't have any other friends."

"For a reason, Becks. She probably drove them all away."

"I know, but I still felt bad."

"You did what you had to do for yourself. And probably for her. Maybe it opened her eyes to the fact that she couldn't treat her friends that way."

She shrugged. "Maybe. I don't know. I hope so, for her sake."

"Me, too."

She leaned in and brushed her lips across his. "Thank you."

"For what?"

"For listening to me, for your empathy. And for coming along with me today. I know it was hard for you."

As usual she thought of him and how he felt. He'd never known a woman with that kind of capacity for empathy.

"Not as hard as I thought it was going to be."

She rubbed her hand along his thigh. "Hey, how about being honest with me?"

"I don't want to be one of those friends that lays all my troubles at your feet."

"I don't think you are. Especially since I just spent all that time whining at you about my ex–best friend. You listen to me, now I listen to you. That's how it works, you know?"

He supposed she was right about that, but digging into today would only bring back memories, and that just wasn't his thing.

"Honestly, it wasn't bad. I liked meeting everyone. But I'd be lying if I didn't say it made me ache feeling that tug of memories."

"It's hard for me, too, Jackson. It always brings dark memories going there. But I feel compelled to give back. I got out and managed to make a life for myself. So many don't."

"You're braver than I am, Becks."

"I don't know about that. Look at what you do for a living. You give back to your community, just in a different way than I do."

He appreciated her compassion, but it was misplaced. "Thanks, but what I do gives nothing to those homeless kids."

She shifted on the sofa so she could grab his face between her soft hands. "Hey, don't do that to yourself. You could have let Josh and Laurel rescue you and done absolutely nothing of value with your life. But did you? No, you didn't. I can't imagine that what you do as a firefighter is easy. So maybe you're not seeing the kids every day, but never underestimate the value of your work."

"Okay." He wasn't sure he bought it completely, but obviously Becks wasn't going to let it go and he needed her to. He didn't need to be anyone's hero. He was fine right where he was.

On the couch with a beautiful woman sitting next to him. He turned to her.

"Know what I think?"

"What?" she asked.

"That we should get naked."

She arched a brow. "Really. And where might we do that?"

"Here. Upstairs. Outside by the pool. Doesn't matter to me. The guys won't be home for a long while."

"I thought we were going to grill something to eat."

"Oh, right. You had mentioned that. And then we started talking and forgot about food."

"Aren't you hungry?" she asked.

"Yeah, but not for food. I'd like to kiss you."

She turned to him and leaned into him. "I'd like you to kiss me."

His lips curved. "I thought you were hungry."

"Yeah, but not for food."

He smiled, cupped her neck and brought his lips to hers.

CHAPTER 17

AS HIS MOUTH MOVED OVER HERS, BECKS BREATHED IN the scent of Jackson, her tongue winding around his. The flavor of beer lingered in his mouth and he smelled like sweat, like a man who'd spent the day outside, which was a bit of a turn-on, she admitted to herself.

She doubted there was much about him that wouldn't hit all her Yes! buttons. She was so tuned into him that she was sure she could differentiate his scent from other men while she was blindfolded.

And wouldn't that be a fun party trick? Though she wouldn't want to kiss anyone else. Not when kissing Jackson was so all-consuming. He had an amazing mouth, and used it with such finesse, moving his lips over hers until she couldn't help but moan in response. She couldn't remember ever being kissed so deeply, so thoroughly.

So damn well. He was really good at the kissing thing.

He pressed her down on the sofa, his body covering hers.

"Mmmm," was all she could manage.

He lifted his head. "Am I too heavy on you?"

"No. I was just trying to comment with my nonword about how now that you're on top of me, I can feel all your good parts rubbing against all my good parts."

He smiled down at her, sliding his hand along her hip and toward her butt. "You have some really good parts, Becks."

She wriggled her brows at him. "Right back at ya, Jackson."

"Maybe we should consider rubbing all our parts together. While naked."

"What a fantastic idea. You should start by taking off all your clothes."

He hopped off the sofa and Becks had never clocked it before, but she was almost certain she'd never seen a man get rid of his clothes that fast.

"Impressive."

He looked down at his erection, then grinned. "Well, thanks."

"I didn't mean that. Though your cock is very impressive. I meant how fast you can get out of your clothes."

"Hey, where sex is involved, I can strip faster than eggs cook on hot asphalt."

She laughed. "Good to know."

"Now, your turn. Though I might want to help you."

She sat up on the sofa. "Why? Do you think I'll be too slow for your liking?"

He shoved all his clothes on the floor, then dropped to his knees between her legs. "No, because it's way more fun if you let me take your clothes off."

"Oh, this is interesting," she said, her thoughts going immediately to all the fun things they could do while he undressed her.

Maybe she'd been too quick about asking him to undress. Because she sure could have a good time revealing all the ideal parts of Jackson's body. Especially since all of him was ideal.

But then she got distracted when he ran his hands over her

ankles, up her calves and toward her thighs. When he reached her shorts, she arched upward, giving him access to pull her shorts and underwear off, leaving her naked from the waist down.

He lifted her shirt and kissed her belly, then rolled his tongue around her navel, making her laugh.

"No tickling allowed," she said.

He lifted his head. "Is that your only 'No' rule?"

She arched a brow. "Just what exactly do you have in mind?"

"Only fun things, Becks."

Maybe his idea of fun meant sucking on her toes. Which would be totally weird. Then again, she didn't see Jackson as a toe sucker. The thought of it made her laugh.

"What?"

"You're not going to suck my toes, are you?"

He frowned. "What? No. Why? Wait. Do you like that?"

"Uh, no. Like I will get up and flee to my room if you get anywhere near my toes with your mouth—or any other part of you."

He rubbed one of her feet. "They're very cute toes, Becks."

She laughed and jerked her foot from his grasp. "Stop."

"Okay, toes are definitely out of bounds. But I'm playing here." He kissed the top of her sex before lifting her shirt to—this time—lightly brush his lips across her belly. She had to admit his mouth on her skin lit a fire inside her.

"And here."

No tickling that time, and she lost all thoughts of giggling when he raised her shirt over her head and unhooked her bra to release her breasts.

"Nothing in that vicinity I intend to say no to." She laid back and sighed. "Have your way with me."

He played with her breasts, sucked her nipples and generally drove her crazy, making her writhe and lift up toward his mouth.

Oh, he was good. So, so good. And as he kissed his way down her body, that taut feeling of delicious expectation grew within her.

He blew a soft, warm breath across the top of her sex. And when the warm wetness of his tongue slid across her tender flesh, it was a sweetly gentle flick, yet so incredibly erotic she trembled from the shock waves it sent across her nerve endings.

She tingled from her hair to her toes and all her sweet spots in the middle.

She rolled from one gentle wave to another as Jackson took her from bliss to torture, those waves gathering in intensity until every muscle in her body tightened in anticipation of her orgasm.

She was so in tune to every delicious movement of his tongue, every suck of his lips over her clit. He took his time to take her right there, to give her exactly what she needed that she didn't have to give him direction, only ahhs and yeses and moans of appreciation.

And when that inevitable burst hit, she arched, pressing against his magical tongue to draw in more explosive pleasure.

After, she felt boneless, and utterly satiated. She felt Jackson move up on the sofa beside her.

She sighed and reached for him. "I'd tell you how great that was, but I'm not sure I'll ever be able to speak again."

"You just did, and I could tell how much you enjoyed that. I think the screaming spoke volumes."

She lifted up on her elbows to look over at him. "I did not scream."

His lips curved. "Yeah, you did."

She climbed on top of him, sliding against his very hard cock. "Prove it."

He grasped her hips. "Well, I didn't record it, but I could probably make you do it again."

She grasped his shaft in her hand and leisurely stroked it. "That confident in your abilities?"

"Yes."

"What if I make you scream?"

He shook his head. "Not possible."

She leveled a determined look at him. "I'm taking that as a challenge."

"You're not going to shackle and torture me, are you?"

She slid off his lap and knelt on the floor between his legs. "Depends on what you mean by torture."

When she cupped his balls, he let out a short moan. "Anything you do with my dick and balls is not torture, Becks."

She lifted her gaze to his and smiled while she gently massaged his balls, watching as his cock grew harder. "Really?"

"Okay, I take that back. I'm pretty vulnerable down there, so my life is in your hands."

He didn't look the least bit nervous as she played with him, teasing his shaft with her fingertip. "Wouldn't dream of hurting you. You're safe with me."

Having control over Jackson's cock was incredibly enticing. Becks wanted to pleasure him, to make him feel amazing in the same way he'd done to her.

She wanted to make him come so hard he'd lose all control.

JACKSON HAD TO ADMIT THAT BECKS KNEELING BETWEEN his thighs with his cock in her hands was the hottest sight he'd seen in a long damn time.

Until she put her mouth on him. Then that was the hottest thing he'd seen. Or felt. Definitely felt, because her mouth was liquid fire surrounding his shaft, and as she wrapped her tongue around the head of his cock, he was sure he was going to die.

If so, it was going to be the best death ever, because Becks didn't let up, sliding her mouth over him, then rolling her tongue over the backside of his shaft.

She had moves he wasn't prepared for, and it took all the will-power he had not to let go right then. But he wanted to hold on, to let this ride last a bit longer, because it felt too damn good to get off now.

Though his resolve weakened when Becks grasped the base of his shaft and began to stroke upward, feeding his cock deeper into the recesses of her mouth.

There was something hot as fuck about a woman who took control over your dick, who knew exactly what she was doing and didn't ask you for direction on how to please you. All he could do was grab hold of the sofa and lift his hips to give up control, because she had him—literally and figuratively—by the balls.

He felt the tremors starting in said balls and knew he wasn't going to be able to hold back.

"Becks. I'm gonna come."

She took him deep, and that was all it took for him to lose it.

His entire body shook as his orgasm erupted, and he couldn't hold back the yell of pure satisfaction. He came hard, leaving him spent and wasted.

He vaguely registered Becks getting up and moving away. When she returned, she sat next to him on the sofa, draping her arm over his shoulder.

She whispered in his ear. "You screamed."

Since he was still trying to find his bones, he turned his head. "Did not."

"Oh, yes. You did. I recorded it."

He frowned. "You took video of giving me a blowjob? Let's see it, because I could relive that every day until I die."

"Okay, fine. I didn't record it. But you still screamed."

He finally found enough energy to push off from the sofa. "I might have made a slight noise."

She went into the kitchen and filled two glasses with ice water. "Grab our clothes, will you? And you did yell."

He gathered up their things and followed Becks up the stairs, enjoying the view of her naked body as he walked behind her.

When they made it into her room, he shut the door behind them and dumped their clothes onto the chair.

He took the glass she offered him and swallowed several gulps of water before setting the glass on the nightstand. Then he grabbed hold of Becks and dragged her on top of him on the bed.

"How about this time we both scream?" he asked.

She rubbed her breasts against him. "I like that plan."

CHAPTER 18

THE SUN BEAT DOWN ON JACKSON LIKE THE SEVENTH level of hell while fire raged all around him. His crew was battling a three-alarm warehouse fire. It was four o'clock in the afternoon, the hottest part of the day, and they weren't getting anywhere managing this fire. This bastard of an inferno was resistant and wasn't going down easy.

When they'd arrived they'd been the first engine on scene. The building had already been blazing hard, flames busting out windows and billowing up black smoke, making it hard to see.

Right now he was managing the scene along with Captain Mathias, who was on the street coordinating with the other stations. Jackson's job was to keep tabs on his station's individual firefighters, their locations and their safety.

"We've got two lines in the main house," Jackson relayed to make sure his captain was kept informed, as well as all his team members. "One team's on the main floor, one upstairs. Ladder squad is on the roof along with Ladder 24."

"Copy," Mathias said.

"Status, Kal," Jackson asked.

"Roof's hotter than Satan's asshole. We're venting it as fast as we can, but we've got concrete tiles and the work's slow going. We're getting there. Should have enough of the roof vented within the next ten."

"Not fast enough. I want all of you off that roof in five."

"Ten-four."

Next up was his inside crew. "Check in, Hendricks."

"Davidson and me have left quadrant covered. We're mixing it in with Engine 15. Getting a handle on this area, sir. Fire's about out."

"Copy. Check in, Rafe."

No answer, which wasn't uncommon since the fire and the water often made hearing difficult.

"Check in, Rafe," he said again.

He heard static, which meant Rafe was trying to respond.

"Tommy here, sir. Rafe's got his hands full right now. We're battling back along with the Engine 24 crew, but this son of a bitch is a fighter."

Jackson took a deep breath. "Need extra hands?"

"No," Rafe finally said. "We've got this. Engine 3 guys are coming in to assist."

"Copy," Jackson said.

Just then a giant flashball of flame burst from the center of the roof.

"Check in, Kal."

"We're on the north side. Saw that, though."

"Get your asses off the roof now."

"Almost finished venting."

"Now, Kal."

"In a minute."

Goddammit. Jackson radioed to the lieutenant of 24. "Your ladder team coming down?"

"Already exiting."

"Copy."

He marched over to the north side, already steaming mad because he had to do this. Pressman and Vassar had already come down.

"Kal still up there?"

Callie Vassar nodded.

Fuck. "I'm going up. You and Pressman hit those northeast windows with a blast."

"Yes, sir."

He climbed up the ladder, cursing his brother the entire time. He had better things to do than babysit his asshole little brother who didn't follow orders.

When he got to the roof, he could feel the heat radiating off the concrete. Kal was right at the edge, using his hook to pull the concrete tiles.

"I told you to exit."

"A few more tiles and I'm done."

"A few more tiles and this whole roof is going to blow."

Kal shook his head. "I've got this. I know the situation."

"So do I. Get your ass off this roof right now."

Kal looked like he was going to argue, then shrugged and headed toward the ladder.

Jackson followed him down. When he got to the bottom, Kal was already at the mechanicals, maneuvering the ladder so he could hit the roof with water.

The one thing Jackson liked about his brother was that he knew how to operate in a fire, had instincts for what came next. The one bad thing was his recklessness. He always put himself in dangerous situations, and he didn't listen.

They'd have a conversation about that, but not right now. Now there were more pressing things to tackle, like getting this out-of-control fire more under control.

And hoping he wouldn't have to pull his attention away again to babysit his younger brother.

It took the entire day to put the fire out. Now all that was left was walking every inch of the building to look for rekindles. Jackson and his engine crew walked through the eastern side, while the other companies took the other portions of the warehouse.

The debris was considerable, so they pried loose any piles of furniture and crates to check for hot spots or hidden flames that needed to be extinguished. Walls were checked and debris torn down to be sure no heat or fire lurked. The last thing they wanted was to be called out again because the fire restarted. They put out a few hot spots, and once they walked through, walked through again, and then again, Jackson was satisfied the fire was out.

No injuries, which was great. They'd been lucky—if a fire was ever lucky—that no employees had been here because it had started before anyone had reported for work. The fire investigation team would come in to determine the cause of the fire. That wasn't Jackson's or his team's job.

They met with the other companies and debriefed, then both Engine and Ladder 6 headed back to the station.

When they got back, trucks had to be washed and tools had to be inventoried and cleaned. Hoses had to be inspected, and everyone was busy. Every person in the station was doing something, including Jackson, who had pages of reports to write.

They were two hours into postfire work when he got to the next item on his to-do list. He called Kal into his office.

"You wanted to see me?" Kal asked.

"Yeah. Shut the door."

Kal pushed the door shut. "Oh, must be serious business."

Kal had a smirk on his face. Jackson intended to wipe it off. He stood up from his desk and stood in front of Kal. "That stunt you pulled on the roof today put yourself and your fellow firefighters in danger."

Kal frowned. "What stunt?"

"I told you to exit the roof. You didn't comply on my first request."

Kal rolled his eyes. "I was still venting. And it wasn't like I stayed up there for an hour. I only had a few more tiles to complete the venting."

"It's my job to see to the safety of my firefighters, Kal, and you know that. Yet you made me come up there and force you down. While I was doing that, I couldn't monitor the rest of the team, which potentially put them in harm's way."

"And if you had just left me up there I would have finished the job and you wouldn't have had to go up there and babysit me. I'm not five years old, Jackson."

He couldn't believe they were having this conversation.

"Lieutenant. On the job, I'm your lieutenant, not your brother."

He could see the anger on his brother's face. But as he told Kal, on the job, Kal was just another firefighter. Not his brother. And he had to treat him just the way he would any other firefighter. No different.

And said firefighter had fucked up today.

"Lieutenant," Kal said, the word dripping with sarcasm. "I know my job."

"Do you? Because it sure as hell seemed as if you compromised the safety of your team by not following orders."

Kal lowered his voice. "And you know as well as I do that I'm the best you've got on Ladder 6."

"Not today you weren't. Today you were careless. Today you acted like a hotshot who wanted to be a hero. Is that the job you're looking to do?"

Kal opened his mouth to say something, then closed it, lifting his chin. "No, sir."

"This is your one and only verbal warning. If it happens again you'll have a written reprimand put in your record. Understood?"

Kal sucked in an angry breath. "Yes, sir."

Jackson pivoted and returned to his desk. "You're dismissed, Donovan."

Kal just stood there as if there was more he wanted to say. Jackson knew there was more his brother wanted to say. But if he did, there was a chance something would be written down on his record. Arguing with your lieutenant was never a good idea. So he hoped Kal would suck it up, take the verbal reprimand and leave the office.

Kal finally turned and opened the door, closed it and walked down the hall.

Jackson felt every one of Kal's angry steps as he watched him disappear around the corner.

He exhaled and leaned back in his chair, dragging his fingers through his hair.

Shit. The last thing he needed was discipline problems with one of his firefighters. The absolute last thing he needed was said firefighter to be his brother.

Desperately needing to get away from paperwork and thoughts of Kal, he got up from his desk and went into the break room.

Since they'd missed dinner, they had to settle for sandwiches tonight. He hadn't gotten around to eating yet, so he made himself a turkey sandwich, threw some chips on the plate and grabbed a soda, then juggled it all on the way back his office, figuring he could eat and get more paperwork done.

When he passed by the battalion chief's office, his dad motioned for him to come in.

"Hey, Chief."

"Rough fire tonight."

His dad had been there overseeing the entire situation, ready to call in more units if necessary and relaying with the other chiefs.

"Yeah, it was."

"You all did a good job out there."

"Thanks." He bit into his sandwich and chewed.

"Any issues?"

He swallowed and took a sip of his soda. "Issues?"

"Yeah. Equipment failures, personnel, anything I need to know about?"

Typically Jackson would report anything to his captain, who would relay it up the chain of command to the battalion chief. So, technically, this was a breach of protocol.

"I'll file my report with Chief Mathias before end of shift."

His dad leaned back in his chair. "Okay, what did one of your brothers do?"

There was no hiding anything from his father. If it was routine, Jackson would have just told his father, no big deal, and he'd read the official word in the report. Dammit.

"Roof was getting too hot. I ordered Kal down. Twice. He didn't comply so I had to go get him."

"Dammit. You talk to him?"

"Yes."

"Verbal or written?"

"Verbal, this time."

Dad shook his head. "You probably should have done written. Not the first time you've had to talk to him."

"Want me to correct that?"

"No. You did what you thought was right. But don't go easy on him just because he's your brother."

Jackson frowned. "Do you think I treated him differently?"

"That's not my call, Jackson. The question is, do *you* think you treated him differently?"

He pondered that question while he ate his sandwich and

chatted with his dad about other things. He tried to let the question go, but it stayed prominent on his mind, as if he had to answer it.

"No, I don't treat him differently."

His dad looked up from his laptop. "What?"

"Kal. Or Rafe. I don't treat them differently. If it had been any other firefighter up there, I'd have done the same thing. I have to give them the benefit of the doubt. I know they're doing their best out there, Chief. I was tough on Kal today. And if he does it again, he'll get a written reprimand in his record. I made that very clear to him."

His dad nodded. "Good enough. And I wasn't questioning your leadership or your impartiality. I knew you were fair when I recommended you for promotion. I just wanted to make sure you knew that."

Hearing that from his dad—from his battalion chief—meant everything. He respected his father more than anyone. "Thank you."

They had three more calls that shift, which meant it was late by the time Jackson fell into his rack. He only had about four hours of sleep before end of shift. Rafe and Kal looked beat, too, and no one wanted to go out for breakfast. He was looking forward to getting home and face-planting in his bed.

They all got home at the same time. He noticed that Becks's truck wasn't there, but something smelled good in the kitchen.

"Hey, Becks left a note," Rafe said, handing the handwritten note off to Jackson.

He read the note out loud:

Saw you all were fighting that big warehouse fire. That looked rough and I figured you'd miss a couple of meals. I'm heading into the shop today to get ready for opening tomorrow, but I made a breakfast casserole. It's in the fridge. Have a good day.

~ B

He smiled.

"Breakfast," Rafe said. "Nice of her to think of us. And I'm starving."

Jackson turned to his brother. "You're always starving."

Rafe patted his belly. "Hey, gotta feed all this muscle."

"You gonna eat, Kal?"

Kal shook his head and went upstairs. When his door closed, Rafe asked, "What's up with him?"

Since personnel issues were confidential, Jackson shrugged. "No idea. Guess he's just tired."

Jackson wasn't going to bring their issues home, so he was determined to ignore Kal's mood. Instead, he went to the fridge and got out Becks's casserole, which looked damned enticing.

Time for breakfast.

CHAPTER 19

IT WAS HER FIRST DAY AT HER NEW SHOP AND BECKS WAS equal parts nervous and excited.

Aria had turned out to be a dream. She'd shown up twenty minutes earlier than expected, her hair pulled back in a high ponytail, a small amount of makeup and lip gloss on. She wore clean black capris and a coral-colored T-shirt, along with black tennis shoes. She looked freaking adorable.

At first Becks showed Aria around the shop so she'd know where everything was located and so Aria would feel comfortable with her surroundings. Then she acquainted Aria with her desk.

"This is my desk?" Aria asked.

"Of course."

Aria smoothed her hands over the surface, staring at all the workspace, and at the laptop computer sitting there before looking up at Becks, her eyes wide with wonder. "It's so big. And a laptop, too. Wow."

"All yours, girl." Though it was an older-model refurbished laptop, she understood Aria's excitement. When you had nothing, everything was a thrill. Becks had been in her shoes before.

And then it was Becks's turn to be surprised. Aria knew computers like nobody's business, so acclimating her to Becks's inventory and appointment systems had been much easier than she'd thought it would be.

She assumed she'd have to spend the entire day with her, but within an hour, Aria had learned the entire system.

She was so damn smart.

"Okay, I have your employee paperwork organized in these folders." Aria came into the room Becks had set up as her workspace and handed her the folders. "Employment applications and all the required government forms."

"Perfect. Thanks."

"Your apprentice applicant Hwan is coming in at one thirty. And you said your potential new tattoo guy Martin will be here at four, right?"

"Right."

She had put feelers out with several of her tattoo peers, letting them know she was looking for an apprentice. One of her friends told her someone had approached him, so he forwarded her the guy's info. Don was an amazing tattoo artist, and he knew of a kid just out of art school who wanted to learn the tattoo business. Don spoke highly of this guy and said his art portfolio was impressive, but since Don was already mentoring someone he didn't have the time to take on anyone new.

She was looking forward to talking with Hwan. If Don recommended him, hopefully he was going to be good.

She wanted to get herself settled in and to work with Aria before Hwan's arrival because once he showed up she'd be busy. Now that she knew Aria could work independently, she wouldn't have to worry.

She picked up her phone and realized it was twelve thirty. "Hey, Aria."

Aria peeked her head in the doorway. "Yeah?"

"You hungry?"

"Um, I guess."

Becks dug into her backpack and pulled out a twenty from her wallet. "There's a sandwich shop around the corner. I'll take a turkey wrap with spinach, tomato and raspberry vinaigrette. And a large iced tea. Get yourself whatever you want."

"I can pay for my own lunch."

She'd wager Aria didn't have extra money for lunch but was too proud to say so. And the last thing she wanted to do was insult her. "When you get your first paycheck here, you can buy lunch. Tomorrow I'll bring us a salad. How's that sound?"

Aria nodded. "Sounds great. I'll be right back."

Becks made a mental note to bring dinner the rest of the week, and to make sure it was something shareable so Aria wouldn't feel bad about Becks buying food for them.

While Aria was gone, Becks answered the phone and made an appointment for a consultation on a tattoo for three o'clock Friday afternoon. She made a note in the master schedule, which would transfer into Becks's phone schedule as well.

Aria returned shortly with lunch, so they sat at her desk and ate. The turkey sandwich was amazing. She noticed Aria had gotten the same thing.

"What do you think?" she asked.

Aria lifted her head. "About what?"

"The turkey sandwich."

"Oh. It's really good. Thank you for lunch, by the way."

"You're welcome. Oh, and while you were gone, someone called and booked a consult for Friday afternoon at three. I entered it in the scheduler."

"Okay. Looks like you're going to be busy this week."

"Yeah. I can't wait."

Aria took a bite of her wrap, chewed thoughtfully, then swallowed. "How long have you been doing this?"

"Tattooing?" Becks took a deep breath, then let it out. "In my head it seems like forever. But in reality, six years."

"Really? So not very long."

"No. I've been drawing as long as I can remember. Even when I was homeless, if I could get hold of a pencil and paper, I'd draw."

Aria swiveled in her chair. "Yeah? What would you draw?"

"Anything that looked interesting to me. Leaves, trees, clouds, buildings, people, a rock I'd see on the ground, a French fry."

Aria laughed. "A French fry?"

"Yeah. It was a unique shape so I drew it. And when I had the chance to go to school and had access to more paper and colored pencils or any kind of drawing or painting medium, I was in heaven."

"So you didn't hate being fostered."

"Mmm, sometimes. My last foster family, the place I stayed before I aged out, they were good people. I went to decent schools and my family made sure I had sketchbooks and pencils to draw with. I was happy there."

"And then you aged out and got kicked out."

"Yeah. Well, you know how it is."

She rolled up the paper from her sandwich. "Yeah, I know how it is. But we're luckier than some. We got educated and we're smart and we know how to survive on the streets."

"You won't always be on the streets, Aria. You have goals and ambition."

Aria gathered up all the trash from their lunch and stood, smiling down at Becks. "And a job, thanks to you."

The day flew by. She had her appointment with the apprentice applicant. Hwan's portfolio was really good, and she had a great connection with him. He was intelligent and eager and friendly. Friendly was important for tattoo artists. You couldn't make it in this business if you were an introvert. Aria liked him as well.

Becks told him she'd let him know. She'd heard of a couple of other artists eager to be mentored so she wanted to talk to them as well, and she told that to Hwan. She'd likely get them in this week if she could and make a decision soon.

Mentoring took a long time and it was a serious commitment. She wanted to make sure to get the right person. It might even take more than one interview. She had to be sure before she invested time and resources into someone. But she also didn't want to leap on the first person she met. Not until she talked to a couple of others.

"Hey, Becks?" Aria stood in the doorway to Becks's work room.

She looked up from her sketchbook. "Yeah?"

"Jackson's here, your friend that was with you at the park."

Frowning, Becks got up and went to the waiting room.

Jackson looked cool and incredibly sexy in his black board shorts and white sleeveless shirt.

"Hey," she said. "What are you doing here?"

He came over and slipped his arm around her waist and tugged her close for a soft but sadly quick kiss, before stepping back. "I wanted to thank you for making breakfast for us."

"Looked like a wicked fire."

"It was. All three of us face-planted as soon as we got home. But we ate the casserole first. It was appreciated more than you know."

She wanted to step into his arms, to touch him, but for some reason it didn't feel right with Aria standing there gawking at them. "You're welcome. Everything go okay at work?"

"For the most part."

He didn't elaborate. It was obvious that there was more, but since he didn't offer, she didn't pry. And then he turned and smiled at Aria.

"How's the first day going, Aria?"

"Pretty good."

"She's just being modest," Becks said. "She's already taken over the computer systems and organized the inventory better than I ever could."

Aria rolled her eyes. "Speaking of inventory, I'm going to go get started on that and make a list of things you might need to get."

Aria headed toward the back, leaving Becks alone with Jackson, which meant she had a minute to run her hand up his extremely chiseled arm.

"Tired?" she asked.

"I got a few hours' sleep, so I'm good."

"I'm glad. Thanks for coming by, but you didn't have to do that."

"I wanted to see you." He looked down the hall, then put his hands on her hips and drew her close. "I needed to see you."

She wrapped a hand around his neck. "Breakfast was that good, huh?"

"Actually, it was more than breakfast. After we visited at the park, I talked to my mom."

She paused, then cocked her head to the side. "About?"

"Lexie."

She dropped her hand. "Oh. What about her?"

"You're close to her. And I know you want better for her. So I was chatting with my mom and she knows this couple that has four kids that range in age from ten to fourteen. They've adopted all of them and are looking to add more within that age range."

"Lexie's twelve."

"Yeah. Mom said she'd love to talk to Lexie if you think she'd want to get out of the park. My mom said these are decent people, Becks."

Her heart started pounding. "You trust her judgement, obviously."

"One hundred percent."

She was almost afraid to breathe. The idea of a forever home for Lexie was almost too much to hope for. "I'll talk to Lexie, and arrange a meeting with your mom."

"Okay."

She reached out and grabbed his arm. "Jackson. Thank you for doing this. You have no idea what this means to me. What it'll mean for Lexie."

"Actually, I know exactly what it means."

Of course he did. And that he thought about her—about Lexie—was almost too much for her heart.

He cleared his throat. "Anyway, no big deal or anything."

"Huge deal." She squeezed his hand so tight she figured she was probably breaking bones.

He grinned, then leaned in to kiss her, and for a moment she forgot all about where she was, who was there. She might have even forgot her own name, because she was lost in the sensation of soft lips, the gentle scrape of beard stubble against her chin and wishing they were alone so they could do more than kiss. Because his body rubbing against hers made her feel hot and tingly all over, and she wanted to explore him with her hands and her teeth and rub her breasts against his naked chest.

Unfortunately, they weren't alone and she had a rather large picture window about three feet from where they stood. So she had to pull some awareness to her sex-fogged brain.

She took a step back and cleared her throat. "Are you going to be around later?"

"Yeah. What time are you planning to be home?"

"I have an interview with my new tattoo artist this afternoon. Then we'll wrap things up around here. I should be home by six."

"I'll make sure I'm home by six."

She smiled. "See you then."

"Okay." He started toward the door. "Later, Becks."

She walked with him. "Bye, Jackson. And thanks again."

She closed the door behind him, lingering to watch him climb into his truck. He definitely looked good in that sleeveless muscle shirt.

"You've got it bad for him."

She whirled around to see that Aria had planted herself back at her desk. She'd been so wrapped up in ogling Jackson that she hadn't even heard Aria come back into the room.

She lifted her chin.

"I do not. We're just . . . casual."

Aria arched a brow. "Casually setting the office on fire, you mean."

Becks frowned. "I have no idea what you're talking about."

She heard Aria laugh as she started back into her office.

It *was* casual. Totally casual. But Aria was right about one thing. It was totally hot, too.

She went back to work with a satisfied smile on her face.

CHAPTER 20

SINCE BECKS WAS ALWAYS DOING THINGS FOR HIM AND his brothers, Jackson figured he'd do something nice for her today.

He stopped at the store on his way home and bought a few things. She'd made them breakfast. He was going to make her dinner tonight.

When he got home, Rafe and Kal were nowhere to be found.

Good. He hoped that he and Becks would have the place to themselves.

His phone buzzed. It was Rafe.

"Hey, what's up, Rafe?"

"Just gonna ask you the same question. Where are you?"

"At home."

"Kal and I are heading to the store to fill up the fridge. Want anything?"

"No, I was just at the store, but thanks."

"Okay. We invited some people over for barbecue and a swim tonight. You game?"

Well, shit. They shared the house, so it wasn't like he could say no. "Actually, I bought stuff to toss on the grill, too."

"Yeah? What do you have in mind? We'll just get extra."

He gave his menu items to Rafe, then hung up.

So much for being alone with Becks. He knew she wouldn't mind, but he was damned disappointed.

He made the marinade, making sure to mix up extra. Then he sliced up the chicken, cut up the pineapple, onions and peppers and put them on the skewers, then slid them into the marinade.

After that, he made himself an iced tea and headed into the game room.

It wasn't long before Rafe and Kal showed up.

"Where you at?" Rafe shouted.

"Game room," Jackson yelled.

"We got the stuff. You want to show us what you want to do with it?"

Jackson rolled his eyes. His brothers were both extremely competent firefighters. They also both knew their way around the kitchen. If he wasn't there, he was certain they could figure out what to do with the ingredients.

He paused the game he'd been playing and went into the kitchen.

"Slice the chicken, pineapple and veggies and slide them on the skewers, then add them into the container in the fridge where the other ones are marinating."

"What, you're not gonna help?" Kal asked.

He noted Kal was speaking to him again. The one thing he loved about his brother—about both of them—was that they could fight and neither of them would hold a grudge. Once the initial mad wore off, the argument was done. Whether it was work or personal shit, once it was over, it was over.

"I think you can both figure it out. Besides, I'm winning a game in there."

"Aww, man," Kal said, eyeing the TV with longing. "I'll be in there to kick your ass as soon as we're done in here."

"Yeah, yeah," Jackson said. "Be sure to clean up the mess you make first."

He went back to his game, feeling no guilt whatsoever for making his brothers do the work. He knew they could handle it, and he wouldn't have to worry about them leaving a mess. They all did their parts about keeping the house clean.

The house had belonged to their grandmother. Well, Laurel's grandmother, who left it to Laurel when she died. Instead of selling it, Laurel had kept it and the guys had all renovated it within an inch of its life before moving in.

Dad had told them they could live there and save on paying rent, though they had to pony up the money for insurance and taxes, and they were responsible for the upkeep and any repairs. It had been a sweet deal and none of them had minded putting the sweat equity into fixing the place up.

Of course, Mom, being Mom, had told them they had to save their money, because someday they'd want to move out and buy houses of their own, so she didn't expect them to show up with fancy cars or stupid toys they didn't need. She had always raised them to become responsible adult men, which meant there were no freebies along the way. Which suited Jackson just fine. The last thing he'd ever wanted—from anyone—was a handout. The one thing he'd always admired about his parents was that they had never treated him or his brothers with kid gloves. They'd given them ample amounts of love, and an equal amount of discipline. Hugs when they needed it, and a good ass-kicking when it was required. Not the physical kind, of course—neither parent ever laid a hand on them. They never had to. Mom was always loving and generous and if you pissed her off all she had to do was look at you a certain way and you knew you'd screwed up. She was so gentle and sweet that you felt so bad if you made her angry that you swore to never do it again.

Dad, on the other hand, was different. He laid down the law in no uncertain terms. He had rules and he expected you to follow them. He was also fun and coached their baseball teams and would laugh with them and play basketball with them. But if you broke curfew or didn't do what you'd been asked to do or broke any of the other rules? You were grounded or you lost privileges. And there was no arguing your way out of it. Rules were rules and you didn't break them.

Jackson's lips curved as he played his way through yet another game. He'd gotten so lucky with his parents. Who knew that almost getting killed in a fire would change his life so dramatically?

"What are you grinning about?" Kal asked as he came in and plopped down on the sofa next to him.

"Thinking about Mom and Dad. About how that fire changed our lives."

"Oh." Kal picked up a game controller and joined in the game. "Yeah, we were damn lucky that night. One, we didn't die. Two, Dad rescued us."

"And then for some reason that still escapes me, he liked you two as much as he liked me," Rafe said, coming over to sit on the other side of Jackson. "Though to this day I still have no idea why."

Jackson shoved his shoulder into Rafe's. "Asshole."

Rafe laughed. "Dickhead."

"No, Mom saw me and decided I was the prettiest thing she'd ever seen," Kal said. "Sweet, too. She couldn't resist me. I had to convince her to take you two. Don't tell her I told you. She made me promise not to."

Jackson rolled his eyes. "You're both wrong. Dad picked me.

It took a lot of finagling on my end to bring you two along. I've been paying them ever since."

"Who'd ever want you?" Rafe asked. "With your ugly face and those skinny white legs."

"My skinny white legs?" Jackson looked up at Rafe. "Look at your fucking hair. Sticks up all over. You're an embarrassment to the Donovan name."

"Please. My hair is luxe, dude."

"No, *my* hair is luxe," Kal said.

"Your hair is wiry and weird."

Kal slanted a look at him. "You would insult a black man like that?"

"No. I would insult my brother like that."

Kal laughed. "I'm killing you in this game."

"We'll see."

The insults went on for over an hour while they played the game. It was the best part of being brothers with these guys. They could offend each other in the worst ways, but Jackson knew— they all knew—that without each other it would be like a part of each of them was missing.

Jackson heard the garage door open and close. Shortly thereafter, Becks poked her head in the game room.

"Hey, I'm home. Oh, hi, everyone. I didn't expect you all to be here."

"Oh, yeah?" Rafe asked. "Did you and Jackson have a hot date planned?"

Becks offered up an enigmatic smile as she exchanged glances with Jackson before turning her attention back to Rafe. "I have no comment. What are you all doing?"

"Insulting each other," Kal said. "Playing a game. Care to join in?"

"Actually, no. I'm thirsty and I had an idea for a sketch I want to do that came to me on the drive home, so I'm going to grab my sketchbook and work on that while I cool down. Lord, it's hot outside today."

Kal leaned back. "Sure is. I mowed the lawn earlier and nearly died."

"Really?" Rafe asked. "You nearly died? Because you look fine to me."

"Whatever, asshole," Kal said. "Hey, Becks, we invited some friends over for grilling and a pool party tonight. You okay with that?"

"Well, first, it's your house so you can always do whatever you want. Second, I'm totally okay with that. It sounds fun."

She started to exit the room, but Kal stopped her.

"Hey, Becks?" Kal yelled over the loud noise of warfare coming from the TV.

"Yeah?"

"It's your house, too, now. So you always get a say in what goes on around here."

She paused before answering, then leveled a warm smile at Kal. "Thank you for saying that. I appreciate it. And I'm looking forward to tonight. See you later, guys."

Jackson wanted to get up and go to her, but his brothers would complain that he abandoned them in the middle of battle, so he stayed put.

"It meant a lot to her that you said that, Kal," Jackson said.

Kal didn't pull his attention away from the screen. "We've all felt unwanted, like we're temporary and didn't belong. She belongs here with us." Kal glanced over at Jackson. "Like family. She needs to know that."

Jackson smiled at his brother. "Yeah."

"Don't think I'm gonna hug you or anything. And pay attention to the game, man. You just got us killed."

"Dammit." It was hard to pay attention to anything when his mind was on Becks.

Guess it was time for him to focus.

BECKS WENT UPSTAIRS TO CHANGE CLOTHES AND WASH up. Summer in Ft. Lauderdale could be so hot, and this summer was no exception. Unless you spent all your time at the beach where the ocean breeze cooled you down, the humidity was unbearable.

She washed her face and wound her hair up into a bun on top of her head, then changed into a pair of shorts and a tank top, making sure to put her bikini on underneath. Now she felt much better. She grabbed her sketchbook and pencil and went downstairs, fixed herself a large glass of iced tea and sat at the kitchen table.

While she'd been talking with Martin, the new tattoo artist who was going to be renting space in her shop, they'd chatted about some of the ink they'd done. She'd looked over his portfolio, falling instantly in love with his work.

Martin's work was incredibly detailed. He was in his midthirties and he'd been tattooing for over fifteen years. He'd started right out of high school. He was like some kind of art prodigy, told her he'd been drawing as long as he could remember. But he never wanted to open his own storefront because he preferred to stay on the move, drawing inspiration from locales. He really liked the location of her shop near the beach, and she was stoked to have him work at her shop. She'd known who he was the minute he'd come into her shop. He traveled all over, but he'd been in Florida for a couple of years now.

She'd run into him a couple of times at some of the local tattoo conventions where he'd put on demonstrations. The guy never had trouble gathering a crowd, not only because of his work but also because he was one of those guys who was incredibly attractive. He was bald, muscular, had big blue eyes and an engaging smile, plus the kind of personality that made people want to spend time with him. Martin always had eager customers.

He also had an adorable pixie of a wife and two beautiful kids. He talked a lot about his wife, who modeled several of his tattoos. The pics he shared were incredible.

And those kids, two boys, were replicas of their dad. With hair, of course.

He was going to be an incredible draw for Skin Deep, and hopefully she could pick up some new business for herself in the process.

She opened her sketchbook, so inspired by talking to him that she couldn't wait to make a few drawings.

"Got some new ideas?"

She looked up to find Jackson standing over her. "Oh. Yeah." She went back to it, her mind overflowing with thoughts of the sand, the way the ocean curled into it when the waves hit the beach. She needed to get her mind straight, to picture it just right at sunrise when the shadows were lifting—

"So what are you working on?"

She snapped her head up. "A drawing. Sorry, Jackson, I'd really like to get this down while the thought is fresh in my mind."

"Oh. Sure."

Jackson walked away and she went back to it. She followed the curve of shadow, using colored pencils to get the coloring right. She often put drawings in her portfolio, because sometimes a customer would have an idea in their head, and a drawing would help them cement that idea, or help her explore that idea with a client further.

She drew the waves as they curled upward, some just flowing over the sand, a few crabs skittering over the beach and the sun rising.

She jotted down a few more sketches. A mermaid on a rock sunning herself, her head tilted back, her hair flowing down her back, the strands so many different colors she couldn't grab enough pencils to shade them in fast enough. It was as if each strand were alive, curling one over the other, nearly jumping off the page with animation.

That one turned out beautifully. She did another one, this time of the park, with the tree limbs bending over in protection of tulips popping up in the grass. And another of a stretch of highway, road signs signaling the start of adventure.

Martin had been so inspiring today. It had been a good talk. Hopefully the first of many.

A new day. A new beginning. After that frenzied batch of sketching, she felt settled. She closed her sketchbook and went to refill her glass of tea. She walked into the game room.

It was empty.

Huh.

She went into the family room, thinking they might have gone in there to watch TV, but they weren't in there.

She made her way back into the kitchen and no one was in there, either. Okay.

She remembered Jackson coming up to talk to her, but she'd brushed him off because she'd been midsketch. She'd been so involved she had no idea what she'd even said to him. God, she hoped it hadn't been something awful. When she got involved in taking an idea from her head to the page, she got so focused she could be blunt about not being interrupted. Jackson wouldn't know that, and she had to find him so she could explain that to him. She looked out into the backyard and saw the guys.

As well as a bunch of other people, too.

Wait. People were here now? How had she missed that?

She knew when she got into her head, the entire world could

pass her by. But had she really been oblivious to people coming in?

Maybe they'd come in through the side gate. That had to be it. Surely she would have noticed—she quickly scanned the crowd. There were about ten people here. She'd have seen all those folks walking by and talking. Wouldn't she?

She started out the French doors, then paused, noticing Jackson sitting off to the side of the main group. He was in one of the chaise lounges talking to a rather beautiful redhead, the two of them nestled up close, seemingly in deep conversation.

Okay. She and Jackson weren't in any kind of exclusive relationship. Or even in a relationship, exactly. They were roommates. Dating. Not really dating. Did dating today even have a definition? She had no idea. It wasn't like she'd had a normal upbringing, so what did she know about anything?

She knew she liked Jackson. She'd always liked Jackson. For the past fifteen years she'd had a crush on Jackson. Though now that they were having sex, she supposed the word *crush* could be tossed out the window in favor of . . .

She had no idea what word or phrase described their situation, and now that she'd had her own circular argument she was right back where she'd started—with no clear answers as to where they stood.

She noticed Rafe heading her way, so she backed away from the door and went to gather up her sketchpad and pencils, hoping he hadn't noticed her gawking at the door.

She was just about to make her way to the stairs.

"You trying to hide from us, Becks?"

She pivoted, planting a smile on her face. "Hide? Of course not. I was just getting my stuff out of the way. I'll be right back down so I can meet your friends."

"You know you could invite some of your own friends. Remember, this is your house now, too."

"Oh. Sure. I guess I could do that."

"Maybe your cute real estate agent friend?"

"Margie?" She gave Rafe a hard stare. "Aren't you dating someone?"

"I'm always dating someone."

"Then I'm definitely not inviting Margie. She's looking for love and forever. Not a serial dater, like you."

Rafe sent a cockeyed grin her way. "That almost sounded like an insult, Becks."

"Not meant as one. But I'm keeping my friends away from you."

He laughed. "Noted."

As she walked away, he yelled at her.

"You're coming back down, aren't you?"

"Just putting my stuff away. I'll be right back."

"Okay. Jackson was asking about you."

She had no idea why he'd do that since he was occupied by the cute redhead.

She closed the door to her room, then stilled, realizing what she'd been doing.

"Okay, Becks. Time to stop acting like the jealous girlfriend."

That wasn't like her at all. She had gone into this . . . whatever it was with Jackson with her eyes wide open, so there was no reason for her to act this way. Time to get her shit together.

She put her sketchpad and pencils away, then started out the door, but paused. Instead, she went into the bathroom and looked at herself in the mirror.

"You look fine, Becks." Her hair was fine, her makeup, though nearly nonexistent, was fine.

She was just fine. Not spectacular, but decent enough.

And no beautiful redhead was going to make her touch herself up, no matter how much she wanted to plump up her hair a bit, add some mascara and maybe a touch of lip gloss. Which would be ridiculous because it was a million degrees outside, her hair was going to fall into a limp mess, and any makeup she did put on would slide down her face and she'd look like a clown.

This wasn't a competition. If Jackson wanted her, he'd have to want her looking like this.

Fine.

With a sigh of disgust at that feeling of worthlessness that never seemed to go away, she went downstairs, sucked in a breath of courage and opened the door to go outside.

She thought she'd find Jackson right where she'd seen him—on the chair with the redhead.

Instead, he was at the grill, beer in hand, talking to a guy she didn't know. When he saw her, he said something to his friend, who looked over at her and smiled, then wandered away.

She walked over to him.

"Hey," he said.

"Hey. I'm sorry about earlier."

He frowned. "Earlier?"

"I was sketching. And I get wrapped up in my own head when I'm doing that. I know you came over to talk to me and I don't know what I said to you, but whatever it was I was probably rude about it. I'm sorry."

"Oh. You were busy. It's okay. It's your work, Becks. Don't apologize for that."

So he wasn't mad. Plus, he understood, which was rare. "Thanks."

"Get yourself a drink and come hang with me while I cook. Unless it's too hot over here. You can always go slide into the pool."

She took a glance over at the pool. The beautiful redhead was in there with Rafe and Kal and a few other guys.

She would not be jealous about that.

"That's Callie, by the way," he said. "She's a fellow firefighter."

"Oh." Okay, so maybe nothing there.

"And an ex-girlfriend of mine."

And now things were even worse. "Oh, really?"

"Yeah." He let out a short laugh. "We dated about four years ago. I wasn't equipped to deal with relationships back then. So we lasted about six months and broke up."

"And she still likes you?"

He gave her a look. "Why wouldn't she?"

"I . . . I don't know. I'm sorry. I don't know why I said that."

This was going well. She should have just stayed in her room.

He grasped her hand and held it up to his mouth, brushing his lips over her knuckles.

"Stop saying you're sorry. Hang on, I'll be right back." He pulled some of the chicken skewers off the grill, laid them on a plate, then took them inside.

She turned to face the crowd, noticing that Callie wasn't the only woman. There were actually two others; she just had been so focused on the cute redhead she hadn't even noticed.

When he came back, he had two beers in his hand. He handed one to her. "Come on. Let's go hang out by the pool."

"Sure."

He took her by the hand, and she hadn't realized how tight she was holding on.

"You know, I bought this food for you and I to enjoy a nice quiet dinner together."

"You did?"

"Yeah. I was going to surprise you. We'd have chicken skewers, some beer, some conversation."

He'd done all that for her? "That's sweet. Thank you."

"You're welcome. And then my idiot brothers invited everyone over."

She squeezed his hand. "It's their house, too."

"I know. Someday I'm going to ruin their romantic plans."

She leaned into him. "You will not."

"Oh, mark my words. I will."

"My man," one of the guys said from the pool. "Chicken smells good."

"Hey, I'm a master cook."

"Is that why you have Kal do all the cooking at the station?"

"No, I have Kal do the cooking because he's on ladder. And we all know the ladder guys don't have enough to do."

"Hey, screw you," Kal said. "I had the fires of hell licking at my ass the other day."

"That's because you didn't get off the roof when I told you to."

"Whatever," Kal said. "I had it covered."

"Yeah," Jackson said. "Your ass was about to be covered with fire."

The guy who spoke up earlier piped up again. "You know you're not going to win that argument, Kal."

Kal tossed a pool volleyball at Jackson, who fielded it easily and threw it back toward his brother. Rafe intercepted it and bonked Kal on the head with it.

"Is it always like this?" Becks asked.

"Like what?"

"You all fighting."

"This wasn't fighting."

Rafe pulled himself out of the pool and came up beside them. "Yeah, when we fight? You'll know it."

"So are all these people firefighters?" she asked.

"Some are," Jackson said. "And some their families or significant others. Let me introduce you."

She met Zep and Mitchell, who Jackson told her rode Engine 6 with him and Rafe. Then she met the beautiful redhead Callie Vassar. She was even more gorgeous up close.

"Callie's on Ladder 6 with Kal," Jackson said.

"Only I'm better than he is." She stuck out her hand. "Nice to meet you, Becks. This is my husband, Aaron."

So she had a husband. Jealousy crisis averted. Becks shook

Aaron's hand. He was fine-looking. Tall, with blond hair and impressive muscles. "Are you a firefighter, too, Aaron?"

Aaron smiled and nodded. "Yeah, I'm a lieutenant at Station 17."

"That must be interesting, the two of you doing the same job."

"I don't know how I could be with someone who wasn't," Callie said. "The crazy schedule, the stress of the job. For me at least, only a fellow firefighter could understand me."

Becks looked around. She'd wager not everyone here was married to or dating a firefighter. But she understood what Callie was saying. For her, that was what worked.

"It's obviously working for you," Becks said.

"For sure. You want to come sit with me in the water, Becks? I'm dying in this heat."

"Sure." She gave a look to Jackson, who had already turned away and was deep in conversation with Aaron, so he clearly had no qualms about her spending time with Callie.

She slid out of her shorts and pulled off her tank top, then slid into the water.

Callie was right. It felt much better to be in the pool. They sat on the steps at the shallow end and Becks sipped her beer. Callie had a large ice water.

"So how long have you been a firefighter, Callie?"

"Five years."

"And do you like it?"

"I love it. I couldn't think about doing anything else."

"The guys all say the same thing. It must be in your blood."

Callie nodded. "My dad was a firefighter. He's retired now, but watching him while I was growing up made me want to do the same thing."

"How does he feel about his daughter having the same dangerous job?"

She grinned. "Oh, he's incredibly proud. I'm the only child, so he figured I'd end up doing something else with my life. When I told him I wanted to be a firefighter I thought he was going to burst, he was so happy."

"Oh, that's sweet. How does your mom feel?"

"She, on the other hand, wasn't as happy. But she understands the desire since she's lived with my dad all these years. It's a calling."

Becks didn't understand that calling, but she definitely respected it. "I appreciate the work you all do."

"Thanks." Callie blew out a breath. "This heat is killing me. Which is crazy since I'm around the heat all the time at my job."

"We could go inside if the humidity is bothering you."

"It's not that. But yeah, let's do that."

"No problem." Becks got out of the pool and grabbed a couple of the towels that were stacked on a nearby table. She handed one to Callie. They dried off and headed inside.

"This is so much better," Callie said as she finished drying off her legs. "For some reason this first trimester is messing with my metabolism."

"Oh, you're pregnant."

"Yes."

Becks grinned. "Congratulations."

"Thanks. I just told everyone at the station this past week. I just passed my twelfth week and everything's good."

"Let's go sit down in the living room. It's really cool in there."

"Sure."

They laid their towels over the leather and took a seat.

"This is probably the least feminist thing I'll ever utter," Becks said. "But do you still get to do your job?"

Callie laughed. "It's okay to ask that. What we do is risky as hell. But yes, I'll still get to do my job, at least until sometime in the third trimester where my center of gravity will make me too top-heavy to drag hose. Then I'll probably have to ride a desk until I go on maternity leave. The current me says bullshit, I can do anything up until the time I give birth. I'm sure three or four months from now I'll be happy to take my swollen ankles to the desk and keep my baby safe."

Becks couldn't imagine being a pregnant firefighter, but at the same time she truly believed women could do anything. "There's no doubt you could fight fires all the way up until you deliver. You seem strong and capable. I mean, look at your muscle definition, girl."

Callie held up her arm and flexed her biceps. "Yeah, firefighting keeps us in shape, for sure. You don't look too bad yourself. And that ink is beautiful."

"Thanks." So, okay, she'd been jealous when she first saw Callie talking to Jackson, which was her own fault because she never judged people on appearances. She should know better. "Jackson tells me you two dated for a while. Is that awkward since you two work together?"

"He told you, huh?" Callie let out a short laugh. "Good for him. I love how honest he is. Sometimes too honest."

"In what way?"

"Working together while we dated was rough. There was no denying it. Fortunately we were both young and just in it for the fun. Jackson knows how to have fun. You know that, of course."

Becks smiled. "Yes, I do."

"But we could both tell after a while it wasn't the right fit. I was looking for something more, and he was up-front and honest about not wanting anything serious. So we agreed it was better if we went back to being friends."

She made it sound so easy. "So it was a mutual thing, then. With no hard feelings between you?"

Callie lay back on the arm of the sofa, yawned and nodded. "Yup. Easiest breakup I ever had, to be honest. He's a great guy, Becks. He's just wasn't my guy. And as soon as I started dating

Aaron, I knew the difference between playing around and playing for keeps. You know?"

She didn't know, to be honest. She'd never been in love. Like Callie, she'd had fun. She'd had sex. She'd been in lust.

But love? Love meant putting your whole heart in someone's care. And that meant someone had the power to throw you away. She'd had plenty of that in her lifetime and never wanted to experience it again.

Yet tonight she'd looked forlornly at the door as Jackson sat with Callie and had felt as if she were being tossed aside, once again. Not Jackson's or Callie's fault, of course, because it had all been in her own head.

Still, she hadn't liked feeling that way. And if this was what caring about someone felt like, she wanted no part of it.

Maybe it was time to back off her relationship with Jackson, start putting some distance between them. She had to protect her heart so she wouldn't get hurt.

She turned to talk to Callie, who was curled up and sound asleep.

She smiled. Yeah, that heat was rough, and pregnancy must be exhausting. She got up and quietly left the room.

Jackson was just coming into the kitchen along with Callie's husband, Aaron.

"Hi. Have you seen Callie?" Aaron asked.

"She fell asleep. She's in the living room." Becks hooked her thumb over her shoulder.

Aaron's lips curved. "She passes out at the drop of a hat as soon as she sits down these days."

"She got hot outside."

"I'll go check on her. Thanks, Becks."

Aaron left the room.

Jackson moved over to the oven and took the chicken skewers out.

"I'm gonna make a pot of rice," Jackson said, smiling as he lifted his gaze to hers. "Keep me company."

Oh, that smile. No wonder she had such trouble keeping her emotions in check around him. She had all these thoughts about big things she needed to talk to him about. Uncomfortable things. And yet, one look from him and all she could think about was wrapping her hand around the back of his neck and drawing him close so she could kiss him.

So much for her distance resolve. Where was her determination?

"I thought I'd put together a fruit salad to go with all of this," she said, hoping to keep her mind—and her hands—out of trouble. "It'll help cool everyone off."

"Great idea."

She had picked up a watermelon yesterday, so she chopped that up, along with oranges, strawberries, cantaloupe and grapes. She stuck the bowl in the fridge to let it get cold, then washed her hands.

Jackson had the rice going in the cooker and was placing plates and utensils on the island. Becks grabbed the napkins.

"I'm sure everyone's hungry," she said. "The chicken smells really good."

"Thanks." He turned to her, surprising her by sliding his hand around her waist and drawing her against him. "Sorry again for turning this into a big party instead of a night for just the two of us."

"Hey, I told you before I had no problem with this."

"But I do." His hands traveled down over her hips, and it was all she could do to remember that whole resolve and distance thing. "I wanted to be alone with you, cook you dinner, mess around a little."

She shuddered as she drew in a breath. It was hard to keep your distance from someone you'd been crazy about for more than half your life. "We can still mess around a little later."

He walked her back a few steps until she was pressed against the kitchen counter. "I'll hold you to that."

And then he kissed her, and just like every kiss he'd given her since the first one, it was melting hot. But not the kind of summer heat you wanted to get away from. This was the kind of heat she wanted to draw closer to, to climb inside it and wallow in it until it liquefied her from the inside out.

When the back door opened and they heard the voices of people coming inside, Jackson stepped away from her. But not before she saw that intense heat in his eyes and knew he felt the same way.

Damn.

She quickly turned and walked away from him.

The crowd piled in and Jackson and his brothers laid the food out. Becks grabbed the fruit salad and a serving spoon and put that out as well. The guys had made plenty of chicken skewers, Jackson'd made a double batch of jasmine rice and she'd made a huge bowl of fruit, so there was more than enough food. She waited along with the guys until each of the guests filled their plates.

"Hey," Kal said, turning to her. "Get yourself something to eat."

She laid her hand on his arm. "I'm good. You go."

"We go after you," Rafe said.

With a sigh, she reached for a plate and placed a couple of skewers on there, then some rice and fruit salad.

She found a spot to sit. Callie had come in with Aaron, obviously having woken from her nap. Becks sat with Callie on one side of her and Rafe on the other. Callie made sure to introduce her to a few other people she hadn't met yet.

"This is Penny Pressman. She's married to Ethan, who rides with me on Ladder 6."

"Nice to meet you, Penny."

"You, too."

"Becks is Jackson's girlfriend."

Ethan, a tall, fine-looking guy, leaned forward on the other side of Penny. "No shit. Jackson's got a girlfriend?"

She was about to correct Callie and point out that they hadn't defined their relationship yet, but suddenly there were about ten sets of eyes all trained on Jackson, who was leaning against the kitchen counter shoveling food into his mouth.

"What?" he asked.

"You didn't tell us you had a girlfriend," Ethan said.

"Wait," another guy said. "You have a girlfriend? Since when?"

Jackson looked over at Becks. She hoped he didn't think she was the one who'd started all of the girlfriend talk. But trying to explain that in front of everyone would be weird, so all she could do was just shrug.

"I told them," Callie said.

Jackson changed his focus from Becks to Callie. "What the hell did you do that for?"

"Because you *are* dating Becks," Rafe said. "Is it some kind of secret?"

He shot a frown over at Rafe. "Well . . . no."

Rafe rolled his eyes. "Then quit acting like we just told everyone you had herpes. Chill, dude."

Becks suddenly wanted to be invisible. Or come up with some kind of excuse to disappear from this house—and from Jackson's life—forever. She'd never been more embarrassed.

"Hey, everyone. I'm dating Becks. She's the beautiful woman sitting next to Callie. I'm sorry I didn't send out a mass text about it. Probably because it's none of your damn business. Now eat and leave her alone."

Callie laughed and nudged Becks with her shoulder. "He likes you."

"I want to die right now."

"Why?"

"Because he's probably pissed off that he was called out about me."

"He's not pissed. Well maybe he's pissed off, but if he is, he's mad at me. And I don't care."

Callie seemed relaxed and not at all concerned about Jackson. Then again, she wasn't dating him.

For that matter, Becks wasn't sure she was dating him, either. And that was the problem. People knew about them when they hadn't even had an opportunity to talk about what was going on between them.

"Slide down, Aaron," Jackson said, easing onto the sofa next to Becks after Rafe got up.

Becks stared down at her plate, at the food that a few minutes ago had looked so appetizing but now seemed impossible to eat because a lump the size of a boulder sat in the middle of her stomach.

She was surprised Jackson even wanted to sit next to her considering all that had just gone down.

"Sorry about all that," he said, leaning over to press a kiss to her cheek. "Some people"—he gave a look to Callie—"just can't seem to keep their noses in their own business."

Callie seemed utterly unaffected by the way he glared at her. "Don't know what you're talking about, Jackson."

"You know I could put you on mopping duty next shift."

She laughed. "You could, but you won't, because you want me on grocery shopping duty so you'll have something to eat besides cereal for dinner."

"Hey, I don't buy only cereal," Kal said. "I buy eggs, too."

Callie leaned her head back since Kal was behind her. "You're a terrible shopper, Kal."

And just like that, they'd launched into another argument, with all the firefighters talking over each other about what they wanted on the grocery list for next shift.

"Anyway," Jackson said. "I hope you're not mad."

She slid sideways to search his face. "You thought I was mad? I thought you were pissed. At me."

"Why would I—?"

He took her hand and hauled her up. She almost dropped the contents of the plate she'd been balancing on her lap, but Jackson scooped it up with his other hand and easily dealt with it.

"You didn't eat," he said, moving her away from the crowd still noisily talking over each other.

"I . . . lost my appetite."

"The chicken was good. You should eat."

She rolled her eyes. "I'm fine."

He slid her plate onto the corner of the kitchen counter on their way out of the room and into the game room, where they were alone. He sat her down on one of the sofas in there and took a spot next to her.

"I'm not mad at you. I'm a little ticked off at Callie for thinking that my relationship with you is anyone else's business."

"I didn't tell her we were dating. Or anything else. She just assumed, I guess."

"It's not hard to figure out we're together, so it's no big deal. It's just that everyone at the station likes to be in everyone else's business. And I like my personal life to stay that way."

"I understand." She made a mental note to try hard to move up her moving-out plans. The sooner it didn't appear as if she were shacking up with Jackson, the better it would be for him. He did, after all, have a position of authority at the fire station. He didn't need the people who reported to him giving him a bunch of shit about housing the chick they'd saved from a fire.

He smoothed a lock of her hair away from her face. "What are you worried about?"

"Me? Nothing."

"You're quiet. Talk to me."

"I just think it would be best if I got out of here sooner rather than later. I don't want to cause trouble for you."

He leaned back against the sofa cushion. "Why do you think you're causing trouble? Because they were teasing me out there?"

"Yes."

"Becks. We all tease each other, especially when one of us is serio— is dating someone. It's all good natured and fun. Especially when we're off duty. When I said I keep my private life private, it just means that at work, my expectation is that we have to take the job seriously."

"I understand that. I don't want to get in the way."

"You're not in the way. And you have a space here as long as you want it."

"I don't know, Jackson. For as long as I can remember, I've made it my personal mission to become invisible when the situation called for it."

He moved forward, taking her hand. "And you think this is one of those situations. Because someone called you my girlfriend."

"I . . . guess so. I don't know. I've never been close to someone before. I never lived with someone. Not that we're living together or anything. I mean, we live in the same house, but we're not." She put her hands over her face. "I'm screwing this up."

He pulled her hands away from her face and tipped her chin up to meet his smiling gaze. "No, you're not."

"And you think I'm funny."

"I do think you're funny. And beautiful. And I'm listening to you. Go on."

She sighed. "I've been on my own my whole life, you know? I don't know how to do this."

"How to do what?"

"How to be with someone. How to be your girlfriend, or to date you, or whatever it is that we're actually doing."

He took in a breath and she could tell she was causing him anxiety, which was the last thing she wanted.

"How about we do this? Let's not put a label on whatever it is we are. Let's just take us a day at a time, enjoy what we have and what we're doing and ignore what anyone else thinks. The only people that matter in this equation are you and me, right?"

"Right."

"Here's how I see this. I like having you here, Becks. I like having you in my bed—or your bed. Or on the couch. Or on the floor. I like seeing your face in the morning before shift, or at night before I go to bed. I like spending time with you. If you left, I'd be upset and worried about you and where you were. So don't leave."

His words caused her stomach to clench, but not in a bad way. It was more in a way that felt warm and comforting. And that was a new kind of feeling. The kind of sensation that made her feel cared for.

She hadn't felt cared for much in her life.

She grabbed his hand and jerked him into the garage, closing the door behind them.

She backed him up against the door and pressed her body against his.

"What are you doing?"

"Just . . . shut up and kiss me."

He wrapped an arm around her and pushed his body back against hers. "Fuck yeah."

His kiss was hot, intense, and her body was on fire in an instant.

She'd wanted this from the moment she'd walked in the door, admittedly disappointed to find his brothers were there, planning a party, when all she'd wanted was some alone time with Jackson.

Now all she could think about were his hands on her breasts, his teeth on her earlobe and . . .

"Oh, shit," she said, pulling back. "No condom."

"Wait." He reached into his pants and pulled one out of his wallet.

She grasped his face. "Yes. Now."

He flipped her around so she faced the door. She heard him rustling with his clothes. Suddenly her shorts and bikini bottom were around her ankles and his hands were between her legs. She shoved the shorts and bikini out of the way to spread her legs.

She moaned as he found her clit, rubbed her right where she flamed hot with need.

"Oh, yes, right there. Don't stop."

She was coming before she could get the words out, biting down on her cheek to keep from screaming.

He stepped between her spread legs, both of them trying to balance on that top step.

She didn't care. She wanted him inside her.

And when he slid into her, she gasped. His hand met hers, his fingers tangling with hers as he drove into her.

She was panting, sweating as he thrust over and over into her, her pussy convulsing around his cock.

"Fuck," he said, licking the side of her neck. "Oh, fuck, I'm gonna come hard inside you."

"Yes. Harder."

She was out of her mind with the need for him. Both of their bodies were slick with sweat as they glided against each other.

She tightened and quivered, so close again. Jackson reached around her to strum her clit with rhythmic, delicious motions. She couldn't hold back the wild spasms of orgasm.

"Oh, damn, Jackson, I'm coming."

He bit down on her shoulder as he came, both of them shuddering against each other as they rocketed through intense orgasms.

Finally, she settled and Jackson withdrew, disposing of the

condom in the garage trash. He bent down and retrieved her bikini bottom and shorts. She held on to his shoulder while she
climbed back into her clothes.

"I'm sweaty as fuck," he said.

She laughed. "Me, too."

"Let's fix that."

He held out his hand and Becks realized at that moment that
she'd follow Jackson anywhere.

CHAPTER 21

"COME ON." JACKSON TOOK HER HAND AND THEY WENT out the side door, around the back.

Becks slipped out of her shorts and they both took a quick dip in the pool to cool down.

As they treaded water, Jackson pulled her against him.

She wrapped her legs around his hips.

"That was fun," she said. "Sweaty, but very fun."

"Definitely hot," he said, brushing his lips across hers.

"By the way," she said, remembering their earlier conversation. "I won't leave. And I like being around you, too."

He nodded. "Good. Then it's settled. Now how about we see if there's any food left so we can feed you."

She did feel hungry. Obviously hot, sweaty sex worked up an appetite. "It's a plan."

They got out of the pool and dried off and went inside. She refilled her plate, and this time she actually ate the food on it. She and Jackson took a seat at the kitchen table. Several people had finished eating and had gone outside to play in the pool. Only Rafe was still inside eating, along with Ethan Pressman.

"How many rounds of food is that?" Jackson asked.

Rafe had just finished off a skewer of chicken and vegetables. "Just two."

"Lying will make your dick smaller," Ethan said, then looked over at Becks and Jackson. "It's four, in addition to the two plates he ate before."

"Hey, I'm a growing boy."

"We really should make you pay at least half the food budget," Jackson said. "Since you eat more than anyone else."

"All muscle, baby."

Rafe flexed his biceps and Becks had to admit, it was impressive.

"Yeah, too bad none of it goes to growing brain cells," Ethan said.

Becks laughed.

Rafe shot her a frown. "Hey, don't go taking their side."

She held up her hands. "I'm Switzerland. You can eat whatever you want."

He took another bite of chicken and pointed the skewer at her while looking at Jackson and Ethan. After he swallowed, he said, "This is why I like having her around."

"You like having her around because she's a great cook," Jackson said.

"That, too."

"Where's your date tonight, Rafe?" Becks asked.

"No date. Not right now, anyway. I'm playing host to all of these fine people."

"Plus, more food for him this way," Jackson said.

Rafe shot Jackson a glare, then laughed. "Rude, but not untrue."

"And now for some strange reason I'm hungry again," Jackson said, shooting Becks a teasing look. "I think I'll get more of that fruit salad." He got up and went over to the island to check out what was left.

"And I'm heading out to the pool." Ethan stood up and left as well.

"Your parents must have spent a fortune on food on all of you," Becks said.

"I seem to recall four or five gallons of milk going into the grocery cart every week," Rafe said. "You know what it was like. When you go from having no food to suddenly being able to eat? It was like we'd died and gone to heaven. And in our heaven, there was pizza and milk and pancakes."

Becks nodded. "Yes. We didn't have unlimited food in foster care, but there was a full plate on the table at each meal, and to me, it was a smorgasbord."

"I started working out in high school. And my appetite grew even more. My parents never complained. Mom just made sure there was plenty in the fridge."

"Your mom is amazing."

Rafe grinned. "Yeah, she is."

The doorbell rang and Rafe frowned. "Everyone knows they're supposed to come through the side gate."

Becks got up. "You eat. I'll get the door."

She went through the living room and by the time she got to the door, whoever was on the other side was knocking in a rapid fashion.

Someone needed that door opened.

She opened the door to a petite, beautiful young woman with raven-colored hair piled high into a bun on top of her head.

"Hi, is Rafe home?"

"He is." She waited, not sure if she should let her in.

"I'm Carmen. I live next door."

Ah, a neighbor. "Hi, Carmen. I'm Becks. I live here."

"That's nice. So is Rafe here?"

Okay, so no pleasantries. "Yeah. Come on in."

She brushed past Becks in a hurry, her tennis-shoed feet squeaking on the tiled floor.

Becks followed behind her as Carmen marched into the kitchen. Obviously she knew her way around the house.

Jackson had disappeared—somewhere, so it was only Rafe in there.

Rafe stood. "Is it Jimmy?"

"Yes. He fell in the bathroom. I can't pick him up by myself."

Rafe wiped his mouth and hands with his napkin. "Let's go."

Not knowing what to do, Becks stepped in line with them.

Rafe paused at the door to look at Becks. "Get Jackson."

She nodded, pivoted and dashed into the kitchen. Jackson hadn't come back, so he must have gone outside. She ran through the doors and searched the pool area, and found him in the corner talking to Callie's husband, Aaron.

She grasped his arm. "Rafe ran next door to help Carmen."

She immediately saw the concerned frown on his face. "Jimmy's in trouble?"

She nodded. "He asked for you to come help."

Not only did Jackson dash through the gate, but Kal did, too. And suddenly the entire backyard emptied, all the firefighters following Jackson out of the yard.

Becks knew there was nothing she could do, but she had her phone on her. So just in case they needed to call an ambulance, she figured she'd come along.

Carmen's house was similar to the guys', only there were wheelchair ramps leading up to the entrance, and once inside, she noticed it wasn't as modern as Jackson's house. There were more walls closing rooms off. But it was clean, nothing strewn on the floors, and there wasn't nearly as much furniture.

She followed the sounds. This was where the floor plan deviated. Straight past the kitchen there was a bedroom, and a bathroom.

And a ton of firefighters helping an older man who was lying on the floor in the bathroom.

"I told you not to try to take a shower by yourself, Grandpa," Carmen said.

Rafe and Jackson were checking him out. "I don't think there are any broken bones."

"I already checked him before I ran over," Carmen said. "Nothing's broken."

"Except my damned dignity. I'm naked here, Carmen."

"You feel okay, Jimmy?" Jackson asked.

"As okay as I'm gonna feel laying here on my side naked with everyone gawkin' at me."

"Then let's get you into the shower," Rafe said. He looked up at Carmen, who nodded.

"Come on, Grandpa. Shower time."

"How about you let me handle this?" Rafe looked to Carmen, who sent a glance to her grandfather.

She gave a quick nod. "Sure. Put him in his shower chair, and his soap and shampoo are on the smaller ledge."

"Got it," Rafe said. "Jimmy and I are gonna get naked together."

Rafe and a couple of the other guys got Jimmy up and into his shower chair. "Don't you think that means we're dating or anything, Rafe," Jimmy said. "I've got a lady friend I see on bingo nights."

Rafe cracked one of his brilliant smiles. "Noted, sir."

Carmen sighed, then turned to the crowd and smiled. "Everybody out. And thank you all for coming over to help. I'll bring an enchilada casserole by next shift."

"Now you're talking my language," Jackson said. Kal had herded everyone else out the door.

After the door closed, Becks lingered while Jackson asked, "But how's he really doing?"

Carmen shrugged. "Good days and bad days. He resists therapy, stubbornly thinking he can do everything for himself. And in the meantime he's getting weaker."

"I'm sorry," Becks said. "That must be so hard for you."

Carmen shot her a scathing look. "Who are you again?"

"I'm Becks." She motioned with her head. "I live next—"

"Oh, right. You answered the door. Well, Becks, you probably have the perfect family so you wouldn't understand. And why are you even here? I'm not after your boyfriend, if that's what Jackson is, so get lost."

Ouch. That one stung. "I don't have a family, I was concerned for your grandfather. And you don't have to be such a bitch to people who are trying to be nice to you."

Tears pricked her eyes and she pivoted and turned, exiting the house as fast as she could without running. When she got back to her house—correction, Jackson and Rafe and Kal's house—she made quick work of getting up to her room. Fortunately, everyone else was outside so she didn't run into anyone she had to talk to, because her throat was thick with unshed tears. Once in her room she closed and locked the door and sat on the edge of her bed, immediately realizing she was breathing too fast.

She slowed her breathing down, slid off the bed and went into the bathroom, splashed water onto her face and gripped the edge of the counter while she stared into the mirror.

Okay, so her next-door neighbor was awful. She could handle that. It wasn't like she was going to be here forever anyway. Once she got some money saved up, she was out of here. She'd get her own apartment, regain her independence and not feel like she was an intruder.

This place was starting to close in on her anyway.

In the meantime—

She heard a knock on the door.

"Becks? You in there?"

It was Jackson.

Maybe if she stayed quiet he'd go away.

"Becks, come on. I just want to talk. I'm sorry about Carmen."

She didn't want him to think it was his fault, so she went to the door. "It's okay."

"It's not okay. She treated you like shit and I told her that. She's upset about her grandfather."

"I know she is. Which still doesn't give her a pass."

"I told her that, too."

Her lips curved. "Thanks."

"Can I come in so we can talk face-to-face?"

If he came in she'd want him to hold her. And then they'd kiss. And probably make love. And then she'd feel better.

So what exactly was wrong with that?

Nothing, except she didn't want to feel like she could lean on Jackson. She wasn't going to be here long, and this thing with Jackson was temporary. She needed to start remembering that.

"I'm kind of tired and I have a big day tomorrow. I think I'm going to bed."

"I could give you a back massage. Help you fall asleep."

She closed her eyes, wishing she could care but not care at the same time. "No, thanks. Good night, Jackson."

It took him a minute to answer.

"Night, Becks. Hope you sleep well."

She'd probably sleep better if he were in bed with her, but wasn't the whole idea to do this alone?

She shuddered in a breath and pushed away from the door.

CHAPTER 22

TO SAY BECKS WAS NERVOUS ABOUT OPENING THE NEW shop would have been the understatement of the century.

On opening day, she was up before dawn, even though the shop wouldn't open until noon. She showered, combed out her hair and went downstairs to make herself coffee. She sipped the first cup while going through her schedule on her phone. She had a fairly full day of appointments, though she had a few gaps between appointments, so if she got walk-ins she could handle it. Plus, it gave her time to spend with Hwan, who wouldn't be tattooing, just observing and working on sketches.

Fortunately, Martin could work independently so she wouldn't have to worry about him.

Since she was heading in early, she'd offered to swing by the park to pick Aria up, so she wouldn't have to walk in the humidity and heat.

At first Aria had declined, saying she could walk. But Becks had convinced her to accept the ride, arguing that if she walked she'd show up sweaty and be uncomfortable all day and she shouldn't suffer just to prove her independence. And that once she got a couple of paychecks under her belt she could start taking the bus.

Aria agreed, so Becks told her she'd pick her up at ten. That would give them plenty of time to stop off to grab a quick bite to eat somewhere before heading to the shop.

"You're up early."

She looked up and saw Jackson coming downstairs, wearing only shorts that hung low on his hips, showcasing his amazing abs, chiseled shoulders and incredible torso. His hair was disheveled from sleep, and all she could think was how nice it would have been to sleep with her body wrapped around his. In addition to how much fun they could have had together before they fell asleep.

But no. She had to get all up in her head about her independence and how she was going to move out, all because the angry bitch next door had insulted her.

She should have jumped all over Jackson, screwed him ten different ways and worked out her hurt feelings that way.

Sometimes you are so dumb, Becks.

She sighed and put on a smile. "Yes. Lots to do today."

He made himself a cup of coffee and pulled up a chair next to her. "Feel better today?"

"I felt fine last night."

"No, you didn't. Your feelings were hurt and I don't blame you. Carmen is very protective over her grandfather. And she was scared. She took it out on you and that was wrong."

Becks shrugged, really wishing they could talk about anything other than what happened last night. "Not the first time someone has judged me wrong. I'm tougher than you think, Jackson."

He leaned over and smoothed his hand down her arm, making her tingle all over and inside. "You're also softer than you think. And you can still hurt, too. We all can."

"Is that why you don't like to talk about the past? Because it hurts?"

He removed his hand and stared down at his coffee. "Partly. And because I don't see the point in it. I like where I'm at now. What good can come from talking about the past?"

"Catharsis?"

He shrugged. "I'm good. I don't need catharsis."

"I don't know if I believe that."

"Believe what?"

"That you don't need to put the past to bed. We've all had ugly pasts. You, me, your brothers. I don't relive mine every day, but I've faced it, I recognize what I went through and I've moved on from it. If you haven't, it'll always haunt you."

He rubbed his thumb over her bottom lip. "And maybe I'm just not as obsessed with the past as you are."

She grasped his wrist, loving the feel of his skin and needing the contact with him. "Come on, Jackson. Don't dismiss it like that. What we all went through is an important part of who we are now. It's like puzzle pieces. You have to fit the past pieces with the present ones to figure out how you became who you are now. And to find your future."

He smiled.

"What?" she asked.

"You're so deep. And smart."

She laughed and shoved at him. "I am not."

"Yeah, you are. Not that you being all the things that turn me on is going to make me delve into my past, but I'm always impressed by how much you examine everything, especially me. I appreciate it."

She wanted to sit there and drink coffee and talk to Jackson all day. Unfortunately, bills had to be paid and there were people counting on her to show up today.

"You're sweet. And sexy as hell and I'd love to drag you to bed right now."

"To talk, right?"

She teased her fingers over his bare chest. "Of course. Unfortunately, I have to go to work. So maybe we can . . . talk . . . tonight when I get home."

He leaned in and brushed his lips across hers. The kiss was soft, but then he deepened it and she found herself leaning in. So did he, his hand cupping her butt, making all kinds of unspoken promises. Her body tingled in anticipation. But she pulled back, smiled and slid out of her chair.

"Gotta go," she said.

"Yeah, I know."

As she went upstairs to get ready for work, she made a mental memory of that kiss, because it was going to have to hold her all day long.

AN HOUR LATER, SHE ARRIVED AT THE HOMELESS ENcampment to pick up Aria. Instead of hanging at the curb, she parked, grabbed a package and made her way to the tents. Lexie spotted her right away and came up to hug her.

"I missed you," Lexie said.

Becks felt the warmth of her hug. "I missed you, too. I brought you breakfast bars and other food and a couple new books and a bag to keep your favorite novels in."

"You did?" Her eyes sparkled with her smile. "Thanks, Becks."

"You're welcome. You're meeting with Mrs. Donovan today, right?"

Lexie smiled. "Yes. I'm excited. And nervous. And excited."

"It's okay to be nervous. But Mrs. Donovan is very nice. And I've heard the Rothman family is wonderful."

Aria showed up, looking cute in her bright flowery capris and blue T-shirt, her hair pulled back in a sleek ponytail.

"Those capris are so cute," Becks said.

"Thanks! I picked them up at Goodwill. They still had the tags on them. Five bucks."

"Really." Becks smiled.

"Yup. I'm amazed at the awesome stuff people give away."

"Aria told me she's gonna take me shopping this weekend," Lexie said.

"Is that right?" Becks said. "Fun."

"When I get back tonight you can tell me all about your meeting," Aria said.

"And then Aria will tell me all about it," Becks added.

"Okay." Lexie grinned.

"I've gotta go, honey. We'll talk soon, okay?"

Lexie nodded. "Okay. Bye, Becks. Bye, Aria."

"I'll see you tonight, Lexie," Aria said.

Lexie gave them a wave and headed back toward her tent.

They stopped and had omelets for breakfast, because Becks knew it might be a while before she had a chance to eat again. Sometimes her schedule ended up being so full she couldn't have any breaks, so she always made sure to fuel up strong at the start of the day.

Of course Aria balked at having Becks pay for her meal, so she let Aria leave the tip, which seemed to satisfy her. She knew what it was like to be homeless but still have a little cash flow. You wanted to feel like you were a contributing member of society.

And hopefully, soon enough, Aria would make enough money to leave the encampment and find a place to live.

And if everything went well, she hoped Lexie would be out of the encampment and on her way to her forever home, too.

When they got to the shop, a buzz of excitement drilled in her veins. Aria settled in at her desk, and Becks was thrilled to see her sitting there.

She had an employee. Three, actually, though Hwan would be an unpaid intern and Martin was only renting booth space. So technically she had only one employee. But it was a start. She'd always run a one-woman shop. Today she felt like an entrepreneur. A boss. For a girl who'd grown up homeless with no prospects for the future, this was a huge jump and a dream come true.

"I have the aftercare sheets printed," Aria said, popping into her work area, handing a folder to her. "I put a folder on Martin's desk as well."

"Perfect, thanks."

Aria started to turn away, but then she stopped. "Oh, and I updated your Facebook page to let everyone know you're open for business today. We should do some Snaps of you working today and put pics on Instagram as well."

Becks nodded. "Good idea. You can do the pics and put them up, but make sure we get permission from the clients, too."

"Okay. I'll print out a release form that we can have the clients sign."

Aria was sharp and always thinking ten steps ahead. Becks had made a good choice in hiring her.

"And see if Martin wants that as well. We can put up a few pics on all the social media accounts."

"I'll take care of it."

Becks had discovered that Aria was a natural at social media, so it would be great to turn all of that over to her, which would save Becks so much time. Typically she was busy and didn't have time to update her social media accounts. But having someone else deal with it would keep things more current. And in this type of market the more you could get out there in real time, the better.

She set out her colors and her machines and organized her

schedule, making sure she knew exactly what her plan was for the day. She liked being organized.

And before she knew it, Hwan had come in. She spent some time talking with him about the responsibilities of a tattoo artist, that it wasn't just the art and the opportunity to put your permanent art on someone's skin, but also you had the care of another human being in your hands.

"There's blood involved in tattooing. You're pricking the skin when you insert the needle, so you have to be careful not only for your client, but also for yourself. Blood-borne pathogens pose a risk to all tattoo artists. Never take that lightly and always keep your equipment, your hands and your environment as sterile as possible. And always wear a mask. Your customers will thank you for it, and you'll be healthier for it."

She'd been around more than her share of inkers who shrugged off precautions. Those were the artists she stayed away from. She took her job seriously. She loved making art, but she also made sure to keep both herself and her clients safe.

"So it's kind of like being a surgeon," Hwan said, studying the precautions booklet she'd handed to him. "Only instead of removing organs, we're leaving art. And we're making sure no one gets sick when we do it."

She smiled. "Yes."

She spent some time going over her schedule today with Hwan so he'd know what she was going to be working on. He'd sit back and observe for a very long time before he'd ever be allowed to work on a person. Plus he'd have to get his blood-borne pathogen certification, and he'd practice on fake skin and fruit and whatever wasn't alive until she was satisfied that he knew what he was doing.

She also intended to keep him drawing. That was how you got better.

She'd been tattooing for years and she still sketched—all the time. In black pencil, colored pencils, ink, watercolor, whatever struck her fancy. But she always had ideas in her head for potential tattoos.

As she'd been going through the different types of ink with Hwan, Aria stuck her head in. "Martin's here."

"Okay, great, thanks."

She'd told Martin when she hired him that she was going to have an apprentice. She wanted to make sure it wasn't going to bother him having Hwan loitering around. Martin was cool with it and had said Hwan could watch him tattoo as well, which would be great for her new apprentice. Learning from two different tattoo artists would definitely help him. Each artist had their own style and did art different ways. Hwan would benefit from being able to watch both Becks and Martin.

Before long, everyone was settled in and their first clients arrived. For the next several hours, Becks was busy with work. Her first client was a repeat customer. She'd done quite a bit of ink on her, so Becks had the opportunity to show Hwan her previous work on Jessie's chest, stomach, back and shoulders and down her left arm. Today they were working on a swan on her right arm.

"Do you intend to go full body ink?" Hwan asked her.

Jessie, a beautiful petite young woman with bubble-gum-pink hair cut in a bob, nodded at Hwan. "I'm an exotic dancer and the ink shows off beautifully under the lights. Plus my body art is a great conversation piece for my clients."

Hwan's eyes widened. He opened his mouth, closed it, opened it again, then finally said, "Oh, that's very nice."

Becks resisted the urge to laugh, but she exchanged a knowing smile with Jessie.

"It's okay, Hwan. I love my work."

"Oh, that's very nice," Hwan said again.

It was clear Hwan had no idea what to do with Jessie.

Most men didn't. Jessie was currently saving up money to go

to law school. And the money she made as an exotic dancer was very good, much better than she'd made as a waitress while getting her bachelor's degree.

"I intend to be the first fully tattooed judge on the Supreme Court," Jessie had told her when they first started working together.

"It's good to have lofty goals," Becks had said in reply. And now, knowing how hard Jessie worked at everything she did, she didn't doubt for one second that someday she'd see Jessie's dream come true.

The swan was a delicate piece and Becks took her time to make sure it was to Jessie's exact specifications. She made sure that every feather, every part of the swan's delicate neck was perfect. When she finished, Jessie stretched and went to look at the swan in the mirror. She lifted her arm and made those elegant strokes with her hand that only a dancer knew how to do.

"Oh, it's beautiful, Becks," she said, turning around to face Becks with a serene smile on her face. "She's beautiful. I love her."

"I'm so glad. Now let me wrap her up and you can be on your way."

After Jessie paid and left, Hwan turned to Becks. "I'm sorry. I have to do better with client interaction."

"You do. You'll find all types of customers come in here. Some are doctors, some are trash collectors. Some are police officers and some are people who have a dark past. And all are worthy of our respect."

"I'll bear that in mind. I'm sorry if I gave the impression that I thought less of Jessie. To be honest, I was kind of dazzled by her and found myself a bit tongue-tied."

Becks's lips curved. "She has that effect on a lot of people. But try to look beyond someone's surface to the person underneath."

"I will. Thank you for that advice. I'll add it to my notes."

Hwan was not only making drawings while he watched her

work—though his drawings were his own and she was happy to see he wasn't copying her—but he was always making notes.

Hopefully he was learning something.

She remembered what it was like to be brand-new, to soak up all the knowledge her mentor had taught her. She'd been raw then as well, so she had to remind herself to cut Hwan some slack.

There was a lot to learn, and they still had a long day ahead of them.

CHAPTER 23

JACKSON PULLED UP IN FRONT OF HIS PARENTS' HOUSE.
Rafe and Kal's trucks were already there.

It was odd for his dad to call a family meeting on their day off.
Typically because his mom was usually at work and family meet-
ings meant the whole family, so Jackson was nervous about what
was going on.

Before he went in, he pulled out his phone and sent a text message to Becks.

Thinking about you. How's your day going?

He didn't expect her to answer because he knew she'd be
busy.

But on his way up the walkway to his parents' front door, his
phone buzzed. He pulled it out of the pocket of his shorts to check
the message. It was from Becks.

Busy but really good. See you tonight. Xoxo

He smiled at that. He was glad she was having a good day. He wanted her to succeed. He tucked his phone into his pocket, then opened the front door. He could hear his dad's voice coming from the family room, so he went into the kitchen and poured himself a glass of iced tea.

First thing every morning in the summer, his mom always brewed a fresh pot of iced tea and left it on the counter. Jackson grabbed a glass from the cabinet, put ice in the glass and poured the tea, smiling as he remembered the first time he'd helped his mom brew a pot of tea.

He'd always been fascinated by everything, especially anything having to do with food. Plus on the weekends, iced tea came with sugar cookies. And anything that added calories to his rapidly growing frame had been good news to him.

Mom had informed all the boys when they came to live with them that they'd learn to be productive members of society. They'd go to school to get smart, and at home they'd had the responsibility of yard work and to take the trash out. They'd had to clean their own bathroom and load and unload the dishwasher. To their horror, they were also taught to cook.

As he grabbed his glass and headed into the family room, he smiled as he remembered the first time he had to make spaghetti and meatballs.

His mother was the most patient woman on the planet. And he'd never made more horrible meatballs in his life.

His mom had been the only one to eat the meal he'd cooked. Dad had taken Rafe and Kal out for burgers.

He'd never loved his mother more than he had watching her smile through her grimaces as she'd eaten those dry, awful meatballs. Even he couldn't stomach them. But she'd told him that he'd done his best, and next time he'd do better.

At least he'd been able to eat out with Dad when Kal and Rafe had tried their hands at cooking. They had all ended up being great at grilling, but Kal had turned out to be a much better cook than Rafe or him.

The bastard.

When he got to the family room, his dad and Rafe were watching a baseball game on television. Kal was pacing behind the couch talking to someone on the phone.

"Hey, what's up?" Jackson asked as he walked into the room.

"Nothing much," his dad said. "Just waiting on you."

Jackson tamped down that nervous sensation in his stomach. "I'm here now."

"Yeah, and you're late," Kal said, tucking his phone in his shorts pocket and coming around to fling himself into his seat on the sofa.

Jackson looked at his phone and rolled his eyes. "Five minutes."

"You're fine, Jackson," his dad said. "I wanted you all here while your mom was at work because I have an idea I'd like to surprise her with for her birthday, and I wanted to know what you all thought about it."

Okay, nothing serious. No one was sick. They weren't getting a divorce. Jackson could exhale now.

"Sure, Dad," Rafe said. "Shoot."

"She's always wanted a garden out back, a place where she could plant herbs and vegetables and stuff. But the backyard is kind of small, as you know."

"Yeah, it is," Kal said.

"So I'm thinking of putting the house on the market and buying another house. One with a pool and a big backyard with a lot of space so she could have that garden she's always wanted. And the pool she never talks about but I know she wants."

"I think it's a great idea, Dad," Jackson said. Though he wondered why he was running it by them.

"Me, too," Rafe said.

Kal nodded. "Ditto."

His dad let out a big breath. "You sure? This is the house where we brought you all to live. For us, it's the house where we became a family, where we have all the memories of tossing a football on the front yard. Where Kal broke his arm falling out of the tree."

"Because he's a klutz," Rafe said.

Kal shot Rafe a glare. "Because you shoved me off the branch, asshole."

"That's because Jackson was chasing after me."

Jackson noticed the tears welling in his father's eyes. "Dad."

"Yeah?"

"Our memories are with you and Mom. Not the house. The house is just brick and wood and glass. We have plenty of pictures. And we have the two of you. Wherever you go, if you're happy going there, we'll all be happy, too."

"What Jackson said," Kal said. "We love both of you. Your happiness is all that matters."

Rafe nodded. "A house is just a thing. It's not our family. You and Mom are our family."

"Besides," Jackson said. "You know Mom has never liked this house. The closets aren't big enough and she's always talked about having that spa bathroom in the master. Plus she wants a home office."

Dad laughed. "This is true. I'm the one who never wanted to move. We bought this house after we got married."

"So why now?"

He shrugged. "Because it's not always about what I want. I kept telling her after you guys arrived that we were making memories here. Family memories."

Now it was becoming clear to Jackson. "So you were the one who wanted to stay. And you used us to make it happen all these years."

His dad gave a half shrug. "*Used* is kind of a harsh word. But yeah, kind of."

"We loved growing up here, Dad," Kal said. "But if Mom wants to move . . ."

"She has never once said she wanted to move. You know how your mom is. She's content here. But I know there are things she wants. A bigger kitchen, for starters. And that garden. And a pool. And like you said, Jackson, the nice big bathroom and an office. But there's only so much renovation we can do here. The house is small. And only two bedrooms. We made do with you guys, but someday there'll be grandkids."

He looked at all three of them.

"I've got nothin'," Kal said.

Rafe raised his hands. "Don't look at me."

Which left Jackson. "Not making any grandbabies for you yet, Dad. Sorry. But I understand what you're saying. Get a new house. A nice big one with a garden and a pool and extra bedrooms and someday we'll all fill the place with annoying grandkids."

His dad beamed a smile. "Great. Your mother will love that."

"What am I going to love?"

Jackson turned to see his mom leaning against the doorway.

"Hey, babe," Josh said. "You're home early today."

She came in and set her bags down on the kitchen counter. "Yes, I had an appointment that was close to home, and nothing else this afternoon, so I figured instead of driving all the way back downtown, I'd just come home. What's this all about?"

His dad looked at all of them, then back to her. "Come sit down."

"Oh, no." She touched her thin gold necklace, the one Dad had given her for her birthday when they were kids. She always fingered it when she was nervous. "Something's wrong, isn't it?"

"Nothing's wrong, Mom," Kal said. "We're all fine."

She slid into the chair next to their father. "What is it?"

"What would you think about a new house?" Josh asked with a huge smile.

She frowned. "That's it? That's the big deal that made my heart flip over with dread?"

"Well, yeah," Dad said.

She let out a sigh. "What's wrong with this one?"

Dad grasped her hand. "It's small. And you've always wanted a garden. And a bigger kitchen. That spa bathroom you've always dreamed about. An office. And a pool."

She pulled her hand away. "Is that right. And you and our sons have been deciding this while I was at work today. Without my input or even asking what I wanted."

Uh-oh. Jackson knew that irritated look on his mother's face. And that meant they were all in trouble.

"Not exactly. I wanted to run it by the boys first. They grew up here, after all. If they were going to be upset by the notion of us selling the house, there'd be no point in even suggesting it to you."

She opened her mouth to speak, then closed it and looked at Dad. It took her a few seconds before she said anything.

"You really want to leave this house? You love it here."

Dad laid his forehead against Mom's. "Who says I love it here?"

"You always talk about those marks we made in the hallway as the boys got taller, and how cozy the living room is, and how much you love working in the big garage, and how convenient the location is to the fire station."

His dad nodded. "Yeah, all that's great, but it's still just a house. Brick and wood. What I love is you, Laurel."

Oh, damn. So that was what love was all about. Jackson knew how much this house meant to his dad. But he'd give that up so his mom could have her dream house.

"That's our cue to get the hell out of here," Kal whispered.

"Yup," Rafe said, and stood. "So, we're gonna go."

Their mom pointed at all of them. "You can all stay right where you are. You're here and we'll all have dinner together and talk about this."

And when Mom said you were staying for dinner, you were staying for dinner.

They ended up grilling pork chops and talking about the possibility of moving. They told their mother the same thing they'd told their dad, that the house was just a thing and she and Dad were where the love and memories were.

Mom said she was hesitant, but then Kal opened a real estate app and they all started house searching. Jackson could see the light spark in her eyes and the smile on his dad's face as he watched her.

It was a done deal. They'd find a new house and put this one on the market. Jackson sat back and thought about what it would mean to never see this house again. He waited for that pang of nostalgia or pain.

Nothing. The house was just a building. And he'd always be a Donovan, regardless of his parents' address.

And he'd still be the luckiest damn kid who ever lived.

CHAPTER 24

THE DAY HAD ZOOMED BY. BECKS'S SCHEDULE HAD FILLED up with back-to-back clients and before she knew it, it was nine o'clock and her last customer was walking out the door, an hour past closing time.

She'd sent Hwan home at six. Martin had finished up and left about thirty minutes earlier. Becks cleaned up her equipment and emptied her trash out back, then packed up her things and headed toward the front.

Aria was still at her desk.

"You don't have to stay just because I'm here late," Becks said.

"I don't mind. Besides, you have electricity. Running water. Internet. And air-conditioning."

Becks laughed. "Okay, then. I'll give you a lift back to the park."

"I appreciate it."

They piled into her truck and Becks headed out. They'd eaten lunch about four, but hopefully Aria would have something else to eat before she went to sleep tonight.

She knew she shouldn't worry, that Aria was likely fine and capable of taking care of herself. But she couldn't seem to help it.

"Do you want to stop for something to eat?" Becks asked.

"No, I'm fine. Thanks for asking."

She pulled up in front of the park. "You did great today, Aria. I'm really happy to have you working for me."

Aria laid her hand on the door handle and smiled at her. "Thanks. I like this job. I'm busier than I thought I would be and it's a lot more interesting than the last job I had."

"Glad to hear that. I'll pick you up tomorrow about eleven."

"See you then. Night."

"Night."

She watched Aria disappear into the darkness, then drove home. When she got there, the driveway was empty. No trucks. Clearly, none of the guys were home.

Interesting. She wondered if they were all out somewhere together. She checked her phone. It was nearly ten. Maybe they'd gone to a bar together. Or out separately.

Not that she cared. She was exhausted. She planned to take a shower, eat something and then crash.

She glanced next door, wondering how Jimmy was doing. She hoped he was okay after his fall last night. But she wasn't going to go over there and ask, considering how rude his granddaughter was.

But then the porch light flew on and Carmen came outside, shocking the hell out of her by heading her way. Becks hoped there wasn't going to be another confrontation, because she was not in the mood.

"Is Rafe home?" Carmen asked.

"No, he's not. None of the guys are."

"Well, damn."

"Is your grandfather in trouble?"

"No. He just wants to go to bed and I've been struggling getting him there lately. I could use some help."

Despite her personal feelings about Carmen's rudeness, Becks couldn't let an old man down. "Hang on. Let me shove my things inside and I'll help you."

She popped the garage door up, tucked her bags inside and dropped the door back down. She shoved her keys in her pocket. "Let's go."

Carmen gave her an uncertain look. "You sure you don't mind?"

"I don't mind. Let's go get your grandpa to bed."

She followed Carmen into the house and into her grandfather's bedroom.

The old man frowned. "You're not Rafe."

Becks put on a smile. "You noticed. My name is Becks. I'm Rafe's roommate. And you're Jimmy, right?"

His frown turned into a smile. "Yes, ma'am. Nice to meet you, Becks. Is that short for Rebecca?"

"It is. Though no one's called me Rebecca in a very long time."

Becks noticed Carmen pulling the covers down on Jimmy's side of the bed, and also giving her the side eye while she did it.

"Becks is a nice name. So what're you doing sharing space with those three crazy young men?"

"My tattoo business went up in smoke, and my apartment above it, too. Since the three of us grew up together, they were kind enough to take me in until I can find a new place to live."

"They're nice boys, those Donovans."

"Yes, sir, they sure are."

"Let's get you into bed, Grandpa," Carmen said.

"You sure you two little things can do this?"

"I'm pretty sure we're stronger than we look, Jimmy," Becks said.

"Lift him under his arms, like this," Carmen said, showing

her by putting Jimmy's arm around her shoulder. "He'll help as much as he can, and I'll take his side that doesn't work so well."

Becks nodded. "Got it."

She slung Jimmy's other arm around her shoulder, and between the two of them they managed to hoist him up and slide him onto the bed. Jimmy wasn't a small man. He was tall and had some weight on him, despite his disability. But he did help and she sensed he still had strength on his right side, which helped. They got him into position on his side, and Carmen tucked a pillow behind his back.

"You okay, Grandpa?"

"Perfect. Don't forget to turn the television on for me, bebita."

"Like I'd forget the classics channel. It's your favorite." Carmen turned the television on, which was already set to the black-and-white movies. Humphrey Bogart was busily romancing Lauren Bacall.

"I love this movie," Becks said.

"Me, too," Jimmy said with a soft smile.

Carmen kissed Jimmy on the cheek. "Good night, Grandpa."

"Night, bebita."

Becks took that as her cue to leave the room. She was on her way out the front door when Carmen said, "Hey, Becks."

She stopped and turned. "Yeah?"

Carmen made her way up to her. "I get frantic when my grandpa is in jeopardy. And because of that I lose my mind. Which was no excuse for me being a rude bitch to you last night. I'm really sorry."

"Don't worry about it. Family is a priority. It's obvious you love your grandpa."

"Thanks. I'm sure you'd do the same for yours."

Becks smiled. "I don't have a family. But I do understand where you're coming from. And anytime you need my help, even if the guys aren't here, feel free to come get me. At least as long as I'm living there."

Carmen gave her a strange look, as if she didn't understand the family comment. Becks wasn't sure why, since she'd told her the same thing last night. Did she think Becks was making it up?

Maybe she did think that. Not that it mattered, since it was doubtful Becks and Carmen would ever be best friends.

"Night, Carmen."

"Good night, Becks. Thanks again."

Becks nodded and walked out, heading across the lawn to her house—correction, the guys' house. It wouldn't do her any good to start thinking of this place as hers when it wasn't. She'd be leaving soon enough.

She'd had a really good day today. Her expenses were up, like higher office rent and paying Aria, but she also had Martin to help pay those expenses. It wouldn't be long before she had money saved to rent her own apartment.

But as she stared up at the cheery house that seemed to smile down at her in greeting, the thought of leaving this place caused a pang of pain in her heart. It was funny how quickly she'd grown to think of this place as her home. But it wasn't her home, it was temporary housing. She should be used to that. She'd had plenty of it growing up.

But it was more than just this house, it was the people who occupied it—Rafe, Kal, and more importantly, Jackson. She liked seeing all of them, liked living with them. It was as if she had a family.

She inhaled and let it out.

Let it go, Becks.

She went inside, washed her dirty dishes from the morning and put them in the drainer to dry, then headed upstairs, stripped and took a long, hot shower, washing away her emotional state and clearing her head. When she got out, she combed out her wet hair, slipped into shorts and a tank top, then went downstairs to make something to eat.

As soon as she hit the landing she saw Jackson sitting at the island looking up at her with a smile on his face. She felt ridiculous about the way her heart leaped in her chest when she saw him.

So much for the washing away of her emotions. Whenever she saw him, there they were.

She also smelled food. There was a bag on the counter.

"Hi," she said. "I didn't know you were home."

"I got here a few minutes ago. You look squeaky clean."

She laughed. "I feel squeaky clean."

"I brought food. I thought you might be hungry. I stopped by the house about an hour ago and you weren't home yet, so I figured you had a late night. I went out and got you some chicken curry and rice." He slid the bag in her direction.

"That sounds perfect. I was just coming downstairs to look in the fridge for leftovers because I was hungry, so thank you. I thought maybe you and your brothers had gone out to eat."

"We went to my parents' for dinner tonight. Dad wanted to talk to all of us."

"Oh? Is everything okay?"

"It's fine. Dad wants to sell the house."

Her hands stilled on the bag just as she was opening it. "Uh-oh."

He laughed. "Go on and eat. It's not a bad thing."

She took the container out of the bag. Jackson handed her a fork and while she ate, he told her the whole story about his dad's suggestion that they buy another house. And then he told her about some of the houses they'd looked at online.

"I think it's incredibly sweet and romantic," she said, as she finished eating and put the top back on the container. She put the leftovers in the fridge and came back to her seat and took a swallow of ice water. "Your dad loves the old house, but he loves your mom more."

"Yeah, it's romantic, I guess."

"You guess? Don't you know what a romantic gesture is all about, Jackson?"

He gave her a hopeful look. "Good sex?"

She laughed. "No. A romantic gesture is when you do something sweet or surprising, or make a sacrifice for someone you love. It's when you make it all about the other person."

"So if I make you come first . . ."

She rolled her eyes. "I can tell you are not taking this seriously."

He leaned over and kissed her, a brief kiss followed by a teasing smile. "I know what a romantic gesture is, Becks. I witnessed it firsthand with my parents tonight."

He pulled her onto his lap, smoothing his hand over her leg. "I've got a few gestures I'd like to try out on you."

"You do?"

"Yeah." He picked her up and brought her over to the kitchen island, sitting her on top of it. He spread her legs and stepped between them, ran his hands up her back, then slid one hand into her damp hair.

Goose bumps skittered across her skin at the feel of his hands on her body. She leaned forward for his kiss. It felt like it had been an eternity since the two of them had been together. She missed the meeting of their lips, the electricity of his tongue at the first touch of it against hers. If she could bottle that delicious lightning, she could retire right now.

Instead, she sank into the feeling of his hands coaxing along her back and his thighs between hers. When he moved in to deepen the kiss, she felt the hard ridge of his erection through his shorts and wanted nothing more than to get skin to skin with him.

She pressed a kiss along his jaw. "Where are your brothers?"

He lifted up to look at her. "We're making out and you're thinking of my brothers?"

She laughed. "No. I want to get naked with you and I don't want them walking in."

"Oh. They went to Tommy's bar. They won't be home for a while."

He bent to kiss her, but she laid a palm on his chest. "A long while?"

"Long enough to lay you back on this counter and make you come. Long enough to slide my cock inside you after that and make us both come."

The images his words evoked elicited waves of need soaring through her. "Let's definitely do all of that."

She lifted her tank top off and tossed it onto the floor. His eyes gleamed in response. He cupped one breast, lifting it to his mouth. She braced in anticipation as he captured a nipple between his lips, teasing the bud with his tongue.

She let out a soft moan, every sexual nerve ending vibrating in response to Jackson's sucking motions. She wrapped her legs around his hips to pull him closer.

He backed up only long enough to draw her shorts and underwear down her hips and over her legs, leaving her naked and sitting on the kitchen island, which was a little odd.

But at this point, she didn't care. All she cared about was having an orgasm. She was pent up, quivering and in need of what Jackson could give her.

When he pulled up a bar stool and sat, then cupped her butt and dragged her toward him and draped her legs over his shoulders, she lifted up on her elbows to watch. She wanted to see what he was going to give her.

He smiled up at her. "Ready?"

"More than." She nibbled on her bottom lip and gave him a look that let him know she wanted what he was ready to give her.

He slid his tongue down one side and up the other, caressing her labia in such a tender way it made her shiver. His tongue was hot and wet and when he circled her clit, she was panting in anticipation. And then he closed his mouth over the bud and swept his tongue over her clit.

She could come right now. Right damn now. The sensations were incredible, and she was taut with the need for an orgasm. But there was no way she was letting go just yet, not when this amazing man with an oh-so-talented tongue was doing delicious things to her. She intended to enjoy this for as long as she could.

Except that he swept his tongue across her sensitized flesh over and over in relentless fashion, sliding a finger inside her to add to the rock-her-world sensations.

She came with an unexpected cry, her entire body shuddering with the force of her orgasm. She rocked through the amazing sensations that seemed to go on and on until she collapsed, those waves of orgasm still undulating within her.

Jackson rose up and pulled her toward the edge of the counter. "I'll be right back."

He dashed upstairs while she took a minute to catch her breath. She felt warm and complete and still turned on. So when he came back, she was more than ready for him.

He pulled off his shirt and dropped his shorts and underwear, depositing the condom packet on the counter so he could draw her into his arms for a blistering kiss that left her senseless. She wrapped her legs around him and the kiss intensified, making her feel weak and hot and quivery.

He pulled back from her only long enough to put the condom on. She leaned back and he slid inside her.

She gasped, holding on to his shoulder as he drove deeper.

"You're beautiful, Becks," he said, looking from her sex to her face. "From the sounds you make to your movements to the way you feel when I'm inside you, everything about you is made for me."

She felt it, too, that utter perfection of him as he moved within her. Her body tightened around him as if to capture him and hold him there.

As if she'd want him anywhere else except right where he was, sliding in and out of her and making her feel things she'd never felt—a sense of rightness, of belonging, as if this man had been made just for her.

She realized she'd echoed the words Jackson had said.

Monumental? Emotional? Or just sexual? She had no idea and she refused to plumb their depths right now, not when every part of her felt so damn good. She was coiled tight and ready to explode.

"Yeah, just like that, babe," Jackson said, the strain on his face evident as his movements increased. "Come on and take me with you."

Her breaths grew more rapid as she raced to the edge of oblivion, held for one beautiful second, then fell.

She took Jackson with her, both of them holding on to each other as they shuddered through the wild storm of their orgasms.

Afterward, Becks laid her head on Jackson's shoulder, licking at the sweat that had formed there. She was perspiring all over as well. When she pulled back, she realized they had stuck to each other.

"Quite a workout, huh?" she asked.

"Yeah. Feel like another shower?"

"Definitely."

He lifted her off the island and they went upstairs to rinse off. Afterward they got dressed, disinfected the kitchen counter and sat on the sofa to watch a movie. It was nice to have a night with just the two of them, alone to hang out and talk.

She didn't make it ten minutes into the movie before she was asleep.

CHAPTER 25

THE LAST SEVERAL SHIFTS HAD BEEN GRUELING FOR Jackson and the entire station. The combination of the epic rainstorms they'd been having and the summer vacation traffic had increased the number of accidents they'd worked the past week. One had been particularly bad, involving a fatality and an ejected passenger. Those incidents were the worst and always brought the entire station down. Their job was to save lives, and when they couldn't, they felt useless.

As a firefighter you could do your best to get the word out to people about fire safety, but there wasn't much you could do to prevent automobile accidents. No matter what the laws were or what people logically knew was right or wrong, people were going to talk on their phones while in the car. Some were going to text. Some would drink and drive. Some were going to lose focus because they were having an argument with their spouse, or yelling at their kids. And like today, some tractor-trailer truck driver was going to fall asleep at the wheel at three a.m., causing him to drift into the adjacent lane and ram into the guardrail, causing his eighteen-wheeler to jackknife, ramming an SUV against the overpass bridge and shutting down the northbound lanes of I-95.

When they arrived on scene Jackson assessed the situation. A family of four was trapped inside the SUV—a couple and their two teenagers. Since both sides of the vehicle were obstructed and the back was pinned as well, they'd have to pull them out from the front windshield.

"Everyone okay in there?" he asked.

"We're okay. No one's hurt," the driver said.

Some kind of fucking miracle there, all things considered.

"Rafe, the Sawzall."

Rafe nodded and ran to the truck to get the necessary equipment while Jackson stayed with the family in the van.

"Okay, I need you all to cover your faces because we're going to pull the windshield to get you out. Do you have something in there to cover yourselves?"

The man looked around, then nodded. "We do."

The kids threw jackets to both the adults in the front seat. The kids had blankets and when everyone's faces were covered, Rafe had returned. He had safety glasses on and the Sawzall in his hand. Tommy Rodriguez was there to help him lift the windshield.

"Okay, we're getting started. You'll hear some sawing noises. Don't be scared. We'll get you out of there shortly."

Jackson nodded at Rafe, who punctured two holes in the top and bottom of the windshield, then started cutting the windshield with the saw. Tommy made sure to slip his hand inside the slightly opened passenger-side window to hold the windshield and make sure it didn't fall inward.

It took less than a minute, then Rafe and Tommy lifted the windshield off. They laid a tarp over the jagged bottom of the windshield and helped extricate the family.

"We've got you," Rafe said, helping the woman out first, then the kids. The dad said he'd wait until last and assisted Rafe and Tommy with helping his family out.

Miguel and Adrienne were there to take them to the ambulance for assessment. Other than what appeared to be some soft-tissue injuries from being jostled so hard at impact, they all appeared to be fine. The parents declined treatment for any of them and said they'd follow up with their family physician.

The truck driver had sustained a broken arm, so he'd be transported.

Tow trucks came and they assisted with the extrication and removal of the vehicles. Which left cleanup, and there was plenty of that. They moved as fast as they could so the highway could be opened quickly. Closing all the lanes of a major interstate wasn't acceptable. They worked with the Florida Highway Patrol to get the tractor-trailer moved as soon as possible, so they could get a couple of lanes open. Highway Patrol handled traffic control while Jackson and his team finished with their jobs.

By the time they got back to the station it was the end of their shift.

Jackson had reports to write, so he stayed behind.

"You coming home?" Rafe asked.

"I'll be there later. I want to get this report filed while it's still fresh in my mind."

Rafe gave a short nod. "Later, bro."

"Yeah, later."

While he wrote his report, he gave a verbal assessment of the accident scene to his next-shift counterpart, Leo Stockton. Leo had been a lieutenant at Station 6 for six years longer than Jackson, so Jackson held a lot of respect for him.

"I'm amazed the family in that SUV got out without a scratch, considering the size of the tractor-trailer that crushed them," Leo said.

Jackson leaned back in his chair in the kitchen, talking over the noise of everyone wandering around fixing food and eating. "No kidding. I guess it just wasn't their day to go."

"You're right about that."

Firefighters often talked about the freak accidents they worked, and how sometimes it seemed as if it was just a person's day to die. And sometimes people survived things that defied explanation. There was no way to fathom it other than either it was your time to go or it wasn't.

The call alarm sounded so everyone disappeared, leaving Jackson alone to finish his report. He liked second team shift, but with them milling about and Leo using his office, he didn't have much privacy to concentrate.

Now, though, it was plenty quiet, giving him time to get his report done.

He couldn't wait to finish so he could get out of there.

When he was done, he filed his report, closed his laptop and slipped it into his bag, then headed out to his truck. It was ten in the morning and he was dead tired. Since that last call came in at three a.m. he'd lost some sleep. He needed activity and caffeine to charge him up.

But he'd wanted to stop by Becks's new shop and see how things were going for her. She'd been open more than a week now, and she'd told him she'd had a full schedule every day. She'd been working well past closing time and had come home late and wiped out. And he'd been busy on his off days, either working at home since it was his week for yard work or doing some things at Mom and Dad's house. Now that they'd agreed to sell the house, Dad wanted to get it done right away. But first they had to spruce the place up, which meant Dad had commandeered Jackson, Rafe and Kal to do repairs and painting.

None of them minded, of course. It just required pitching in on off days.

He stopped by the coffee shop, grabbed a large coffee and a couple of breakfast sandwiches, then headed over to Becks's place.

The rain had stopped, making it even more hot and humid. There was nothing worse than Florida in the summer. Though as he parked and got out of his truck, he could smell the ocean.

Maybe after he visited Becks he'd make a stop at the water and do some boarding. It might wake him up enough to keep him going until his regular bedtime tonight. The worst thing about a twenty-four-hour shift was the havoc it played on your sleeping hours. If you had a middle-of-the-night call, the last thing you wanted to do was pass out during the daylight hours, then end up staying awake all night long, no matter how much you wanted to sleep.

In the meantime, he was hoping this large coffee would help.

He walked inside. Aria was busy on the phone; she made eye contact, smiled at him and held up a finger to let him know she'd be right with him.

There wasn't anyone in the waiting area, but he heard Becks's voice so she obviously had someone in the back.

Aria put the phone down. "Hi, Jackson."

"Hi, Aria. How's it going?"

"It's busy here. Which is good."

"Sounds great. How are you liking the job?"

"I'm loving the job. You look like you just got off work."

He was still wearing his uniform and hadn't had a chance to shower, figuring he'd do that once he got home. "Yeah."

"How's your job?" Aria asked.

"Busy. Which in my line of work isn't always good."

"I guess you're right about that."

"What's Becks up to?"

"She's doing a piercing. She should be finished soon."

"A piercing, huh?" He'd talked to her about her tattoos, but he didn't know she also did piercings.

She came around the corner with a young girl who looked to

be in her late teens. She was wearing a crop top and looking down at her belly, where there appeared to be a brand-new piercing.

"Okay, Hailey, Aria will give you a sheet containing your aftercare instructions. Follow them closely, because the last thing you want is an infection."

Hailey nodded.

"And if you have any problems or any questions, call me. Aria will give you my card."

"Thanks, Becks."

"You're welcome. The piercing looks good. I think you'll like it."

Hailey stared down at it, then up at Becks with a happy smile on her face. "I know I will. I already do."

After Aria motioned for Hailey to come to the desk, Becks stepped over to Jackson, and the sweet smile she laid on him made his day.

"This is a nice surprise."

"I was going to head home after my shift, but I wanted to stop in and see how you were doing."

"You came by at just the right time. I have about a half hour before my next client comes in. Let's go back to the break room."

He followed her down the hall. She'd done a lot with the space since the last time he was here. More equipment, more people for sure. She stopped in a doorway where a tall, bald, muscular guy whose arms were covered in ink was sitting and working on tattooing another guy's shoulder.

"Hey, Martin, this is Jackson Donovan, my . . . my roommate."

Jackson noted the hesitation.

Martin swiveled around in his chair and cast some serious blue eyes and a smile at Jackson. "Hey, buddy. Nice to meet you."

"Same."

She tugged on the sleeve of his T-shirt. "Come on."

They'd taken a small space in the back of the shop and set up a mini-fridge and microwave as well as a small table and a couple of chairs.

"Cozy."

She shrugged. "It works as a spot for breaks and to eat. And speaking of eating, you brought your breakfast?"

"A couple of egg sandwiches, because I got out of the station late. I brought extra, you want one?"

She shook her head. "I made some toast and eggs before I came in this morning."

He got up. "Maybe Aria will want the extra sandwich. I'll just tuck it in the fridge and you can let her know it's here. She can microwave it if she gets hungry."

"You're sweet. I know she'll appreciate it."

He closed the mini-fridge door. "Hey, we know what it's like to be hungry."

"Yes, we do. And speaking of being hungry and homeless . . ."

"Yeah?"

"It went well, as you know, and Lexie was very excited about meeting the Rothman family. So yesterday, your mom took her to meet them."

"Is that right?" He was relieved to hear it. It wasn't often kids like him and Becks got a break.

She nodded. "Yes. Aria filled me in on what happened. I guess Lexie and the Rothmans connected right away, and the other kids in the family grabbed her and took her upstairs and showed her which bed would be hers. It was like she was already a part of the family."

"Aw, that's great."

"Yes. I hope it's going to work out. She's a sweet kid."

"Yes, she is. And it's one less kid on the streets."

"That's right."

He ate his sandwich in about three bites. He could have eaten the second one easily, but he'd grab something else after he got home. It was important that Aria got to eat.

"So, you do piercings, huh?" he asked.

"Yes. Why, do you want one?" She arched a brow.

He laughed. "No, just asking about your business. Do you do all kinds of piercings?"

"Yes."

"Yet you only have piercings in your ears and the one in your nose."

She smiled at him. "So far."

He arched a brow. "So far, huh?"

"I might get more at some point."

"That has my imagination working overtime."

"Why? Are you fascinated at the thought of me getting nipple piercings? Or maybe a clit piercing?"

His dick twitched. "Are you trying to get me hard?"

She leaned forward and brushed her lips across his. "Do I have to try?"

He laughed, then pulled back, knowing this wasn't the time or place, despite really wanting to explore the kiss. "Tease."

"So why were you stuck at the station late?" she asked.

"We had a call in the middle of the night that took a while to work. We didn't get back to the station until after end of shift, and I stayed to write my report."

She swept her fingers over his forehead. "Must have been a bad one."

"The wreck was bad. Surprisingly, no major injuries."

"That's good to hear. You're probably tired."

"I am."

"And yet you took the time to stop by here."

He leaned in, his lips so close he could almost taste her. He really wanted to kiss her again. "I wanted to see you."

She tangled her fingers in his hair and bridged those inches to kiss him again. He breathed her in, losing himself in the softness of her lips, in the way she moved her mouth so eagerly over his. If they were alone, he'd pull her onto his lap and deepen the kiss, put his hands all over her and before long they'd end up naked.

But they weren't alone, and the thoughts in his head were only going to get him hard and in trouble, so he pulled away.

Becks drew in a deep breath. "I'm glad you stopped by. We've both been so busy lately we haven't spent much time together. And I know it's mostly me. I've put in some late hours."

"You have. But that's good for you, isn't it?"

"It is. I had no idea the change in location would bump up our walk-ins so much, but we're getting a lot more business. And having Martin here has really helped because he brings in a lot of repeat business. More than he can handle, actually, which means I'm getting some of his overflow."

"I'm glad to hear that, babe. Growth is a good thing."

"Yeah." She propped her tennis-shoed feet onto the chair next to her. "I think it's just because we're new. Surely it'll calm down once we're established."

Jackson finished off his coffee. "Or maybe it won't. Maybe it'll build."

Her eyes went wide. "If it does that, I'll have to add another artist."

"That wouldn't be a bad thing, would it?"

"No. It would be a great thing. Though I'd hate to grow out of this space so fast."

He looked around. "You have room for one more artist, right?"

"Yes. We could fit one more. Any more than that and I'd have to move."

"Or bust into the space next door."

She laughed. "Sure. I'll just boot out the yogurt shop."

He shrugged. "Hey, yogurt places come and go. Or you could make them an offer they can't refuse."

"Ha. Like the Godfather, huh?"

"Yeah. You could be the mobster of Ft. Lauderdale."

She laughed. "Yeah, that's me all right. I like how you think I'm going to become this tattoo mogul, so rich I'll be able to take over this entire shopping strip."

"Hey, you never know. Or maybe you'll just branch out. Open up Skin Deep Two or Skin Deeper or something."

She stared at him. "Now you're giving me ideas."

"Good ideas, though, right?"

"Very good ideas."

He grinned. "I have many ideas in regard to you."

"You do? I'd like to hear some of them."

He looked down the hall, then leaned in to whisper. "Most of them require you to be naked."

"Okay. I like where this is going. So far I'm scheduled to finish up here on time tonight."

"Sounds good, but hey, you do what you need to do for work. Building up your client base is your priority. And if you want me to bring you some food, text me."

She rubbed the side of his face with the palm of her hand. "You're too good to me."

Her touch was driving him crazy, so that was his cue to leave. "I'll let you get back to work."

"Okay." She stood and walked with him to the front door.

He picked up her hand, noticing that Aria was staring at them. He wanted to put his mouth on Becks, to draw her into his arms and kiss her for a long time. So long she'd know how hard it was to leave her. Instead, he brushed his lips across hers in a quick kiss. "See you later."

"Okay."

After he got into his truck he drove down to the ocean, his initial plan to face-plant and get some sleep replaced by the need to cool down his heated body.

He'd crash later. Right now those salty waves were calling his name.

CHAPTER 26

BECKS SHUFFLED HER SCHEDULE AROUND SO SHE COULD be out of her shop by one on Saturday. Martin was working and so was Aria, and Martin promised he'd drop Aria off at closing. She also brought in food and told Aria there was extra food in the fridge in case she got hungry.

Since it was also Jackson's day off, she was hoping they could spend some time together.

They had nights together whenever he was off, and those nights had been getting hotter and hotter, and it wasn't just the steamy summer nights making her sweat. It was his touch, the way his hands roamed her body as if he'd memorized every inch of her and knew exactly what it took to send her soaring right over the edge. And then he'd kiss her. Starting with her mouth, moving to her neck and making his way ever so slowly south.

It didn't matter to her how late they stayed up, because every night was a trip to heaven.

She couldn't get enough of putting her hands—and her mouth—on him, either. His scent was embedded in her and on her. Often during her workday she'd find herself stopping just to close her eyes, take a deep breath and remember the night before.

Oh, she had it so bad.

She was just finishing cleanup in her room when Aria came back.

"Someone named Margie is here? Said she's a friend of yours."

"Oh, great, thanks, Aria."

She went out to the front to find her friend standing there wearing a sundress and the brightest smile.

"You look happy."

"I'm always happy."

That was true. Margie was never in a bad mood. When Becks had first hired Margie to find rental space for her tattoo shop, Margie had been this fast-talking bundle of energy and Becks had been subdued and nonverbal and had no idea how to handle this strange, gorgeous, vibrant girl.

But Margie's joyful attitude was infectious and she'd found the perfect place for Becks where the rent for the studio and the apartment were combined. And despite Becks not wanting or needing friends, Margie had decided right then that they'd become friends.

And so it had been decided. Because once Margie Vasquez decided you were her friend, there was no backing out.

"I'm on my lunch break," Margie said, "and I was wondering if you had some time to get something to drink."

"Actually I'm finished for the day, so I'd love to."

"Awesome. We need to catch up. It feels like it's been forever. Oh, and this place looks fabulous."

"Come on, I'll give you a quick tour, since you need to eat. Then we'll go."

She introduced Margie to Aria and Martin as she showed her around the offices, and then Becks locked her room and they headed out. Martin had a set of keys to the shop, so he'd lock up when he left for the night. She knew Aria liked to stay until closing, because the shop was air-conditioned and much cooler than hanging out at the park, and Becks totally understood that. Summer could be rough months for the homeless. It was so hot and you could easily get overheated if you didn't know the tricks to keeping yourself cool.

At least she had a spot in the park where it was shady.

She and Margie left and walked across the parking lot to a great Mexican restaurant.

After the week she'd had, Becks was dying for a margarita, but she held off and decided on an iced tea. Margie had the same. They ordered guacamole for an appetizer and Margie decided on the taco lunch special.

"I'm moving into real estate sales," Margie said.

Becks's eyes widened. "Are you serious?"

"Yes. My boss at the real estate office loves how outgoing and take-charge I am. He thinks I'm underutilized in commercial rentals and wants me to try my hand at home sales. He also said with my personality and the way I go after new business I'll be making tons of money in no time."

Becks knew how ambitious Margie was, how much she wanted to grow in her profession. "Oh, honey, I believe that. You are so great with your clients. And you're not pushy, but you have an uncanny knack for knowing exactly what people need. I think it's a perfect job for you."

"Thank you. Me, too. I'm going to start training next week. Home sales are quite different, but I know I can do it. It won't take me long to get up to speed. And then I'll beat everyone's sales at the office."

Becks laughed. "Of course you will."

They dug into the guac the server brought. In between bites, Margie asked, "So how's the new shop doing?"

"Crazy busy. The location is perfect and I couldn't be happier."

"I'm so glad to hear that. I knew it was going to be a good fit, even if the rent was a little higher."

"It helps to have Martin there to share the expenses."

Margie took a sip of her tea, then said, "Who's a total hottie, by the way."

"Yes, it doesn't hurt to have a good-looking artist there. Female customers love him."

"Hey, everyone loves you, too. I know I talk about my tattoo all the time."

Margie turned over her arm to reveal the bright red-and-yellow butterfly Becks had tattooed on her inner arm.

"It's one of my favorite tattoos," Becks said. "And it looks beautiful against your skin."

"Thank you. I love it so much."

Margie's tacos arrived, so she started to eat. She offered one up to Becks, who tried to decline but Margie insisted on sharing, so she ate part of one.

"Tell me about the roommates," Margie said. "Are you going to stay at the house with the three delicious firemen?"

"I don't think I'll stay there. But I am sort of kind of seeing or maybe just having sex with Jackson."

Margie held out her hand. "Wait. You're sleeping with Jackson? The tall, lean, dark-haired, gorgeous, steely-gray-eyed one?"

"Yes. That one."

Margie fanned her hand back and forth over her face. "Girl, that man is so hot he could *cause* fires."

Becks smiled over her glass of tea. "He causes a fire in my panties."

Margie laughed. And when Margie laughed, you could hear it six tables away. "I'll just bet he does. Aren't you the lucky one? He's the one you had a crush on when you both were homeless, right?"

"Yes, but that was an adolescent kind of crush."

"Oh, and now it's an adult, let-me-strip-for-you-so-you-can-do-naughty-things-to-all-the-parts-of-my-body kind of crush?"

Becks laughed. "Yes. Just like that."

"Hmm," Margie said, leaning back in the booth with her glass of tea in her hand. "Or maybe it's more than just a crush and sex?"

"I don't know what you mean."

"You know exactly what I mean. How do you feel about him?"

"I feel like he gives me shivers when he kisses me. And when I'm not with him I miss him. Other than that, it's just . . . fun, you know?"

"Oh, I know, honey. I've dated my share of guys who set my panties on fire. But I've never fallen in love with any of them."

Becks lifted her chin. "I never said I was in love with him."

"That's true, you didn't. Just . . . be careful, Becks. I worry about your heart."

Margie always watched out for her, which was one of the reasons she was Becks's best friend. They looked out for each other, especially as it related to guys.

"I've got hold of my heart, don't you worry."

"Uh-huh. That's what we all say, right before we tumble straight into love land."

"I'm not going there. I've got too many other things planned for my life."

Or at least she didn't think that was what was happening. She hoped it wasn't.

She left Margie confused about how she felt. She knew better than to think there was a happily-ever-after in her future. Sure, her job was great, and she had a best friend and right now she had a roof over her head.

And at one time in her life she had parents she thought loved her. And then one day all of that changed, when they left her alone and never came home.

And she never, ever saw them again. So she'd always had a hard time believing things people told her, and an even harder time believing that anyone could ever love her.

But she did believe in herself, because she'd always only had herself to rely on. And she was damn good at handling life. She was talented, tenacious and a survivor.

That she could always count on.

Anything else wasn't a guarantee.

She ended up back at the house in a thoughtful frame of mind. When she went inside, Rafe and Kal were in the pool with a couple of women.

She popped her head outside to wave hello and they waved back.

Jackson came downstairs just as she was going up.

"Hi," she said.

He slid his arm around her waist and tugged her close. "Hey, yourself. How was your day?"

"Short, finally."

"Good. Still feel like going out with me today?"

"I do. What did you have in mind?"

"Well, first I need to ask you for a favor."

"Okay." Now she was curious.

"My parents are doing some house hunting this afternoon and they asked one of us to come along. Since Rafe and Kal have dates over, I was wondering if you would mind coming with me to look at houses with them."

"That sounds fun. I'd love to."

He gave her a quick kiss. "Thanks. I know this won't be fun."

"Are you kidding? I spent the first twenty years of my life homeless. Looking at houses is like a fantasy."

"A fantasy, huh? I doubt that."

"Hey, you might not think of it as fun, but I do. Give me a minute to freshen up and I'll be ready to go."

"Okay."

She went up to her room to change clothes and brush her teeth and hair. She opted for a pair of orange capris with a white short-sleeved shirt, then slid into a pair of white sandals. When she came downstairs, Jackson was looking down at his phone. When he saw her, he smiled.

"Damn, you're beautiful."

"Oh, come on. I'm casual."

"Casually beautiful." He got up and swept her into his arms, then kissed her. "You always take my breath away."

And he always knew exactly what to say to make her feel swept away. "Thank you."

"We'll meet my parents at the first house. They sent the address and they're already on the way."

"Exciting. Let's go."

This would be exactly what she needed to get her mind off the future. What she needed was to stay in the present, and away from thoughts about herself and how she grew up. She'd already made peace with her past. She couldn't change what had happened to her, and she'd decided not to let it influence her future. She was worthy, and her parents hadn't been worthy of her. So she had to get rid of the negative feelings that occasionally cropped up.

What could be more fun than house hunting?

"Did you have a bad day?"

She looked over at Jackson. "No. Why would you ask that?"

"You're really quiet. We don't have to do this, Becks, if you don't want to."

"No, actually I was thinking how much I want to. I got deep in my head thinking about the past today, and house hunting will be a really good distraction."

"The past?"

"Yes. You know. Parents. How I became a homeless kid. Things like that."

"Oh." He made a turn onto the highway and sped up to catch up with traffic. "Yeah, well you know how I feel about that."

"I'm sorry. I shouldn't have brought it up."

"Not about you, babe. You can talk to me about anything having to do with *your* past." After he merged into traffic, he gave her a quick glance. "Tell me what's bugging you."

She inhaled and let it out. "Sometimes I just get angry."

"About?"

"My parents. They just left me at that apartment and never looked back. I was their child and they just walked away from me as if I were a piece of old furniture they didn't care about. Who does that?"

"Shitty parents. People who should have never had the responsibility of caring for a kid."

"Like yours?"

He paused, changed lanes. "My parents died."

She gasped. "Oh, Jackson, I'm sorry. I didn't know."

He shrugged. "No way for you to know since I don't talk about it."

She waited, knowing talking about his past was a sensitive subject. "What were they like?"

"I don't remember much. I was six when they died. There was a car accident. Winding back roads and it had been raining really hard. I guess my dad didn't negotiate the curve well and the car went off the road and down a ravine. They'd been driving some older-model compact car and it didn't save either of them."

"How awful."

"Yeah. Anyway, there was no other family, so it was the foster care system for me."

"No grandparents or aunts or uncles or any distant relatives?"

"Nope."

"Not even any friends of your parents willing to take you in?"

"Nope."

"Yeah, same for me."

"It sucks, doesn't it?"

"It does."

She could tell from the way his fingers clung to the steering wheel that she needed to end this conversation.

"It doesn't matter. Look where you ended up. With incredible parents who love you and your brothers."

He smiled and relaxed his death grip. "Yeah, they're pretty amazing."

"I think it's pretty amazing that they want to move into a new house after all these years."

"I do, too. It's a big deal for my dad. He really likes the old place."

She was glad he'd let go of whatever pain from the past had made him so tense. "It's obviously true love if he's willing to give up the house he loves for the woman he loves even more."

He glanced at her. "Does love always have to be about sacrifice?"

She stared at him. "I . . . have no idea."

"So you've never been in love."

She stared out the windshield as he exited the highway. "Not that I know of."

"You don't know if you've ever been in love?"

"No. I mean, how do you know if you love someone, Jackson?"

"I don't know." He shrugged. "I know I love my parents and my brothers, but I've never been in love with a woman before. I know that kind of love has to feel different from how you love your family, but I've never felt deeply enough to tell someone I loved them."

"Me, either. So I guess you have to feel it, and when you do you'll know."

"I think so."

Well. Weren't they a fine pair. Two clueless, never-been-in-love people. The problem was she *was* having feelings. *Those* kinds of feelings.

For Jackson.

And the one person she wanted to talk to about them was Jackson. So what was she supposed to do? Because she sensed that if she tried to approach that particular conversation with Jackson right now, he'd run like hell.

They pulled down a street that contained mature trees and houses that didn't look new but were well maintained. The front yards were spacious, but not overly large.

The house they stopped at was a one-story, very pretty Spanish-style home.

"This one looks nice," she said.

"We'll see what it's like on the inside."

They got out and Jackson's parents were waiting at the front door. They both hugged Jackson, which Becks thought was so sweet.

"Our agent is already inside," Josh said. "We told her we were waiting for you."

"It's good to see you again, Becks," Laurel said, giving her a hug.

"You, too, Laurel. Thank you so much for what you did for Lexie."

Laurel smiled. "She's settling in happily with the Rothmans. And they adore her. So do her new siblings. I think the placement is going to work out perfectly."

"I'm so happy to hear that." There was nothing better than a happily-ever-after. To know that Lexie was going to have hers filled Becks with joy. She looked over at Jackson, who made eye contact with her as he was having a conversation with his dad. She cast a grateful smile at him.

"It was all your son's doing, Laurel."

"So I understand. He's a good boy."

"Yes, he is."

Jackson and his dad came over.

"Nice to see you again, Josh," she said.

Josh smiled at her. "We're happy you decided to come along, Becks."

She always felt welcome in the presence of Jackson's parents. Which meant she could be herself and didn't need to have her guard up or feel as if she wasn't going to be accepted.

"The outside of this place looks nice, Mom," Jackson said.

"I think so. Your dad doesn't care for it, though."

"Yeah? Why not, Dad?"

"The trees are overgrown and it looks like the roof might need replacing."

"Something you can talk to the agent about," Jackson said. "And you can always make roof replacement a condition of the sale."

Josh looked the place over. "I don't know if I like it."

Laurel looped her arm in Josh's. "How about we at least go inside first?"

"You're right. Sorry."

Laurel cast a smile over her shoulder at Becks. "No home will ever measure up to the one we have now. I'm not even sure why we're bothering to look."

Becks suppressed a smile of her own at Laurel's comment, then looked over at Jackson, who shrugged.

They went inside. The foyer was open to a beautiful staircase. There was a chandelier overhead that was a little blingy for Becks's tastes, but it wasn't her potential house, so she'd withhold judgement.

"Josh, Laurel, so glad you're finally inside."

A well-dressed woman who looked to be in her forties came walking down the hall.

"Jackson, Becks, I'd like to introduce you to our real estate agent Ellen Grayson," Laurel said. "Ellen, this is our son Jackson and his girlfriend, Becks."

Becks blinked. Just like that, without hesitation, Laurel had assumed she was Jackson's girlfriend.

Though she and Jackson had decided not to put a label on things. And Becks was fine with that.

"It's nice to meet you," Jackson said.

Becks forced herself out of her weird state of shock. "Nice to meet you, Ellen."

"Welcome," Ellen said. "I'm so glad you both came along to see the homes I have on today's tour. Let's get started."

"This is nice and open," Laurel said to Ellen, then turned to Josh with a smile. "I like the floors."

"Uh-huh," Josh replied, following them down the hall. "There's that weird wall between the kitchen and living room."

"Yes," Laurel said. "I don't like that too much."

There was a partial wall that separated the kitchen from the living area. But the walls were painted a beachy turquoise, which Becks liked. The floors were large white terrazzo tile and absolutely gorgeous but would probably show every speck of dirt and have to be constantly cleaned.

Who would want to do that?

They walked from the living area into the dining area, which had a table and four chairs along with French doors that led out to a nice Florida room.

"We'll go outside in a minute," Ellen said. "Come see the kitchen first."

"Oh, a galley kitchen." Laurel pursed her lips. "And it's so closed off from the rest of the house."

Josh put his arm around Laurel. "It's not the best option, is it?"

"No. I so want something that's open and spacious, especially the kitchen. I don't want to be stuck in here cooking while everyone else is out in the living room. I do like these white cabinets and new appliances, though."

"Noted," Ellen said. "I just thought you'd like the pool."

As Ellen walked off with Laurel and Josh, Jackson and Becks lingered.

"There's a lot more to a house than just the pool," Becks said. "And more to pleasing a woman than what's in the back-yard."

Jackson gave her a knowing smile. "I know how to please a woman."

She nudged him with her shoulder. "Not at all what I'm referring to and you know it."

"Huh. I thought you were asking me for sex when all you're really interested in is a fancy kitchen and stainless steel appliances."

She nuzzled her chin against his shoulder. "A woman has priorities."

He looked over the top of her head, then grasped her hand and placed it on the ridge of his zipper.

"I've got a priority for you."

She quickly snatched her hand away. "Oh my God, Jackson. Your parents are in the next room."

He laughed. "We're not sixteen, Becks."

She narrowed her gaze at him. "You must have been horrible at sixteen."

"Wrong. I was a freaking angel."

"I do not believe you." She pivoted and hurried to join the rest of them. She caught up to Laurel and Josh in time to see Laurel shaking her head at the master bath.

"This house needs too many renovations, Josh," she said. "If we were going to do that we could just stay in our house."

"I agree," he said.

Laurel turned to Ellen. "We need a more updated house, Ellen."

"Of course. And I have just the thing. It's only a mile or so from here."

They all piled into their cars and followed Ellen.

"What's your dream house?" Jackson asked as they trailed behind Josh and Laurel's SUV.

She glanced over at him. "Honestly? I've never thought about it."

"Really."

"Yes. Why? Does that surprise you?"

"Yeah. Don't most women have the house of their dreams already made up by the time they hit puberty?"

"Jackson. By the time I hit puberty I had been homeless for three years. My dream was just a roof over my head. Any roof. Decent shelter was always my dream."

"Yeah, but that was when you were thirteen. And you've had a roof over your head for—what?—nearly ten years now?"

"Yes. So what's your point?"

"My point is that maybe between the homeless years and the roof-over-your-head years, you might have had some time to dream, Becks."

She was getting a headache. Between her conversation with Margie and now this one, she was more confused than ever. Why couldn't they just have some fun looking at houses?

"Well, the truth is, I haven't dreamed."

He made a right turn and entered a gated community. Nice, with well-manicured lawns and some beautiful homes. Now maybe they could focus on the fun stuff.

"Why not?"

"What? Why not what?" She dragged her gaze away from the pretty houses and shot a questioning look at Jackson.

"Why no dreams, Becks?"

"Because the only things I dreamed about were making rent and hoping my business would stay afloat, so I could pay my bills and never have to worry about being homeless again. Those were my dreams."

"Yeah, but those are practical things. How about something frivolous and fun or a reach-for-the-stars kind of dream?"

She shook her head. "I can't afford to think beyond practical."

"Sure you can. You've got a great job and your business is growing." They pulled in front of a gorgeous two-story contemporary home that looked brand spanking new. "It's okay to dream, even if that dream is never realized."

She grabbed the handle to exit the car and looked over at Jackson, sending him a shrug. "Then what's the point of dreaming?"

She needed out of that car, away from the tight space with Jackson. Away from the thought of dreams and the future and a pretty house. Because she was already in emotional trouble, and she didn't need a pile-on.

She headed toward Laurel, who was already beckoning to her with a wave.

But Jackson caught up to her, leaning in to whisper in her ear. "Our conversation isn't finished."

As far as Becks was concerned, it was.

Dreams were for suckers. She was way too grounded in reality to be waylaid by fantasy.

Like this house, for instance. She was in love with this house. It wasn't super fancy on the outside, but there was something about it that seemed perfect for Laurel. Maybe it was the slate gray roof in contrast to the dark blue painted wood and dark gray shutters on the sides of every window. The large porch had wide pillars and enough space that it contained a small table and a couple of oversized, cushioned chairs. There was even a ceiling fan on the porch.

It was pretty without being ostentatious, yet also had that homey feel that she thought might appeal to Josh.

"What do you think?" Laurel asked.

"I like the outside. It's unique, yet also feels like home, if that makes sense."

Laurel slid her arm into Becks's. "It makes so much sense, because it's the exact thing I said to Josh when we pulled into the driveway."

Becks smiled at her.

"Okay, before you start moving our furniture in, shouldn't we see the inside?" Josh asked.

"There you go, being all practical," Laurel said.

Becks laughed.

"If you like the outside, you're going to love the inside," Ellen said. "It's modern and beautiful and only three years old."

Josh leaned over to Laurel. "That means expensive."

She rolled her eyes. "This is not my idea, mister. I'm happy with our current house."

Ellen stepped between the two of them. "And I'm fully aware of your maximum budget, so don't worry. This fits."

Becks looked over at Jackson, who shrugged. "We'll see," he said.

Becks just wanted to get a peek at the inside, because the outside was pretty.

Ellen opened the door and Josh and Laurel walked in. Jackson and Becks followed, and to Becks, it was like someone had read her mind.

If she had a dream house—which she did not—this might come pretty close to being it.

Planked tile floors were shaded gray, lending them a woodlike appearance. The entire living room and kitchen/eating area were open, making the space look huge.

Okay, it didn't just appear to be huge, it *was* huge. The kitchen was expansive and bright, and there were windows everywhere. The kitchen had modern appliances and a large island, and there was a lot of cabinet space.

Laurel wandered through without saying much or asking questions. No one spoke because they could tell she was seriously inspecting every corner of this house, from the downstairs bathroom to the laundry room to the bedrooms.

The bedrooms upstairs were spacious and had plenty of room for whoever wanted to sleep there. The master was huge, had a gorgeous, extremely roomy walk-in closet and an amazing master bath with an oversized shower and an extremely tempting soaker tub.

Laurel's eyes seemed to gleam with pleasure.

"Shall we go take a look at the backyard?" Ellen asked.

Laurel looked over at her and smiled. "Yes. Let's."

Becks thought this place was amazing, and so far Laurel hadn't said much.

"What do you think?" Jackson asked after his parents went downstairs.

"Honestly? I love it."

"Yeah, me, too. It's a great house. Though I'd change a few things if it were my house."

She leaned back. "Really. Like what?"

"Wood floors instead of tile. Bigger shower and no tub in the master."

"Huh."

He cocked his head to the side. "What does 'huh' mean?"

"Just thinking about what you said. By the way, I disagree."

"Which part? Or all of it?"

"I agree about the wood floors. But I like taking a bath."

"That's what the other bathroom is for."

"No. That's the kids' bathroom."

He laughed. "What kids?"

She was about to say *our kids*, but caught herself. "The kids I'm going to have someday."

"By yourself?"

She lifted her chin. "Maybe. Women can do that, you know."

"Really. In what magical way can women have kids by themselves?"

They made their way slowly downstairs. "Come on, Jackson. You're smart. I can get inseminated. Or I can adopt. In fact, you want to talk about my dreams? If I were to have dreams, that would be one of them. I do plan to adopt. God knows there are plenty of kids out there in foster care who'd love to belong to a family."

"I don't disagree with you there. But tell me you're not planning to do that alone."

This conversation wasn't going places she wanted to go right now. "I don't know what my plan is. I've never thought that far down the road."

She paused. "Have you?"

"Not before."

She stilled on the bottom step. "Before what?"

"I was just hoping that maybe—"

"There you two are," Laurel said. "I thought maybe you lost yourselves upstairs in that amazing bathroom."

Becks wanted Jackson to finish his sentence, because she needed to know what he'd been hoping. But instead she smiled at Laurel. "I have to admit that soaker tub was tempting."

"I know, I loved it," Laurel said. "I love everything about this place. The location is perfect for both Josh and me. It's close to work for both of us, and oh, you have to come see the backyard."

Now Laurel was talking. She liked the place. Really liked it. And, for some reason, that made Becks extremely happy.

Laurel took her hand and led her through the kitchen and toward the sliding glass door.

"Wow," Becks said. "This is like an oasis."

Laurel grinned. "Right?"

There was a good-sized pool centered in an even bigger yard. One side of the pool was shaded by palms and beautiful bushes, giving it a tropical feel. There was also plenty of grass and entertaining space.

"I like it," Jackson said. "You could have some serious parties out here."

Josh nodded. "We're already planning on it."

Becks turned to Laurel. "This is the place?"

Laurel nodded. "There's no point in looking at anything else. The location is ideal in terms of Josh's work and mine. There's plenty of space, and I'm in love with every room. Other than some minor changes like painting a few rooms, I'm ready to move in tomorrow."

Josh laughed. "We've gotta sell our house first, babe."

"I know, but our house should sell easily."

"It should, Mom," Jackson said. "You're in a prime location and the house is in great shape. A few repairs and some paint and it'll be ready to sell."

"You and your brothers have done a fantastic job helping us to get the house ready to sell."

"Which we'll do right away," Ellen said. "Once you spruce up your existing house and get it ready, I'll organize an open house and I can guarantee we'll get offers that day."

Becks loved Ellen's positive attitude. She reminded Becks a lot of Margie.

They all walked out front.

"Come by the office tomorrow and we'll get the offer in," Ellen said.

"We'll do that," Josh said. "Thanks, Ellen."

After Ellen walked away, Laurel turned to Becks and Jackson. "We need to celebrate. Come to the house for dinner."

"Oh, no," Becks said. "You should go out to celebrate. Just the two of you."

"No. We dragged you along with us," Laurel said, "so we all go out to celebrate."

"Okay," Becks said.

"I'm kind of in the mood for Thai food," Josh said.

"How about Asia Bay?" Laurel asked.

"Sounds good to me," Jackson said, then turned to Becks. "What do you think?"

"I think it sounds perfect."

They climbed into their cars and drove over to Las Olas Boulevard. By the time they parked and went inside the beautiful restaurant, Becks's stomach was rumbling.

They were seated with a view of the canal. Becks ordered an iced tea and Jackson and his dad ordered beer. Laurel opted for water.

"Excited?" Becks asked.

Laurel shook her head. "Feels like a dream. I thought we'd live in that old house forever."

"You know, you could just move into the house we're living in," Jackson said. "It's big and spacious and has a pool. And it was Grandma's house."

Laurel laid her hand over Jackson's. "No. You and your brothers put a lot of sweat equity into remodeling that house. And the location is perfect for all of you, being so close to the station."

"But it's your house, Mom."

"It belongs to the family. Aren't you happy there?"

"I like it there just fine. I just thought before you go investing more money in buying another house, you might want to consider one that's already paid off."

"That's sweet, Jackson. But, really, your dad and I like the new place, don't we, Josh?"

"Yup."

Becks fought a smile. Josh was a man of few words, and it was obvious that whatever made Laurel happy was good enough for him.

They ordered sushi appetizers, and Josh and Jackson went outside to look at the canal.

"That means Josh wants to smoke one of his cigars," Laurel said. "I'm after him all the time to get rid of those things, but since it's only once or twice a day, I let it go."

Becks smiled at the sweet way Laurel looked out the window at her husband. She could tell how much she loved Josh. "You two seem so happy together."

Laurel pulled her gaze away from the window. "It's been a great life."

"About to be greater, I think."

"You would think after twenty-five years together, there wouldn't be any way he could surprise me. And yet he still can. I had no idea he wanted to sell the house. But either way, I'm thrilled to death."

"I don't blame you. The house is beautiful."

"Thanks. I think so, too. But enough about the house. Let's talk about you and my son."

Uh-oh. "Is there a problem?"

"Lord, no. I've never seen him so relaxed. And happy."

"You think so?"

"I know so, honey. I've noticed the difference in him since he reconnected with you. He smiles more, jokes more with his brothers. He's more talkative and expressive."

She didn't want to ask the question, but curiosity got to her. "Has he said something to you about . . . us?"

Laurel laughed. "Of course not. Boys don't typically share relationship information with their parents. But I can tell there's something special going on between the two of you. Do you feel it?"

"I . . ." She'd been in denial for so long, had tried to come up with any excuse or explanation for how she was feeling. But hearing Jackson's mother talk about her son's behavior opened something up inside her, made her feel warm and happy in ways she couldn't begin to explain. "I feel a lot of things where Jackson is concerned."

"But neither of you have talked to each other about your feelings."

She looked down at her glass. "No. Not yet."

"What do you think is stopping you?"

She inhaled a deep breath and let it out. "On my part? Fear. Love hasn't really been in the picture for me throughout my life."

"So you're afraid if you tell him you love him that he won't return your feelings."

Jackson's mom sure cut to the chase. "Yes."

Laurel gazed a sympathetic smile at her. "I understand. I can't speak to Jackson's true feelings, only my own observations. My best advice is for you to talk to him."

Easier said than done. "I'll do my best."

The guys came back inside, so conversation about her relationship with Jackson was put to rest. Not that Becks had stopped thinking about it. She kept shooting glances toward Jackson, who obviously had no idea what was on her mind.

He kept smiling at her and sliding curious glances her way.

And she couldn't say anything to him. She just smiled back at him and tried to communicate her thoughts to him psychically.

We have a lot of stuff to talk about, buddy, she thought to him. *A lot of "feelings" related stuff.*

But later. When we're alone.

CHAPTER 27

AS MUCH AS HE ENJOYED SPENDING TIME WITH HIS PAR-
ents, Jackson was happy to say good-bye to them and get back
home with Becks.

Fortunately, Rafe and Kal and their dates had disappeared,
which suited him just fine, because he wanted to be alone with his
woman.

His woman. Whenever he thought about Becks lately, that was
all he thought about. Not that she belonged to him, but that he
wanted her to stay in his life. Because when he wasn't with her,
he missed her. And though their housing arrangement was supposed to be temporary, he wanted it to become permanent.

He knew how independent she was, and he respected that, so
he was going to have to approach the topic cautiously.

He should probably start by telling her how he felt about her.
These feelings were all so new to him he wasn't sure he could put
a name to them. All he knew was he cared for Becks and wanted
her to know his feelings ran deep. Why was it important to name
them?

Becks had gone upstairs. When she came down, she'd changed into loose shorts and a tank top. He had pulled two beers out of the fridge, so he handed one to her. They went into the living room and she slid on the sofa. He sat next to her.

"Alone at last," she said.

"Thanks for coming with me today."

"Are you kidding? I had a great time. Your mom seems so happy about the house."

"Yeah, she does. I'm happy for both Mom and Dad that it's all working out, house-wise."

"Me, too." She took a pull of her beer.

"So how about a movie?" he asked.

"Sounds good."

They cuddled up together and picked out a movie, a mystery suspense that had a little romance in it. They argued over who the baddie was, agreeing halfway through and then diverging on their guesses three quarters of the way.

They were both wrong at the end.

"I hate being wrong," Jackson said.

Becks laughed. "I love being surprised like that. When you've got the plot figured out halfway through the movie, it ruins everything."

"I guess." He finished off his beer, then set it on the side table and turned to her.

"So I need to talk to you about something," she said.

Okay, so he'd let her go first. "Sure."

She took a deep breath, then let it out, and he could tell she was nervous. He picked up her hand and covered it with both of his. "Is everything okay?"

"Yes. It's just that there are all these feelings that have been building up inside me for a while now, Jackson."

"Feelings about?"

She lifted her gaze to his and he felt that gut punch that always seemed to hit him every time she leveled her beautiful eyes on him.

"About you."

He couldn't help but smile. "Good feelings?"

"Yes. Good feelings. Like I know I'm falling in love with you."

He exhaled, realizing he'd been nervous, like he'd been expecting something bad. This definitely wasn't bad. In fact, it was just what he wanted. He kissed her, and everything in his world felt right, perfect and exactly as it should be. Becks in his arms, her mouth on his, and getting lost in the taste of her and the feel of her warm body against him.

When he pulled back, she was smiling, and her cheeks were pink. He rubbed her bottom lip.

"You make me happy," he said. "Like, happier than I've ever been."

She cocked her head to the side. "Why do I feel as if you're holding back?"

"I don't know. Why do you feel that way? I want the same thing you want. I feel the same way you do. I care about you, Becks. I want you in my life. I want us to be together."

She crossed her legs and turned to face him. "I'm going to be honest here."

"Okay."

She squeezed his hand. "I love you. I just said that. But I wouldn't be honest if I didn't say that I feel like you're not all in."

He had no idea where this was coming from. "What do you mean?"

"I've been open with you about everything. My past, my feelings, pretty much everything. I don't hold anything back from you, Jackson. I never have."

And there it was. "And you think I do."

"I know you do."

He started to look away, but she palmed his face and forced him to look at her.

"I know you don't see it, but I do. And I can't help but feel it has to do with your past."

Goddamn. "Are we doing this again? Come on, Becks."

"Hey, I get it. The past hurts. It hurts me, too. But I think it holds you back from saying what you really feel."

"Like what?"

"Like . . . I love you?"

He hadn't said the words back to her. He didn't know why. He felt them. He couldn't say them. But they didn't have a damn thing to do with the past.

"It's not that. It's not the past. It's never the past. I told you my parents died. It was shit and I got sent to foster care."

"Yes. It was awful and I know how hard that was for you to tell me. But what about that night we all got separated? The night of the fire? Have you ever talked to anyone about that night?"

This wasn't how it was supposed to go. He stood, needing distance. "No. No point. It's over. We got rescued and everything turned out okay."

"Except you have nightmares, Jackson."

He looked down at her and frowned. "No, I don't."

"Yes, you do. When we sleep together, you don't sleep peacefully. You thrash around in the bed and mumble, as if something is troubling you."

He didn't believe her. "Why do you feel this need to drag it out of me, Becks? I've told you I don't want to talk about it. Yet it seems like we keep having this same conversation over and over again."

"I know." She stood and faced him. "But I love you, Jackson, and I want you to be happy. And whole." She laid her hand on his chest. "And I just don't know that you can be happy—that we can be happy together—until you deal with those ghosts of your past."

"So is this some kind of ultimatum? I talk to you about that night or we're through?"

Her eyes widened. "Of course not. I just told you I loved you. I would never do that to you."

"But you just did. Here I thought I was going to tell you I cared about you tonight. That it was going to be great. Instead, you start nagging at me to talk about the past. That's not love."

"There are those words again. You care about me? Is that all you've got?"

"What do you mean?"

"I told you I loved you, Jackson. Can you say it back to me?"

He stared at her. Part of him was pissed, the other part confused. "I said I cared about you."

"You can't say it. Is it because you don't love me?"

"I . . . I don't know how I feel right now."

He saw the hurt on her face, but goddammit he was confused.

"Talk to me, Jackson. Tell me what you're feeling."

He dragged his fingers through his hair. "I just . . . I can't believe you're laying all this down on me tonight of all nights."

Her gaze drifted down to the floor for a few seconds before she lifted it back to his face. He thought he saw the sparkle of tears in her eyes, but he couldn't be sure.

"I'm sorry, Jackson. I can tell I put too much pressure on you and I didn't want to do that. You need some time to think things over. When you get it figured out, or if you want to talk to me about it, let me know."

She left the living room and he followed, watching her climb the steps and disappear into her room.

He wanted to follow her, but something kept him rooted to the floor, his feet unable to move.

Talk to her? About what? He'd already told her everything he had to say. So he went to the fridge and grabbed another beer, but after two swallows he realized it didn't taste good.

It wasn't what he wanted. What he wanted was to rewind the entire conversation he'd had with Becks.

He ran it all over again and again in his mind, trying to map out where it had gone wrong.

He knew where it had gone wrong.

With getting in too deep, with letting their emotions get involved. When they'd been having fun, everything had been fine. As soon as it had gotten serious everything had gone to shit.

But the alternative would have been letting her go, and he couldn't imagine his life without Becks. So what the fuck was he supposed to do?

Maybe by tomorrow he'd have it figured out.

CHAPTER 28

JACKSON WAS JOLTED AWAKE BY SOMETHING SHOVING at his shoulder. He sat bolt upright in bed, only to find both of his brothers glaring down at him.

"What?"

"She's gone," Kal said.

His mind was still filled with sleep fuzz. "Who's gone?"

"Becks," Rafe said.

He blinked and rubbed his eyes. "What do you mean she's gone?"

"Like packed up her shit and left, gone," Rafe said.

Kal shoved him back against the mattress. "What did you do?"

"I didn't do anything. And get the fuck out of my room."

"We'll be downstairs," Kal said, narrowing his gaze.

They both left, Rafe slamming the door shut behind him.

He threw the covers off, went into the bathroom to take a piss, then slid on a pair of board shorts and went downstairs.

Rafe and Kal were waiting for him in the kitchen, glaring at him as if he'd just killed someone.

"What the fuck, man?" Rafe asked.

"Don't even talk to me until I've had coffee."

Kal slid a cup across the island to him.

"Thanks." He took a couple of sips, hoping the caffeine would help clear the cobwebs.

They'd talked last night, but it hadn't exactly been an argument. At least not on her part. She'd been upset, but not angry.

"She left this," Kal said, sliding an envelope in front of him.

It had his name on it, so he opened it and read it.

Jackson,

I'm sorry I pressured you into doing something you aren't ready for.

I don't think this is going to work out.

I had a great time with you.

Thanks for letting me stay here.

Love, Becks

What the actual fuck? She left?

"So?"

He lifted his gaze to look at Rafe. "So what?"

"So what does the letter say?"

"None of your business."

"It *is* our business," Kal said. "Becks is family. You had something good with her. And you obviously fucked it up."

"What he said," Rafe added.

Jackson turned his back on his brothers and focused instead on his cup of coffee.

"Seriously, Jackson," Rafe said. "What happened with the two of you?"

He sighed, then sank into one of the chairs. "Hell if I know.

Everything was fine last night. She told me she loved me. And then we started talking and things went downhill."

"You told her you loved her back, right?" Kal asked.

"Not exactly."

"So you don't love her?" Rafe asked.

"I do. I just didn't say it."

"Well, why the fuck not?" Kal asked. "Are you stupid?"

"I said I cared about her."

Rafe laughed. "Yeah, because that's exactly what a woman wants to hear after she tells you she loves you. No wonder she left."

"No, that's not why she left. Or maybe it's partly why she left." He grimaced at the ache forming between his eyes. "I don't exactly know."

"Or maybe you do know and you just don't want to face it," Kal said.

He'd had enough of this inquisition. He whirled to face his brothers. "Oh, right, because you know me and my relationship with Becks so well."

Kal held his palms out. "I didn't say I knew your relationship. I just know you. And if there's a way for you to avoid getting close to someone, you'll figure it out."

Jackson narrowed his gaze. "What the fuck does that mean?"

"It means you avoid getting close to anyone," Rafe said. "You always have. Ever since the fire."

Again with that night. "I do not."

Kal nodded. "Yeah, bro, you do. Don't get me wrong. You've always been there to look out for Rafe and for me. And since that night, maybe more so. But we're not your responsibility anymore, ya know?"

"Yeah," Rafe said, coming over to grab Jackson by the shoulder. "We made it through the fire that night. All of us."

Jackson looked up at Rafe, the pain of almost losing him that night still fresh, even though it had been years. "But we almost didn't. And it's all my fault."

"No, it's not."

"Yeah, it is. Don't you remember? You guys didn't want to go into that house. I made you."

Kal frowned. "I don't remember that."

"Rafe, you said the house looked unsafe, like it could fall down on top of us. Kal, you said it looked haunted and you'd started to cry. And I was pissed because we had food to eat and I'd found this great spot for us to get out of the rain and neither one of you wanted to go inside."

Rafe dragged his fingers through his hair. "We were kids, Jackson. We were always complaining."

"But that's the thing. I made you go in. You getting trapped in that fire was my fault."

Kal came over and sat next to him. "No, it wasn't. You can't blame yourself for that."

"But I do. If it wasn't for Dad finding us, I might have lost both of you."

"Jesus, Jackson," Kal said. "That's a heavy load to bear. Why didn't you ever talk to us about it?"

He shrugged. "I never wanted to think about it again. I was just damn happy we got out."

"So were we," Rafe said. "But Kal and I never blamed you for choosing that house. It was just circumstance."

"Kal's right," Rafe said. "You're our brother. No one took better care of us than you did."

"I didn't that night."

"Bullshit." Rafe glared at him. "Don't you ever blame yourself for the fire in that house. You've got to let that shit go, Jackson."

His shoulders sagged. "I'm sorry. I'm sorry I made you stay in that place and put you both in danger."

"Stop it," Rafe said. "Not your fault. How many times do we need to tell you that?"

He felt his brothers' arms around him. Not judgement. Not condemnation. Just love.

"You saved us, Jackson," Kal said. "So many times. You always kept us safe. You were just a kid yourself. I think sometimes you forget that."

Maybe he had forgotten that.

"Let it go, bro," Rafe said. "No one here has ever judged you for that night. No one ever will. We all made it out that night. We're safe. We're all safe."

Rafe was right. He had to let it go. The guilt, the feelings of responsibility that he'd held on to for so long. He drew in a shaky breath and looked at his brothers, felt their love pouring into him. "Thanks. For always being here for me. I don't know what I would have done without both of you. It's not a one-way street, you know?"

"Yeah, we do," Rafe said, taking a step back to give Jackson some air. "Which means you need to go fix this mess you made with Becks."

Oh, God. Becks. "I really fucked that up."

Kal slid into the chair next to him. "Dude, you can't hold back on feeling something for someone just because there's a chance you could lose them."

"Kal's right," Rafe said. "Time to fix this with Becks, because maybe you don't see it, but Kal and I do. She's the best thing that's ever happened to you."

"Besides us, of course," Kal said, grinning, breaking up the tension that had grown so thick around them.

Jackson laughed, then got out of his chair and put his arms around both of his brothers.

"I love you guys."

"Love you, too, idiot," Rafe said.

"Ditto," Kal said. "Now go get Becks back."

He went upstairs to shower, trying to figure out how exactly he was going to repair what had gone wrong between Becks and him.

And there was only one way to do that.

First he was going to have to fix himself.

CHAPTER 29

"HEY, BECKS, CAN YOU SQUEEZE IN ANOTHER APPOINT-ment today?" Aria asked. "I've got a guy on the phone who'd like some ink done."

Becks looked up at the clock. It was already seven thirty and what she thought had been her last client of the day had just left.

"How big a tattoo?"

"He said it isn't a big one."

She rolled her eyes. Then again, what else did she have to do? It wasn't like she had anywhere else to go. She was already sleeping at the shop and showering at the truck stop.

It helped to have experienced years of being homeless, so she knew where she could shower and eat on the cheap. No one but Aria knew she was bunking at the shop. She'd rented a storage locker for all her other stuff, and kept a few days of spare clothes stuffed in a duffel bag with her. Plus she had a sleeping bag so it wasn't so bad.

And soon enough she'd have enough money saved up for

first and last months' rent on an apartment, so this was just temporary.

Temporary. The word of her life.

She'd certainly had worse.

The sleepless nights the past few days had been the hard part. Because all she'd done was lie awake and think about Jackson, about how much she missed him and how she'd screwed everything up. She'd pushed and pushed, because she thought she was helping him. Helping them. And all she'd done was ruin the best thing in her life. So he couldn't tell her he loved her. Was that so bad? It wasn't like anyone had ever loved her anyway. She could have dealt with that. She could have lived with that.

Bullshit. You deserve to be loved.

She shook off the voice in her head. There was nothing she could do about that now. It was over.

She blinked back the tears that pricked her eyes.

"Fine. Tell him to come on in."

She spent the next fifteen minutes cleaning up her work area and getting her equipment ready for the new client.

Work was going to keep her busy and keep her mind clear.

She heard the door jingle, so at least the dude was timely.

Aria stuck her head around the door. "Uh, Becks? You might want to come out here."

Now what? She got out of her chair and went around the corner to the front. The jeans-wearing dude looking out the window didn't even have to turn around for Becks to recognize Jackson.

She'd know his exceptionally fine ass anywhere.

"Jackson."

He turned and smiled at her, and her heart lurched.

Oh, how she'd missed his smile. And his face. And his hair. And his everything.

"Hey, Becks."

"What are you doing here?"

"I'm your eight o'clock appointment."

She arched a brow. "You want a tattoo."

"Yes."

She crossed her arms. "Why?"

"Because I feel something emotional inside me that needs to be inked on my skin."

She should walk away, refuse to do it. But something compelled her to ride this out. "Okay. Come back and we'll talk about it."

"You want me to stay, Becks?" Aria asked.

Martin had a date tonight, so he'd left an hour ago. And, surprisingly, Aria also had a date tonight, who was picking her up in about ten minutes. The guy who worked at their favorite sandwich shop had asked her out. He was cute, too.

"No, you can go, Aria. Have fun. Make sure to lock the door behind you."

"No problem. I'll see you tomorrow."

"Okay."

Aria cast a distrustful glance at Jackson, which made Becks smile. She hadn't talked to Aria about what went down with Jackson other than to tell her they weren't seeing each other anymore.

Obviously that was all Aria needed.

It was nice to know someone had her back.

"Come on back," Becks said.

She felt his presence behind her, so close to her, and yet they were miles apart. It made her sad to know they were over when all she wanted was to hug him.

She shouldn't have agreed to do this, not when she'd have to touch his skin to do a tattoo, and be close enough that she'd be able to breathe in his scent.

Dumb idea, Becks.

"Take a seat in that chair," she said, then slid into her chair and grabbed her sketchbook and pencil. "Tell me what you want."

"I want a lot of things," he said, his voice low and sexy, the kind of voice he always used when he was whispering in her ear when he was inside her.

She cleared her throat and gave him a direct look. "Tell me about the tattoo you'd like."

He pointed to his biceps. "Flames. With words above them."

"Okay." She started sketching. "How big do you want the flames?"

"I have no idea. I guess you can decide that."

"How much verbiage do you want? Like a couple of words, or a paragraph? That'll determine how big to make the flames."

"Just a few words."

She nodded and put her focus back on her sketchbook. "And what words do you want above the flames?"

"Rise above the fire."

Her gaze shot up. "Jackson."

"I want to tell you about that night."

She laid the sketchpad in her lap. "You don't have to."

"Yeah, I do, because you're right. If we're not open and honest with each other about everything, then we're not meant to be with each other."

"I pushed you. I shouldn't have. No one who loves you should push you to relive something you're not ready for. Or that you may never be ready for. I was wrong."

"You weren't wrong. I've pushed the memories of that night away for all these years, and all it's done is stifle my emotions, made me unable to get close to anyone I cared about."

"But you love your brothers and your parents."

"To the extent I was capable of loving anyone, yeah. I always knew I had the capacity to feel more, but I never allowed it because loving someone meant I could lose them."

Her eyes filled with tears. "I understand that feeling. I feared that myself."

"Falling in love with you was the biggest risk I've ever taken. I couldn't even say the words to you, and I'm sorry for that. But I love you, Becks."

She shook her head. "You don't have to say it."

He took her hands in his. "I *love* you. I love your independence, your bravery, your fire and the way you make me feel as if I can do anything."

She swept her palm across his cheek. "Because you can. I believe in you, Jackson."

"Let me tell you about that night."

She shook her head. "You don't have to."

"Yeah, I do."

She sat back in her chair. "All right."

Jackson took in a breath. He had to get through this. For Becks, sure, but mainly for himself.

For so long he'd avoided memories of that night, but after talking to his brothers he knew he'd never be whole again until he really relived it.

He looked at Becks, but his mind had traveled back to that night in the house.

"I thought we were safe in that abandoned house. You know how it was. Getting shelter like that was so rare. I checked everything out. No one was in there, and we had a roof over our heads. It was a bad storm. Lightning, thunder, hail. God, it rained for hours that night, remember?"

"I remember."

Her voice was soft, a balm in the midst of his tortured memories.

"Rafe and Kal didn't want to go in at first. Rafe thought the house was unsafe, and Kal was worried someone would find us there. I pushed them. I made them stay there. I had scored us a pizza and all I wanted was a warm, dry place where we could eat it and then sleep."

"Jackson, you didn't know what would happen."

"I know. But maybe I should have listened to Rafe and Kal. Their instincts about the house." He shuddered in a breath. "Anyway, our bellies were full after eating the pizza, and we had a roof over our heads. Once Rafe and Kal were asleep I did a walk-through, checking the windows and doors. We were secure. I figured we'd all get the best night's sleep we'd had in months.

"And then I woke up in a room filled with smoke and panicked. I had to get to Rafe and Kal, but I couldn't find my way to the door."

He was staring at the wall, seeing through it to that fucking awful night. If not for Becks grabbing hold of his hand to ground him in reality, he wasn't sure he'd be able to keep reliving the nightmare of that night.

"I thought I was going to die in there. But even worse, I thought Rafe and Kal were going to die in there."

She smoothed her hand up and down his arm. "I can't imagine how that must have felt, Jackson."

"I was scared. Despite all the shit I'd been through in my fourteen years of life, I'd never been scared before. Until that night. Until all that smoke. I panicked. I couldn't remember the layout of the house or where the guys were. I crawled around on the floor trying to find the door. Smoke burned my eyes and I couldn't see.

"I'd always been the guy in charge, the one who'd get us out of trouble. We were in serious trouble that night and I couldn't see a way out. I couldn't get to Rafe and Kal.

"I failed them. I was supposed to take care of them and I failed them."

He felt her hand in his, felt her squeezing his fingers, and she was his lifeline to the present. Because he was back in that room, seeing everything clearly for the first time since that night fourteen years ago.

"Nothing ever scared me before. Not the cops, not social services, not even the possibility of dying. But that night I thought Rafe and Kal were going to die. That I'd led them into this horror show and I was going to be responsible for their deaths. And there was nothing I could do to save them. I was coughing hard and the smoke burned my eyes and my throat was so raw I couldn't call out to them anymore."

"Oh, Jackson, I'm so sorry," she said, stroking his arm, keeping at least a part of him in the here and now. But he had to remember the worst night of his life. Had to remember what that felt like. He had to see this through.

He felt the burn of tears in his eyes, just like the smoke had burned his eyes that night so long ago. He swiped at the tears, and then felt Becks's soft fingers swiping across his cheeks.

"It's okay," she said, her voice a soft whisper. "I'm here with you."

He nodded and knew he could get through the rest of it.

"And then my dad—only he wasn't my dad yet, he was just this dark vision—he busted through the door. He was so tall and so formidable. He was all in black and with a mask and a helmet and he was carrying an ax and wearing boots and he scooped me up like I weighed nothing. He got me out of that house and I swear it was like God himself had saved my life. He carried me outside, and sitting there in the ambulance were Rafe and Kal. They were alive and they were okay.

"I cried, Becks. I cried so hard when I saw them. And I put my arms around Josh Donovan and sobbed against his chest, and thanked him for saving all of us. And when he showed up at the hospital that night with Laurel, and said we could all come home with them, I thought I really had died, because good things like that didn't happen to kids like us, you know?"

"Yes. I do know. It must have felt like a miracle."

He smiled. "It didn't feel real. I didn't believe him. But Laurel convinced me it was real, and the next day after we got released, we went home with them."

"It must have been so nice to be like a family."

He looked at her, part of him still living in that dream. "It was amazing to get fed regularly. To be able to take a shower and put on clean clothes. To know you were loved. That was the best part."

She smoothed her hand over his jaw. "You were saved in so many ways the night of the fire; why have you blocked it out all of these years?"

He looked pained. "The guilt of making Rafe and Kal stay in that house that night. God, I've held tightly to that guilt for so long."

"Oh, Jackson. You had to know the fire wasn't your fault."

"Did I? I always had to be in charge. I always knew what was best. Except that night I made the wrong decision and it almost cost my brothers their lives. I almost lost them."

"Without the fire you never would have been taken in by Josh and Laurel. In a weird way it was the best thing that ever happened to the three of you." She smiled at him, her tone warm, gentle.

Jackson's smile was self-deprecating. "Logic has no place in my guilt—or my terror from that night. Emotion rules.

"It's like every time I try to hold on to something—to someone, I lose them. First my mom and dad in the car accident. Then I almost lost Rafe and Kal. It took me a long time to trust in Josh and Laurel, to believe that this time they were going to stick, ya know?"

She nodded. "Yes, I know."

"I remember my parents, but all these years later, it's more of a vague feeling of loss, of knowing that I had something that was precious and lost it. Rafe and Kal are tangible. We might not be blood, but we are brothers and we're gonna stay that way. So that night in the fire? That memory's always the worst.

"The nightmares began after we started living with Josh and Laurel. Every night I'd wake up screaming. The dreams were vivid as hell. Flames licking all around me, and a wall of fire separating me from Rafe and Kal and all of you guys, too. And the flames would devour you all, and you'd disappear. I could feel the heat of the fire in my dreams. It was so damn intense. I'd try to get past the wall but I couldn't. It was too hot. No matter how hard I tried, the wall was blistering and impenetrable. And then it would come for me, like this living, breathing . . . monster. And as soon as it caught up with me, that's when I'd wake up screaming."

He saw the look of horror on Becks's face.

"Oh my God, Jackson. I can't imagine having that dream every night. It must have been terrifying for you."

"Yeah. Laurel wanted me to go to therapy, but I refused. I said I could handle it and I did."

"By pushing the memories down and refusing to remember the past."

"Yeah."

"And here I've been pushing at you to remember." She leaned against him. "I'm so sorry, Jackson."

"No, it's okay. That catharsis you talked about? I needed it. I needed to remember, to talk about it, to bring it all out into the open. That fear can't hurt me anymore if I face my memories."

"Are you sure?"

"I think I'm sure."

She laughed. "Okay. But maybe you should talk to your mom and dad about it."

"I probably should. They've never pressured me to talk about that night. I never wanted to relive it and no one made me."

"Except me."

"Babe, you didn't make me do anything I wasn't ready to do. I'm sorry I didn't tell you I love you first. In my heart I knew I loved you, but I couldn't get the words out. Because saying the words meant I could lose you. And then I lost you anyway."

"You didn't lose me. I just thought I had pushed you too hard and you needed some space to sort things out. I already knew you loved me. You didn't need to say the words."

He laughed. "You are an amazing woman, and I'm so damn lucky to have you." He picked up her hand and kissed it, so grateful that she'd stuck by him, that she was willing to forgive his stupidity.

"I love you, Becks. I hope you don't get tired of hearing that."

"People like us never get tired of hearing that we're loved."

"You got that right."

"I love you, too, Jackson."

Her words made his heart want to leap out of his chest.

"So, you still want the tattoo?"

"Hell yes, I do. I've been thinking about it ever since I woke up and found out you had left. I knew I had to do something to fix what was broken inside me. And the only way to do that was to walk through the fire, to see what I had refused to acknowledge all these years. I had to deal with it and make it a part of me, so it couldn't haunt me anymore."

"I hope it helped."

"It helped a lot. Thank you for being here."

"You do realize ink is permanent."

He leaned over and brushed his lips across hers. "Like you and me."

"Oh, Jackson." She climbed over onto his lap and kissed him, and that passion, that love he always felt whenever he was with her, surrounded him.

Jackson realized that with Becks, he felt whole. Becks was the piece in his life that had always been missing.

That was what love was all about.

EPILOGUE

BECKS PULLED THE CASSEROLE OUT OF THE BACK OF HER truck and carried it through the front door of Station 6.

The first person she ran into was Josh Donovan, who looked so sharp in his blue pants and white shirt.

"Hi, Josh," she said. "Or should I call you Chief?"

He laughed. "Since you don't report to me, Josh is fine. Are you looking for Jackson?"

"Well, this casserole is for all of you, but yes, I'd like to see Jackson if he isn't too busy."

"You can drop the casserole in the kitchen, and tell anyone who's in there that I said it's for dinner."

"Duly noted. Sir."

He laughed, then leaned over to brush a kiss to her cheek. "Nice to see you, Becks."

"You, too."

She went into the kitchen and ran into Rafe and Kal and a few of the other firefighters.

"Hi, everyone. I brought a chicken enchilada casserole."

Rafe got up and took it from her. "You're the best, Becks."

"Yeah, we're starving," Kal said.

"The chief said to tell you to leave it alone, because it's for dinner."

"Dammit." Rafe took it and put it in the fridge. "Jackson's in his office."

"Okay, thanks."

She went down the hall and stopped at the window, watching as Jackson worked on his laptop. His brow furrowed as he concentrated on whatever it was he was doing.

He looked hot and she couldn't believe he was her man.

The past several weeks since they'd spoken their love for each other had been nothing short of a fairy tale.

She'd moved back into the house, though not really back into her room since she spent every night in Jackson's room, and all her toiletries now sat prominently on his bathroom counter.

She kept asking him if she was crowding him and all he'd do was pull her into his arms and tell her he liked her in his space.

She definitely liked being in his space.

She knocked on the window and he turned around. He smiled and motioned for her to come in.

He stood and she closed the door behind her.

"This is a nice surprise."

"I brought a casserole."

"Did you tell those heathens not to eat it?"

"Your dad gave orders that it was to be saved for dinner."

"He's the best chief."

"Isn't he?"

"Have you got a few minutes to sit?"

She pulled out her phone. "Yes. My first appointment isn't until one."

"Good. Too bad we don't have any privacy here. Otherwise we could make out or do some other things."

She arched a brow. "Other things, huh?"

"Yeah." He looked out the window, then slid his hand up her thigh. "You know, those things that make you scream."

"I think me screaming might bring some of your coworkers running."

"I could kiss you while you were screaming and then no one would hear. Did I mention I have a private bathroom?"

She took a deep breath. "You're making this very hard."

"You're making me very hard."

He leaned in to kiss her but then quickly leaned back and frowned at the window.

Becks shifted and then laughed as she saw Rafe's and Kal's faces pressed against the window, making goofy faces at them.

They came into the office.

"I expect both of you to clean that."

"Yes, Lieutenant," Rafe said, winking at Becks.

"Did you show her the drawing?" Kal asked.

Becks looked at Jackson. "He did not. What drawing?"

"The guys and I have an idea for a tattoo."

"Another tattoo?"

"This time all three of us want the same ink," Kal said.

"That's exciting," Becks said. "Show me."

Jackson opened his desk drawer. "Fortunately Miguel is a better artist than any of us, so we gave him the concept and he drew it out pretty well."

He handed it to her and she gasped.

It had the Maltese Cross and Fire and Rescue written on it, just like their badges, but nestled within that design were three male fists grasped onto each other.

Because Jackson, Rafe and Kal were all so different in coloring, Becks could easily see the three fists belonged to them.

And underneath, in bold letters, was *Brotherhood by Fire*, with flames licking all around the tattoo.

She looked up at them and smiled, realizing the bond the three of them shared. A bond that could never be broken.

"Perfect. Let's do it."

FLAMES LICKED ALL AROUND RAFE DONOVAN, THE HEAT from the house fire causing sweat to drip down his face and inside his SCBA mask. Since he couldn't wipe his face he blinked instead, clearing the perspiration from his eyes.

Rafe firmly gripped the lead hose to douse the flames threatening to drop the ceiling on their heads. Tommy Rodriguez had his back, feeding him more line. They soaked the fire in the living room, pushing through the dining room and into the kitchen, driving the beast back.

"It's wearing down," Rafe said, watching as the flames tried to roar, then inched back into the walls as he blasted them with water. "You don't win today, you bastard."

"You tell that fucker, Rafe," Rodriguez said.

Fire was his nemesis, the thing that had almost killed him back when he was a kid. It had also saved his life, turned it around and given him a new beginning. But it still had to die. Every day he faced it, it had to die.

When the flames were finally extinguished, he exhaled. The Engine 6 team did a walk around, pulling down walls to make sure the fire didn't lurk in the sheetrock, waiting to reignite. He made his way outside and pulled off his mask, sucking in a deep breath of Ft. Lauderdale hot summer air.

It might be humid as hell, and he might be drenched under his turnout gear, but he'd survived. No one was inside the house when the fire broke out, so he'd call this one a success.

He looked at the one-story ranch, charred but still standing. The fire had beaten it down a bit, but the old house would come back.

"Nice job in there." Jackson Donovan, his brother and his lieutenant, patted him on the back.

"Thanks."

He grinned and headed back to the truck, elation blasting through him as it always did when they defeated a fire.

He loved his job. If he could do it every day, he would.

They began to wrap up, folding the hoses and packing up equipment, when smoke started pouring from the roof.

"Dammit," Rafe said. How had they missed that? He heard Jackson's voice yelling at them to get back into the house. He loaded a fresh tank of oxygen on his back and put his mask on, then waited for his backup.

Rodriguez was right behind him as they returned inside.

"Be careful in there, all of you," Jackson said. "I don't like the looks of that smoke."

"Yeah, got it," Rafe said. He didn't like the skittering feeling crawling down his back. He had a sixth sense about fire, and which scenes posed a danger. This one didn't feel right to him. Something was off.

Inside looked clear, which meant the smoke was hiding in the walls somewhere. Hendricks and Richards were inside, too, helping them inspect. They'd broken off, going in the opposite direction.

"There's no heat, no smoke," Rafe said as they made their way around the house, testing more walls for fire. "So where's the smoke coming from?"

"Attic, maybe," Rodriguez said.

"Already up in the attic and cleared it," Hendricks said into his radio. "So whatever we saw, it isn't up here."

Damn. It wasn't unusual for a fire to snake along the walls, lurking, moving from one location to another. Which meant they'd have to check behind the drywall in every room until they found it and extinguished it. Rafe used his drywall hook to cut open a section of wall, checking for smoke in one of the smaller back bedrooms.

"Anything?" Jackson radioed.

"Still looking," Rafe radioed back. "Not finding anything."

"I don't like this," Jackson said. "Keep a sharp eye."

Rafe was already doing that. The whole team was in here now, cutting through and dragging down sections of walls to search for smoke, looking for hot spots.

When Rafe got to the closet in the hallway, he felt the door. It was hot, and the paint on the outside of the door was bubbling.

"There you are," he whispered to the bubbling closet door, then turned to Rodriguez. "We need to vent this through the roof."

He was about to notify Jackson that they were exiting and to bring Ladder 6 up on the roof to vent when he was knocked back on his feet by an explosion.

And then everything went dark.

BUSY DAYS IN THE EMERGENCY ROOM AT FT. LAUDERDALE Medical Center were Carmen Lewis's jam. If she stayed busy the entire shift, before she knew it she'd be off duty. Of course, demanding days meant sick and injured people, and that part wasn't great. Then again, the ER was always full.

She was charting in the station when her friend and coworker Tess Blackstone stopped by. "The patient in room seven is ready for discharge, according to Dr. Lange. Scrip for pain meds and a follow-up with his personal physician in a week. Room six is still waiting for someone to take her up for a CT scan. I just administered another bolus of morphine to room eight with Dr. Chan's approval."

Carmen nodded and updated the patient charts, signing off on the discharge for room seven. "Call CT—again—and tell them we've been waiting an hour and a half for that scan. What's the status on the patient in room three?"

"Waiting to be taken up for an angiogram."

"Okay, thanks."

"I'll make that call to CT—again," Tess said, picking up the phone and rolling her eyes at Carmen.

Carmen grinned, confident Tess would do her job well. All her nurses did. She had the best staff in the hospital, in her opinion. As triage nurse and supervisor of the department, Carmen had her hands in everything in the ER, which meant she was always managing chaos. Just the way she liked it.

EMTs came in with a firefighter strapped to a stretcher, bringing Carmen to instant alert. She recognized Rafe right away since he and his brothers lived in the house next door to hers. As a nurse, she didn't panic, but she hated seeing someone she knew on that stretcher.

His face was covered with ash and grit, but she was happy to see he was awake and seemingly alert as the paramedics took him into room five.

The attending physician came into the room at the same time to do an assessment.

"Explosion at a house fire," EMT Miguel Acosta said. "He took a pretty good blast that knocked him unconscious."

Acosta and his fellow EMT Adrienne Smith unstrapped Rafe and moved him from the stretcher onto the ER bed.

"But as you can see," Rafe said, "I'm not unconscious now."

"Patient was down for approximately three minutes, but roused quickly," Miguel said.

"And then he was a royal pain in the ass in the ambulance all the way here," Smith said, glaring at Rafe. "So he's alert and oriented times three."

"Any vomiting?" Dr. Lange asked.

"None," Smith said.

"Thanks, Adrienne," Carmen said. "We'll take it from here."

Miguel smiled at Rafe. "Behave yourself."

Rafe tried to sit up but Carmen laid a firm hand on his shoulder. "Nope. Stay put until we assess you."

Dr. Lange did a physical and neurological exam.

"No burns, but he does have a bump on the head. No external injuries. Get him set up on an IV and EKG and do his vitals and bloodwork," Dr. Lange said. "Let's order a CT scan."

She nodded and Dr. Lange stepped out. Carmen went to the cabinet to get the leads and everything else she'd need, then alerted one of the other nurses to bring her IV fluids.

"I shouldn't even be here," Rafe said.

"You know the protocol, Rafe," Carmen said, giving him her standard nurse stare. No one ever argued with her stare. It was pretty fierce.

Rafe, apparently, wasn't fazed by her glare.

"Whatever, Carmen. I'm fine."

"Sure you are. Let's get you out of that turnout gear."

He grinned. "Getting me naked. Now we're talkin'."

She laughed and shook her head. "Can you sit up?"

"Yeah, sure."

She held out her hand. He grasped it and sat up, much too fast for her liking.

She noticed he winced, and then he wobbled on the table a little.

"Head hurt?"

He reached for his forehead, cradling it in his hand. "A little. Damn backdraft caught me unaware and the door knocked me backward. And out cold, I guess."

She'd known Rafe and his brothers since they moved next door to her four years ago. Rafe helped her all the time with her grandpa. Over the years they'd grown close, and the thought of him being hurt made her hurt.

She helped him unlatch his jacket and slide it off. "You're lucky it wasn't worse."

He shrugged out of his coat and Carmen couldn't help but admire his broad shoulders encased in his tight T-shirt, something she shouldn't be noticing right now.

"Can you stand so we can get the rest of your turnout gear off?"

"Yeah."

"Hold my hand."

His lips curved, revealing his amazing smile. "Carmen, I never knew you were interested."

She rolled her eyes at him. "Up. Hold my hand."

But he took her hand and dropped his suspenders, letting the pants fall while he stepped out of his boots.

The hottest man she knew was undressing in front of her. At least partially undressing. Even in his T-shirt and standard uniform pants, standing this close to him made Carmen feel things she hadn't felt since—

Longer than she'd like to admit. Which she wasn't going to think about because right now Rafe was a patient. And that's all he was to her.

"Come on, climb back into bed."

"See, you flirting with me like this makes my head feel a lot better."

She shot him a look. "At least your sense of humor is still intact."

He gave her a lopsided grin. "Always."

She got him hooked up to the machines so they could chart his vitals, all of which were ridiculously normal. She checked his eyes, which were dilating normally as well—a very good sign.

Amy brought Carmen the IV fluid, so she started the IV. Rafe didn't even flinch when she inserted the needle, which wasn't a surprise. The guy was tough. She wet a washcloth with warm water and brought it over to clean the soot and grime off of his face.

"I didn't know a bath was included," he said, his warm brown eyes studying her the entire time.

Heat sang through her body. Normally cleaning a patient was an emotionless task. She did it because it was part of her job. But with Rafe it felt . . . different. Intimate. Unnerving.

"I thought you might want to get some of the residue from the fire off."

"A nice hot shower would feel really good about now."

She swept his thick dark hair away from his forehead and finished cleaning his face. "Can't do that for you, but does this feel better?"

He reached up and wrapped his fingers around hers. "You touching me feels good."

That heat she felt earlier was replaced by an incredible tingling sensation that settled somewhere in the vicinity of her sex.

Whoa, girl, back up.

Which she did. "Okay, I can actually see your face now."

He smiled, as if he knew exactly what he'd done to her.

She needed to remind herself that Rafe Donovan was a patient, and her neighbor, and that nothing was ever going to happen between the two of them.

Ever.

No matter how many times she'd fantasized about him.

JACI BURTON is the *USA Today* and *New York Times* bestselling author of the Brotherhood by Fire series, the Play-by-Play series, the Hope series and the Wild Riders series, and the coauthor of several anthologies with Lora Leigh.

CONNECT ONLINE

jaciburton.com
facebook.com/authorjaciburton
twitter.com/jaciburton